Prais

. an ominous tale populated by characters caught up terrifying journey through a series of lawless, amoral erlands: between adolescence and adulthood; city streets open countryside, and crime and punishment. With its ing insistence, though, Polley's tale stands out, most ptionally because of the way in which his language hich seems to crackle with electricity – conjures up a ening sense of unease and the sense of being trapped in ady borderland between all sorts of certainties'

Metro (review)

ey unflinchingly patrols the moral borders – and bore- – at which vulnerable young minds might be tipped violence, as Chris finds himself almost literally on a e's edge and must learn what it is to feel pain.'

Anita Sethi, *Independent*

rucial new voice' *Herald*

well as this vivid visual imagery, the novel has wide ry reach: an adolescent intensity conjures up a sense of . . . Carlisle and its hinterland is depicted as a bleak, n giving environment that nevertheless retains an unusual beauty . . . the verve, invention and reach of Polley's prose lends the story its richness.' *TLS*

'This is the first novel by the Carlisle-born poet, and the story follows Christopher Hearsey's painful and often amusing quest to find his missing mate as the summer holidays draw to a close. The setting is bleak, but there's something uplifting about this coming-of-age tale.' ***Esquire***

'It is one of the many achievements of *Talk of the Town* that, as we read, we hope [Chris] will emerge, if not physically unscathed, then at least not so emotionally damaged that he sinks permanently into the grim rictus of cool'

John Burnside, *Guardian*

'A brilliant evocation of a particular time and place from a new author who deserves a wide readership.'

Waterstone's Books Quarterly

'And finally . . . the **Most Impressive Debut** award. The Cumbrian poet Jacob Polley's *Talk of the Town*'

***Independent on Sunday*, Books of the Year**

TALK OF THE TOWN

Jacob Polley was born in Carlisle in 1975. He is the author of two poetry collections, both published by Picador. *Talk of the Town* is his first novel. For more information visit www.jacobpolley.com.

Also by Jacob Polley

THE BRINK

LITTLE GODS

JACOB POLLEY

TALK OF THE TOWN

PICADOR

First published in paperback 2009 by Picador

This edition published 2010 by Picador
an imprint of Pan Macmillan, division of Macmillan Publishers Limited
Pan Macmillan, 20 New Wharf Road, London N1 9RR
Basingstoke and Oxford
Associated companies throughout the world
www.panmacmillan.com

ISBN 978-0-330-44545-0

9 8 7 6 5 4 3 2 1

A CIP catalogue record for this book is available from
the British Library.

Printed in the UK by CPI Mackays, Chatham ME5 8TD

Visit **www.picador.com**
and to buy them. You w
news of any author even
so that you're always fir

for Ian and Janni and Richard

Talk of the Town is a work of fiction.
Characters, events and place names
are products of the author's imagination,
or, if real, not portrayed with geographical
and historical accuracy.

ONE

Town stinks. If I woke up on a street in Carlisle and didn't know how I'd got there, what time it was or where, I'd tell yer by the smell what time it was at least. The affternoon if there was the smell of biscuits bakin, cus a shift comes on and the ovens fire up, two till six, at the bicky works. This mornin there's a sooty smell, I wouldn't know what from, but as if last night's dark had settled like smoke ovver town and I can still smell the last of it this mornin, before it's all blown away.

I never drink tea, but me mam doesn't like us ter have coffee. It meks yer twitchy, she says. I've med this one on the sly, with two spoons of coffee and three sugars, and smuggled it up from the kitchen, inter me bedroom. I've bin stirrin it madly, cus I didn't dare wait fer the kettle ter boil and just med it with hot watter outta the tap. But the watter wasn't hot enough ter melt the sugar, so now I'm scrapin the runny crystals up off the bottom of the mug with me spoon and then lettin em slip back off inter the black.

I've bin sippin me coffee but the smell of the smoke's got us thinkin about the nutters and where they might be. Yer see the nutters at the weekend in the city centre. One's a shouter and a swearer and can't stop himsel. Yer hear him comin down the street, fuckin and cuntin, and the people with their shoppin bags cross the road ter get outta his way, and he shouts directly at people standin at the bus stop, right inter their faces, and they just turn away, cus maybe they know he can't help it and there's nee arguin with someone who's got nee sense. Then there's the mutterin smiley man who walks with a dog on a string and a radio under his arm, always talkin ter himsel. Yer wouldn't know there was much wrong with him but fer his look if yer catch his eye.

I've bin wonderin what'd happen if they met up, the two of em. Would they both know they weren't right is what I wanna know, and if they didn't then how d'yer stop em, the one of em shoutin fuck this and fuck that, and the other on the turn, cus he'd be smilin but part of what meks him a nutter is that his smile wouldn't be fer owt and any minute it'd come off his face and summit worse'd tek its place. I wanna know whether if there was nee one there ter watch em they'd recognise the nutter in each other and pass on by. Cus if they didn't pass on by, the one liftin his manky old hat ter the other, then how would they get out from under each other, the one roarin *cunt cock twat*, and the other with his radio under his arm and his smile with its missin teeth? That'd seem dynamite ter me, trouble yer wouldn't wanna see, if they kem together, each with their own mad path through the world and neither able ter mek room in their mind fer the other.

Where I live, on Scalegate Road, they're buildin a new close ovver the way. From here at me bedroom winder I can see the slick of oil on the road outside where me dad parks his cab. At the road end there's a Spar where packs of lads hang about in the evenin with their furry hoods up and the blazin yeller winders mekkin em nowt but shadders – anyone. And anyone could be Carl 'the Black' Hole and his crew, so I never risk moochin ovver and gettin offered out and havin ter run. On the corner there's a phonebox yer can bang till yer money comes out but yer credit stays in. The trick's ter not dial up till yer've fed a fifty in and banged, fed then banged, fed then banged, so yer've got three or four pun credit in there and yer can ring who yer want. I ring me best mate Arthur or when Arthur was with us, before he ever got his name in the newspaper, we'd both ring America and speak ter anyone.

Two weeks ago there was a tramp set on fire in Bitts Park, squirted in lighter fluid and his big coat lit, so he went up like rubbish, like the swept-up leaves. The talk's bin of nowt else, on the telly and pinned ter the boards outside the papershops, all the whys and what-fors and what-must-be-dones, and this last week, every time me dad's driven off, the black slick under his car's looked more and more like the outline of a body left scorched inter the road. I wouldn't know where the nutters live, whether they live under the Eden Bridge, in the city, or in one of the parks affter the gates have bin locked and the parkies have thrown everyone else out, whether they hide in a bush with their carrier bags, then sleep in the parky's shed. But I can't stop thinkin about the man with the gappy smile, smilin at his radio in a shedful of rakes and signs. Cus ter burn someone where they lie in a heap isn't a nutter's work. It teks more than one ter gang up and decide what's rubbish and deserves ter gan, and I'm thinkin of the lads like shadders outside Spar, all ganged up ter agree ter owt.

I tek another slug of cold coffee. It tastes black and reminds us of everythin else black, like the plastic of the phone handle and the black soles of me new school shoes, stowed in their box. I grab the old stubby bullet off me windersill and hod it till it warms in me hand. I shudder, and then I have ter turn from me winder and start gan back and forth from me wardrobe ter me Lamborghini poster on the opposite wall. Five steps it is between the wardrobe door and the Lamborghini, four and a bit if I tek big steps.

Chris! What yer doin up there? me mam shouts.

Nothin! I shout down, though I stop stompin.

It doesn't sound like nothin!

What can yer say ter that? I spose that now she won't be able ter hear owt she'll think I *was* doin summit that I'm not now I've stopped. I'm stood totally still, the half-drunk coffee in me hand. I'm guessin that she won't come up ter check if she can just shout from the bottom of the stairs, but I'm totally still anyhow, and knowin exactly where I'll stash the mug if I hear her start up the first few steps.

Seconds gan by.

Mebbe if I'm too quiet she'll start up, cus if yer gan too quiet it's almost as bad as when yer were mekkin noise, as if yer hidin summit in yer quietness.

I tek a coupla strides.

I pull oppen me wardrobe door and rattle the hangers hangin there, ter mek it sound as if I'm on with summit useful, like tidyin up.

I stand and listen.

I reckon I'm probly listenin ter me mam standin and listenin, but she could still come upstairs outta pure spite, just cus I was yawnin before when she was showin me and me sister our baby photos.

Yer can't be tired, she said, on the sofa. Why're yer so tired?

I'm not. I'm just yawnin.

Well stop it. Nobody wants ter see what yer had fer breakfast.

Me sister giggled. Me mam turned back ter the album on her knees.

Do we have ter do this?

Do what, Christopher? Keep yer mother happy? Yer don't have to, she said, and flopped ovver another big slippery page. If yer too tired ter do a little thing like this, I'm sure yer sister'll sit with her mother, won't yer, Fiona?

I'm not too tired, chirped me sister, and I just got up off the sofa without sayin owt and stomped up here ter me room, which is why me mam's probly stood at the bottom of the stairs now, gettin ready ter come up and catch us at summit.

But me mam's right. I'm knackered, knackered and twitchy, cus I'm thinkin about the city tomorrer, when I have ter gan back ter school, and how different it'll be ter the quiet Sunday city I've bin watchin outta me bedroom winder, though the streets'll be the same and the houses'll be in the same order. Tomorrer there'll be kids in their uniforms, and buses and cars on the move, and people all stridin along. And I'm thinkin about how it'll all gan on, like a pure silver wheel gettin spun, even if Arthur still hasn't turned up.

I shut me wardrobe door loudly and shuffle round in a circle. Then I stop and listen.

Nowt.

I put the mug ter me lips and tip the last of the coffee inter me gob, keepin the mug tipped right up till the warm unmelted sugar's slid from the bottom and onter me tongue. I run me finger round the inside of the mug and suck the sweet grit off it, then I get down on me hands and knees and push the empty mug under me bed, behind the new shoebox. I look at the hand I'm leant on, at the skin ruckin ovver me knuckles and me fingernails pressed white. I tilt me head and listen, all the while thinkin of me other hand like a live thing, separate from us and cowerin on its own in the fluff under me bed. I'm whisperin ter mesel, Yer have ter look, yer have ter look. Me heart's pulled through itsel like a slipknot and before I know what I'm doin me blind hand's found the newspaper and I'm draggin it out inter the light, unfoldin it and smoothin it flat with me fist. I lift the first sheet oppen slowly, so it hardly crackles, and me eyes gan straightaway ter the black words.

> Police are becoming increasingly concerned about the whereabouts of Arthur William Grieve of Edenton, near Carlisle. The 14-year-old has not been seen since Thursday

Me eyes slip down the page like spit down a winderpane.

> William

I didn't even know till yesterday that Arthur had a middle name, and now I'm readin without readin, cus every word's the same as the words that were squirmin through me skull as I lay on me bed in the dark last night, not sleepin.

> brown hair brown eyes medium height black jacket quilted lining contact the city police on Carlisle two eight one nine one

There's nee mugshot, but I've got one already, me own movin clip of Arthur reachin down ter give us a hand up off the deck, the sun comin out from behind his head, dazzlin away his face. I whip the paper shut and shove it back under me bed, further back than the empty mug, behind the shoebox. I get ter me feet, wipin the sweat off me palms on me jeans. There's nowt else fer it. I reckon I have ter gan and see Gill Ross, cus it's her who might know where Arthur is, cus of what fat Booby said yesterday on the Arches.

I shut me bedroom door softly affter us. Before I gan downstairs I peep through the banisters. I can hear me mam sprayin her hair in the mirror on the mantle. She was probly never standin and listenin at the bottom of the stairs, and I was stood so still and listenin fer nowt. The hairspray gans *Shhhh Shhhh*, cus me mam gets her hair rock-hard in the mornin. I tread quietly. I can hear the radio burblin from the kitchen as I avoid the creaky stair. I cross the hall, grabbin me jacket off its hook, and gan straight outta the front door inter the day.

TWO

I knew Arthur'd be in the Saturday late edition, so yesterday I stood on the doormat and waited ter nick it. I was wound so tight I'd jumped when it kem pokin through the letterbox, but then I'd pulled it gently through.

Is that the paper? me dad had yelled from the livin room as I started up the stairs.

No, I shouted. Just me.

I heard his chair tek a breath as he stood up out of it. I climbed faster.

I've told yer, he was sayin, his voice gettin louder as he moved inter the hall. What've I told yer?

I was safely at the top though, lookin down ovver the banisters at his black hair, me eyebrows lifted and me face emptied out, the paper behind me back.

What? I said.

How many bloody times? Keep yer fingers outta that letterbox.

The blue shadder of me dad's beard was runnin from his upturned face down the front of his neck. He pushed his fingers through his hair. I looked down and he looked up.

Okay, I said, and he looked harder and then turned away. I watched his bright black hair as the top of his head disappeared under us.

I knew he'd be in the affternoon paper cus I'd bin out on Saturday mornin, yer see, and rang Arthur's house.

His mam told us he hadn't bin home fer two days.

But he's got ter be back at school, I told Mrs Grieve from the phonebox.

There was a silence when I could just hear Mrs Grieve's ragged breathin.

I know, Christopher. I know he has to go to school, she said at last, her voice wobblin and risin higher, as if it was only just balanced on her lip and might fall and gan ter pieces any second.

Well, is he alright? I asked, cus I reckoned Mrs Grieve'd have ter know whether Arthur was alright or not.

There was a sound like a held-back sneeze.

In me mind I had a flash of Arthur, sniffin in the dark, and of the fields around the village where me and him had lost oursels that night he cut his hand.

He's fine, Christopher. We've reported it, but we're sure he's absolutely fine, she said. Okay?

Okay, I said as the phone went dead at me ear.

So I'd stood on the doormat yesterday and waited fer the paper, and as soon as I'd got it up ter me room, I'd oppened it and found Arthur's name.

Arthur William Grieve.

I couldn't breathe. Suddenly I wanted outta the house, away from me sister, and me dad as he killed time in his chair before startin out on his shift. I was wantin out under the oppen sky, well away from the neat black print that med Arthur's goin missin so true it choked us.

I rolled the paper up and shoved it under me bed. Then I snuck downstairs. I heard me dad clear his throat from the sittin room, but I was away through the door before he could yell. I pelted down our road and kept runnin, gan left under the narrer, riveted railway bridge and joggin down the potholed lane that leads ovver the wasteground. The high purple flowers left white fluff wisped onter me kegs. There were nee birds singin, not even seagulls meowin ovver the rooftops. The river was unravellin and brown. I slowed down ter foller it, then climbed the steps onter North Rise and crossed the roadbridge. I walked up past the pie factory, beside the main road, where the houses got further from the kerb and the streetlights stood taller and more lonely with the grass beginnin to stretch behind em on a summer's early evenin. There's usually someone on the scrub, either ridin on the dirt track so many bikes have worn outta the grass, or just havin a smoke where the trees stand, so I struck out across the green, twards the hill that climbs the Arches.

They haven't fallen down. It's more like the ground's risen ter cover em up. Yer can still see the red bricks and mek out the Arches themselves, but there're scrubby trees and bare earth grown ovver em. They and the ground, like a big park with nowt in it, separate our estate and the North Rise. I could have walked ovver the flat, but all the empty grass would've med us feel like I was bein watched from far away with a telescope or binoculars, caught out between either estate.

There was the whine of a scooter from outta sight and I could see a man follerin a black dog across the park. Booby Grove was at the toppa the rise, an aerosol in his hand.

Alright, Chris.

Alright, Booby. What's doin?

Nowt's doin, man, apart from what's already fuckin done. His face folded up, silent-like and laffin, tears squeezin out of his creased-up eyes. The smell of petrol was hangin on him, and he had a glassy look ter him and a red mouth from sniffin. Yer can call it sniffin, but I reckon he'd had his mouth ovver the mouth of a petrol tank, givin it lungfuls of fumes.

Who's on the bop? I asked, cus I could see someone bouncin ovver the rough ground on a moped, then topplin ovver, as if they'd keeled off a chair, and the machine lyin screamin on its side, its throttle stuck wide oppen in the earth.

Oh fuck. He can't fuckin walk straight, said Booby. Tek out the key! he shouted down. Don't fuckin pick it up, yer dense twat!

But whoever it was was flappin about, and then lifted the screamin bop upright by the handlebars so it flew out from under him, jerkin him runnin along with it till he let go and flopped onter his face. The bop wobbled on a few feet then pitched ovver. Booby watched this and his big body shook. He'd got his meaty hand on me shoulder and he could hardly stand up fer laffin, though he med nee sound, as if all the laffter was muffled in his belly. Whoever was on his face in the grass was still on his face and I was beginnin ter feel the weight of Booby bearin down on me ankles.

Some people can hod yer with what they say and others it's the pure size of em that keeps yer drawn up ter them. Booby's one of them. He swaggers with his weight and yer interested in him cus he does, cus his body's all his, like a king's, and there's nowt embarrassed about him and his size. He weighs more than most people, and knows it and uses it, lookin down at yer ovver his big tits and belly, weighin himsel against yer, and winnin. He was shoutin.

Cmon! Git the fuck up! Right, Chris lad, he said, looks like we're on a stroll down ter that sillyarse with his mouth fulla grass. And we started down the bank, me behind Booby as he took it slow down the steep side, firmin each foot on the slope before he'd put his full weight on it. Me, I dotted down, wonderin what it'd be like ter have Booby's body when I get ter his age, what it'd be like ter sleep with that weight on yer, or ter climb inter the bath and have the watter ride so far up the sides. But yer can never get inside anybody else. Yer yersel and all yer can do is change what yer've got, and yer can't even easily do that.

We'd lost the bop and the rider, outta sight now we were down off the toppa the Arches and were in the green dip.

Have a blast, lad, said Booby, hoddin the aerosol out ter us as we walked. Give it a squirt inter yer sleeve, then getta good deep breath off the spot. It'll be chilly, like.

I was imaginin Booby on the scooter, like a gorilla on a trike, not easily believin he'd ever get on it. I was thinkin he'd be more likely ter pick the whole machine up and drink the petrol tank dry.

Nah. Yer alright, I said.

No?

Yer alright.

Booby shrugged. There was a khaki stillness as we walked, with the blue night stood just a little way off from the sky. Across the park the pink streetlights of North Rise were poppin on, one by one.

Talkin of chilly, Chris lad, what's this I hear about yer mate Arthur and Gillian Ross?

I could see Booby's face from the corner of me eye, his little eyes sizin us up.

Yer what? I said.

Aye man, Arthur and Gill in the cemetery, givin it a wee bit chilly on the stones.

Booby took a few big gulps of air. He face was bulgin, bloody-cheeked, like a slab of cling-filmed beef.

Not a place yer'd have thought popular with the ladies, but yer man Arthur's got ideas of his own, asn't he? And whatever cranks his handle. If he can shag Gill Ross on a gravestone, and it isn't me own Nana's fuckin stone, then good luck ter him. But if I've heard it then Carl's sure ter have wind of it.

Booby paused and looked across the grass.

I felt like I was fallin ten floors through meself, but I kept me face gormless-lookin.

What d'yer reckon, Chris? Never an easy rider at the best of times, our Carl, and there's bad enough blood between the pair of em. It's no wonder yer man's tekkan hisel off, said

Booby, and silently creased up again, hoddin his sides just like yer read about people hoddin their sides in books, but never see it.

I swallered, me throat thick as an old sock. Who's on the bop, Booby?

Aw, cmon Chris, said Booby. Don't be a ballsack. And I knew then that it was Carl lyin on his face in the grass – Carl Hole, the Black Hole – who Arthur'd crossed already. And Booby had got us held in his huge gravity, so if I turned heel I'd be admittin summit, like I was scared or I knew about Arthur and Gill, and I didn't wanna know about Arthur and Gill and have the Black Hole look us in the eye and see Arthur, cus me and him knocked about so closely that we'd be nigh on the same person ter Carl. We walked on, Booby and me.

Yer a bit quiet, Chris lad, he said.

But we were climbin the next rise and Booby was too outta breath ter carry on raggin us, and I was racin through what might happen, how far I'd have ter run ter get safely away or how I could cover me face and head if the Black Hole caught up with us and I found mesel on the deck, on the end of his shoe. Booby had stopped on the rise and was starin across the grass. The Black Hole was crouched ovver the wee red scooter, a thread of smoke risin from his hands. It took us a minute ter work out what he was doin, I was so fulla runnin and the thought of Arthur in the graveyard and tryin not ter know it in me eyes when the Black Hole looked inter em. But then I realised Carl wasn't smokin a fag or just sittin firin dry grass. He had an almost invisible flame – just a patch of heat shiverin in the air – on the end of a rag. He'd got the seat of the bop lifted, where the petrol tank was, and he was feedin the rag inter the hole. Booby was swearin under his breath.

It's no easy thing ter get a petrol tank lit, but the Black Hole was intent on it, the bop layin on its side so some fuel must've spilled out, and him coaxin the flame ter scurry inter the tank. Then suddenly he sprang back on his haunches and the whole bike shivered with heat and he was laffin and stampin one smokin foot where a flame had caught.

Shite, said Booby, and I knew this wasn't part of Booby's grand plan, and I thanked fuck when he set off twards Carl across the grass, his big strollin body pushed out in front of him, leavin us free ter stand fer a second lookin affter him before I turned and walked quickly back through the green dip and ovver the Arches, me back all the while feelin as wide and bare as the park itsel. And I was hatin Arthur fer not tellin us he'd done what he'd done, so that I was walkin the town, half-blind and stupid. But Booby had given us a clue ter Arthur's disappearance, a clue that hardly let us sleep a wink last night.

THREE

Plastic bitsa sheet held down with bricks are lyin ovver the unbuilt parts of the close ovver the road. There's nee one climbin about with trowels and yeller hardhats, cus they're all playin footy or waitin fer their Sunday lunch. As I pull oppen the phonebox door, I'm wonderin what'd happen if nee one ever kem back ter work, and how long it'd tek anyone ter notice if the houses never got slates on their roofs or glass in their winders. I wedge me feet on the sill round the inside of the phonebox. The slow door seals us in.

I like that I can be outta the house and in the box, so I'm inside and outside at the same time. And the voice in me ear can be tekkin us further away, right the way down the flex, away from me road and the town. The phonebox is like me own wee room, even more me own than me bedroom where I've bin stompin and frettin and chuggin sly coffee all mornin, expectin me mam ter come chargin upstairs ter ask us about the paper. I lift the black handle and dial.

Through the smeary sunlit winders I see deaf Mr Banks step outta the front door next door ter ours and hobble down ter his front gate. I watch him get ter the gate and hook his old brown hands ovver the top of it. He looks left and then right, up and down the road, and then his face points twards the box where I'm wedged listenin ter the voice say, At the third stroke the time sponsored by—

Mr Banks turns and starts ter hobble back. I time him ter his doorstep. Forty-seven seconds. I'm wonderin why the gadgee in me ear calls a pip a stroke. I click down the clicker, cus stoppin the speakin clock speakin is like lettin Mr Banks off, cus if I'm not timin him then it doesn't matter how much time he teks. This lets me off in all, cus it's best if yer don't know the time.

That's one of the first things Arthur ever told us, in the corridor outside the Headmaster's office while me whole face rang from gettin punched in the gob.

Stop twinin, he hissed at us, cus I was shufflin me feet and wipin me nose with the back of me hand, then checkin the back of me hand fer blood. It doesn't matter how long we're stood ere, does it, he said, as long as we don't know how long it is.

I said nowt. I'd told him ter fuck off four times by then.

Aye, he said, summit's only a chore if yer told it's gonna be a chore fer a length of time. If time doesn't come inter it, then yer can't be wastin it. Why d'yer think all the lessons are divvied inter hours and minutes and seconds?

I must've bin gawpin at him as if I wouldn't ever guess.

Ter mek it worse, of course, he said, shekkin his head at us. It's just best never ter know.

Mr Banks braces his palms on his doorframe and pushes himsel up and through his door. I've got the phone handle crooked in me neck, watchin him. I don't need the phone-book hangin off the scratched shelf. I feed a ten inter the slot and dial the number I know by heart. I bring the handle ter me ear just in time ter hear the first ring. But it only rings twice before Arthur's mam says, Hello, exactly the same as she did yesterday, as if she's bin sittin beside the phone since then, just waitin fer it ter ring.

Hello, she says, even keener.

Mebbe it's cus I'm twitchy. Mebbe it's cus I've spent so long lettin me mind wander about while I watched Mr Banks and listened ter the speakin clock. Mebbe it's cus I already know that Arthur's not there by the sound of his mam's voice. Whatever the reason, I say nowt. I just lean and listen ter Mrs Grieve's breathin, me feet shiftin on the sill of the box. Me jacket rustles loud in me ear.

I can hear you, she says suddenly. I know you're there. I slam the phone down, cus she sounds so sure that it's me who's here.

Me ten pence falls through inter the safe and I stand, feelin miles from anyone.

When I push out the door of the box, it tries ter push back against us.

I stand on me street and look up and down, like old Mr Banks.

I feel filled with charge, like a new battery, so before it all leaks out of us I flash a quick look at me house, where I reckon me mam'll still be doin her hair, and I head fer Gillian Ross's.

FOUR

Arthur and me first met at school, at the toppa the stairs outside Chemistry, on the landin where yer wait fer the Chemistry teacher Dennis the Menace ter let yer in. The landin smells of the inside of an old hot-watter bottle or the rubbery air from an inner tube when yer changin a tyre. Ter get ter it yer gan up two flights of stairs, so everyone leanin ovver the railin on the landin has a spittin-view of the toppa yer head.

At school yer have ter think about everythin. It's a wonder yer can hod sums and sentences in yer mind when yer have ter decide how ter climb the stairs or which walk is the one that'll stop yer gettin kicked about the cloakrooms, but doesn't mek yer look like a spacka, a puff or just soft.

Me, I tek long strides and don't hurry. I keep me hands outta me pockets and swing me arms. Mrs Drake, me History teacher – known as Cannonball-nostrils fer her nostril width – is always tellin us ter put the ears of me turned-out pockets back in.

So I was tekkin the stairs two at a time, but slowly, and not lookin up at the Chemistry landin. There's a big winder in front of yer as yer climb the first flight, one of the few yer can look out of onter the empty playground. I was lookin outta that, so nee one would think that I had a strategy, that I was thinkin about how not ter get gobbed on, which is all about lookin like it's the last thing yer expect. If yer look up and cringe and cover yer head, some fucker'll just oblige yer and unload from the back of his throat. Cus yer askin fer it if yer flinch before someone's even thrown a punch. That'd show yer'd thought enough ter imagine how much it might hurt, not just how much yer were gonna hurt someone else, and yer'll've already bin punched in yer mind. First punch ter the softest bit – yer brain – before anyone's even tekkan a swing.

So I'd turned the first flight and was climbin the second, facin the landin where two classes were stood waitin ter be let in. And now I had ter look, I had ter hod whoever stared cus they were in me way. I had ter watch em and expect em ter mek way fer us on the top, as if owt else – any body in the way, any hands held out ter stop us, any shufflin ter their right as I stepped ter me left, then shufflin ter their left as I shuffled ter me right – had never crossed me mind. There was nowt in me face but cast-iron casualness, fixed there in me eyes and me mouth.

All that effort to mek all yer do look like yer doin nowt.

But I'm good at it. I don't care. And if yer don't care then nee one can give yer what yer care about, so yer owe em, and nee one can spot what yer care about and hod it from yer till yer beg em.

I got onter the landin, nee bother, and there were bags all ovver the deck, the huge sports bags with their tags and labels and the girls' drawstring sacks and wee satchels, and I wasn't lookin at me feet and the straps were all coiled about the floor and then me ankle gets caught in one, doesn't it?

And I'm doin a wee off-balance hop and a skip, shoulderin inter the bodies about us, and I was nearly ovver, which would've bin so much fer us not lookin like anythin but a twat, but I recovered. I caught mesel and just staggered a wee stagger and got ready ter hoof whoever's bag had bin dumb enough ter tangle with us, cus it's the done thing ter be sorry fer nowt – even when yer staggerin about like a blind man – and part of the who's who and who's hard is who says they're sorry, who rolls ovver fer yer, even if they've got nowt ter be sorry fer. So I was expectin ter be said sorry ter till some fucker proved it otherwise.

Then Arthur Grieve punched us in the mouth. Ter prove otherwise, good and proper.

I spose it's the one thing I wasn't expectin in all me expectin, cus I didn't even fall down, as if me body hadn't caught up with what it ought ter have bin doin, which was keelin ovver and not knowin owt about nowt any more.

I spose I just stood there.

I spose, cus I wasn't there. Yer can walk in yer sleep, can't yer, when yer don't remember, when yer mind's gone out, but yer arms and legs still carry yer about and yer eyes might even be oppen. It was like that. Arthur Grieve had swung a sweet one, hard as fuck, and everyone had gone quiet, or I was too far away ter hear em.

I kem round ter me nose ringin and me jaw numb. But the ringin was in me ears as well till I realised the school bell was ringin, bang on the wall above the landin, a round red fire-bell, as bright as the blood I thought I could feel runnin outta me nose, and I took a swing at Arthur Grieve, an off-balance wee swat, and I caught Dennis the Menace, didn't I, on his tweed shoulder. Where he'd kem from I'd no idea but I should've known, should've known that all me walkin slow and not gettin gobbed on and thinkin so much about owt but what I was sposed ter be thinkin about would have us fallin ovver mesel and inter fuckin bother.

Mr Menace looked like he had an ice cube up his arse. I spose he was busy in all, expectin what he thought he should've bin, with his teacher's face on and his teacher's walk and teacher's leather elber patches. I hardly touched him and didn't mean ter anyhow. But that counts fer nowt. I'd like ter know what does count if what yer've done is hardly owt and yer didn't even mean ter do that. What was I gettin done fer but fer the fact that Mr Menace had got a goggle-eyed look on his face and had ter save his face affter that by liftin me and Arthur by the scruffs of our jumpers and pushin us down the stairs in a great huff and hurry? On through door affter door he pushed us, with Arthur and me pushin them oppen in front of him, our collars up round our throats. And the Menace had a fury on that wasn't just his teacher's bluster but summit with less control and none of the jabber. And on inter the corridor, twards the Head's office, he half lifted, half pushed Arthur and me, and it was bright and silent in the corridor, cus nee one but teachers are allowed ter cut through it, and there're doors at either end ter shut out the kerfuffle and babblin of all us as we fire from class to class, humpin bags and gettin bottlenecked in the doorways.

And there he left us, stood outside the Headmaster's door with our backs ter the wall. I was touchin the knuckles of me hand ter me nose and then checkin em fer blood, me eyes on the Deputy's door and the doors of the heads of the departments along the corridor. It was lesson time, just begun, so it was deadly quiet, and me and Arthur were stood there fer any righteous fucker ter ask what we were stood there for. Cus if yer out of a lesson it's pure fluke who'll come walkin by and either keep on gan, eyes straight ahead, mindin their own business, or if they're Mr Britain or Pubic, the head of Maths, stop and start pokin their beak in and dolin out their own bollockin, separate ter whatever yer already gettin bollocked fer. So yer fair game on the corridor, which hardly seems fair. But we were saved, at least, Arthur and me, from the fury of the Menace, who'd stormed off ter give the lesson I should've bin in, his tie askew and his mouth a crack in his plastery grey mask.

What d'yer hit him fer? whispered Arthur. I was busy runnin me tongue up round the inside of me mouth, round the inside and outside of me teeth, and pinchin the gristle of me nose, tryin ter getta feelin fer me own face again.

I hissed, Fuck off, as best I could, wantin ter look at meself in a mirror, ter know where I was at with the world and how much I could risk splutterin ter anyone through me swollen lips.

If yer were gonna hit him, like, yer could've smacked him in the mouth and med it worth it. Yer may as well'ave. If the roof's gonna come down, there's nee point sweepin the floor.

Fuck off.

It's true enough though, isnnit? If yer gonna nick a bit, might as well nick the lot. If yer gonna piss yersel, yer may as well shit yersel in all and get it ovver with. Or d'yer think it's less of a shan to piss yersel than it is to piss *and* shit yersel?

Arthur swung a look up and then down the corridor and I took a sly look at him. His white school shirt was sailin untucked from his kegs. He had the beginnins of scrawly sideburns creepin down his long face. When he turned back ter us, he was grinnin.

I reckon it would be about the same either way, he said.

I could hear the striplights hummin in the quiet.

If yer stood in yer pissy kegs, nee one's gonna be layin off yer, are they, sayin give him a break cus at least he hasn't shit himsel in all? No. So yer might as well tek it all at once. It's just unlucky if yer don't need a shite at the same time that yer happen ter've pissed yersel. That'd be just bad luck. A right waste.

I see what yer mean, I said, and I did, cus the thing I'd learn about Arthur was that he could talk a good talk and mek yer see summit from a place yer hadn't seen it from before, like lookin up when yer swimmin underwatter and seein the watter's surface, solid silver all of a sudden and not watter at all.

How am I lookin? I asked him in a whisper.

What am I? Yer boyfriend? Yer lookin bad, though. They'll probly have ter amputate yer fuckin head. Yer'll be alright without it, won't yer? Less dead weight. Probly speed yer up. But yer'll have nowt ter scratch when yer vexed. That'll be the big loss like, that and there bein neewhere fer yer mam to clip the back of. She'll be confused, if she isn't already. Affter all, she squeezed yer inter the world and yer were probly enough ter send her round the twist. I'd be fuckin surprised if she didn't ask them in the hospital ter sew her right up affter you and have done with it. Did she?

Yer what?

Have yer gotta wee brother or sister, yer mong?

Fuck off.

Aye. Fuck off. Yer a witless wonder, you are. Me dog's got more ter say for himsel and he can lick his own balls. If yer could dee that it'd be nee surprise, yer havin nowt ter say fer yerself. Can yer lick yer own balls?

No.

Well, what d'yer say?

Fuck off.

Aye. I thought yer would, said Arthur, and brushed his school tie with his knuckles, as if I was summit spilled down his front that he could just flick off.

The drill is that yer stand in the corridor till whoever it is that's med yer stand there comes back ter bollock yer. So the bell went again and Arthur and me stood there. There's some uncertainty in this, like, and sure enough Mr Justice, the Head himsel, Judge Dredd, pushed crookedly through the doors at the far end of the corridor and crookedly kem soft-shoein it down the corridor twards us.

There're some teachers who like the tip-tap of their polished shoes ter get ter yer first, but the Judge wears Hush Puppies and just appears among the bickerin or the foolin and snips all inter silence. Yer feel guilty just fer havin bin watched by him without knowin it, as if not knowin is proof enough that yer an idiot, and bein idiots is what most of us feel most guilty about. Most of us, that is, but not Arthur.

Me and him straightened up and looked ahead. Judge Dredd was all arms and long legs, a pair of scissors in a suit.

And what seems to be the problem, lads, he said. And it's always what seems and what might be with him, as if there's plentya scope fer the inbetween.

An accident, sir, piped up Arthur straightaway, and laid out fer the Judge how I'd tripped on his bag, which, true enough, we're always bein warned ter keep off the floors and landins, and banged mesel, and Mr Dennis had come in on the tail-end of this wee bitta carelessness and caught me dazed and confused, and he hadn't had the time ter properly appraise the situation, which was fair enough, but he hadn't waited fer an explanation before he marched us down here furiously, sir, which Arthur wasn't, with all due respect, sir, used to at all.

I could've saved him his breath if he'd given us half a chance.

We got two weeks' dinnertime detention and letters home.

Fer detention yer shut in a classroom and med ter write lines, lines like 'I must learn to obey when those around me depend on my obedience', or essays with titles like 'What I have learned from my time in detention' while everyone else is outside. It'd be alright if yer were let out when yer'd written a thousand lines, but yer just given another thousand till the time's up, so yer may as well dawdle through the first thousand yer given. People knock on the winders while yer in, their blurry hands loomin up on the other side of the cobbly glass, and yer can hear the voices, which is the worst, the shouts and the fizzy chatter.

The Menace popped in ovver the two weeks Arthur and me were cooped up, ter see we were keepin pace. What me and Arthur were doin was gettin acquainted ovver Hangman and Battleships, which Arthur showed us how ter draw out and we played, him on one side of the room and me at a desk on the other side. We were in nee hurry ter shade in our aircraft carriers and gunboats. Arthur told us how the cows swung past under his winder, so his days started and ended with the sound of splatterin shit, and how outta town, where he lived, there was anyspot ter gan if he just took it inter his head ter climb a gate and walk. He let us hod the bullet he'd dug outta the old rifle range ovver the fields from his house.

The metal targets're still there all stacked up, rusty and shot fulla holes, he said, and yer never see nee one down there. Yer stand on the toppa the range and yer can see straight ovver the Solway ter Scotland. Yer can swim there in all but nee one does anymore.

Why not?

Cus of the radiation, yer dipshit. Yer gan in ter cool off and come out glowin.

I thought about the empty country, imaginin meself standin lookout on the rifle range.

Have yer ever caught a rabbit?

Nah, I said, cus I hadn't.

Ever buried a sheep's head, then dug it up when the skin's rotted off it?

Nah.

Ever sin a cow-fuck?

Nah.

D'yer wanna?

Yeah, I said, noddin me head, serious like.

Yer wanna see a cow-fuck?

Yeah.

Really badly?

I watched Arthur's mouth twitchin at the corners.

Not really badly, I said slowly.

But fairly badly? Arthur said, but he couldn't hod it together and fell back laffin in his placky chair.

Yer a hoot, you are, now give us that back, he said.

I looked at the blunt cone in me hand. It was flattened and greenish, but it was a bullet, pure and simple. I put it back on Arthur's palm.

I learned that by the playin of Battleships, an hour's detention was fairly whittled away, and two weeks of em were enough ter see Arthur and me mekkin plans ter mooch about together at the weekends.

FIVE

A few weeks later I was smokin the first fag of a new pack of ten while I sat on a wall round the corner from Arthur's, a carrier bag at me feet. Arthur was inside, tellin his mam he was off ter mine. I'd told me mam I was off ter his, so we were each off ter neither place and were gonna be somespot inbetween instead, somespot right off the radar. The evenin sun was still hot in me hair. When I put me hand on me head, me hair felt glossy, as if there was nowt on top of me head but the crackly heat.

Me fag was smoulderin blue smoke, and hardly any, as if even it couldn't be arsed in the heat to mek more heat by burnin. Wee red mites were crawlin the wall-top, though crawlin's the wrong word fer the speed of em. Like dots doodled from an invisible red pen, they were scrawlin about around me hands where they were clamped. The little road-chips and pebbles and the weeds squeezed up from the cracks at the pavement's edge were all growin their own shadders as I sat, so the pavement was its own world laid out and I was lookin down at it, huge, and I squirted some spit without hardly tryin, to see how long it'd tek ter dry.

There're worlds and worlds, I was thinkin, all laid ovver the top of each other. There was the pavement where me spit was dryin in a dark badge, and the road where the cow shit from the cows' comin home had bin baked a yellery-green.

There were the summer's noises, wee buzzes and clicks, as if I could hear all that was growin around us bein dried out. I was thinkin that these worlds were all boxed away in me own head when Arthur suddenly said from beside us, Ey up. He toed the carrier bag with his trainer so it chinked, bottle on bottle, and we were off, down the lanes and across the fields, seein nee one, tekkin turns ter lug the bag of booze.

On toppa the rifle range, Arthur twisted the cap off the first shekkan-up bottle and the fizz kem foamin out. The wind was rollin through the grass and yeller cornfields. I told yer we'd find yer one, Arthur said, passin us the drippin bottle. The estuary crinkled. The unmovin hills across the watter loomed. I swigged and passed the bottle back, lickin me thumb and rubbin some orange crusted dirt off the stubby bullet on me palm.

The night kem down without us even noticin. Me fingers were round the cold glass cider bottle again. Arthur was whippin the foam off the cow parsley with a stick, roarin, Yahoo! – Luke Skywalker with the stick cuttin through the air with a whippy sound there was nee word fer, and there was nee word fer the sound I blew from the bottle-neck by breathin ovver the hole before I upended the bottle and drank the last of it, sour from the bottom. There were goosebumps on me milky arms, and Arthur's face was a mask of glimmer, the whites of his eyes glintin, so he might just have bin smilin ter himsel at the state of us.

So this is pissed. Easy as owt, I was thinkin, the cow parsley all around us, its yeller-white flowers like foam. We were pissed and shouldn't've bin fer years yet, them years yer count from where yer are till when yer'll be eighteen, wonderin what yer'll be, pissed just ter see what it was like.

Shush man, I said.

But Arthur shouted, Who's listenin! and I threw me head back ter look at the stars, which seemed loud, not bright, there were so many of em, mebbe cus me own head was runnin like a motor and it was only cus the night was so clear that I could hear me own head. Far off, town was an orange stain on the dark.

Shoutin, There's nee one here! and kickin dust up from the dry lane, Arthur was what I was, reelin and shaddery. But I wanted the quiet. I didn't want us standin out, the two of us, frighteners of the hedgehogs and foxes that might've come out with the stars.

I remember tryin ter mek a list, ter steady mesel.

There were village houses lit up in the direction of Arthur's village, the village we had ter keep out of. There was the bunker we were headin fer, down on the marsh, where the farmers kept their feed, where Arthur had said we should sleep.

There was the time, but what was it, cus neither of us was wearin a watch, cus neither of us wanted the feelin of a watch sweatin on our wrist.

There were stars, and a long way off the chill on me bare arms.

There was an owl I knew by its *who-who*-in, whose secret shape I wanted ter see for mesel, but there was just its *who-who-who* comin outta neewhere, askin us. And I was missin a bitta time everytime I turned, and had I dropped the bottle?

Aye, and hadn't noticed, so it was like I was flickerin, or the night was. Nowt was gettin inter me brain complete. I'd lit a fag, but had I put me fagbox back, and me Clipper? I patted down me pockets but I'd forgotten I had a fag in me hand and it scuffed on me T-shirt and orange sparks kem trailin out – Whoah! – like I was on fire or I was a fuse ter a firework, just lit. And Arthur had got the bottle I'd dropped and he chucked it straight up so it might have kem down on me head, but didn't, and landed instead with a dusty unbroken clump. He snatched it up by its neck and skebbed it back up inter the night sky where it was lost in the dark, but kem down again and smashed this time inter pieces that all took ages ter stop tinklin apart. And then Arthur was on his knees, a lump of dark that was him.

Art, what yer doin? I said.

He was moanin, Oh fuck, fuck, fuckin hell, but laffin as well. I could tell cus his teeth were glitterin in his face.

Fuck, Chris. Give us some light, he said. I'm fuckin bleedin.

I could mek out his hand in his other hand, slick-black as he kneeled ovver the glass he'd fallen on in the dark.

I slotted me hands under his armpits ter drag him up. He sniggered at the touch of me cold hands under his arms.

Help us out, man. Cmon, I was sayin, dead calm, sayin cmon ter mesel more than ter him. Cmon. Stop bein pissed. We've gotta sort yer out, I said.

But where was there ter gan? Not Arthur's, where his mam thought we were in town at mine. Not mine, which was miles away along the country roads, then on through the outskirts of town where we'd be stickin right out when cars beamed past. And then there'd be me own mam ter wake up from thinkin I was at Arthur's.

Oh fuck. Tek us home, he said when I flicked the flame of me Clipper alive and it stood still in the windless dark. There wasn't much ter see by it but the wetness all ovver both his hands before the heat of it was too much for me thumbnail and we were left ter adjust all ovver again ter the blackness.

We can't, man. How far's the bunker? We're fucked if we gan ter yer house, I said.

I'm not gan all the way down there. It's a fuckin shed in the middle of neewhere, Chris. It's startin ter hurt and I'm fuckin freezin.

I could feel him shiverin through his T-shirt as he pulled himsel up, still hoddin one hand in his other. The bottleglass crunched under his trainers. It was then I started talkin mad.

We'll have ter gan if we can't get outta this. We'll gan ter London, I was tellin Arthur, blinkin till I could see a bit more of the blue behind the black dark. We'll just tek off. We can't get fuckin caught fer this, can we? What'll happen? We may as well just gan.

Don't be a plum, Chris. Just fuckin get us back ter mine.

No. Listen ter us. If we gan back, yer mam'll ring mine. Me mam'll tell me dad. Me dad'll fuckin belt us, and that'll be us fucked fer doin owt together. They'll never let us out again. And this'll be my fault, yer hand. They'll be blamin me fer lettin yer fall, cus we're not where we said we were gonna be.

I'm not runnin off. What'd we do, man? What'd we do in

fuckin London? Where'd we sleep? What d'yer wanna run off for and get fuckin lost? It's not as if it's like this, Arthur said, and swept his arm round at the dark. There's neewhere empty in London fer us.

We'll just walk, then. We can't stay here, I said, cus it was as if I'd just realised we were stood deep in the country, in a lane, in the night, with the owl askin us again who we were, and nee one around and neewhere ter lie down till mornin kem.

We'll just walk and find some more light ter look at yer hand.

So we set off walkin between the fields around Arthur's village, down the lanes that Arthur knew, even in the dark. I remember the sound of our feet scuffin in the dust – silver then by the moon that was up – and Arthur sniffin, as if he was cryin.

Fuckin hay-fever, he said as we walked.

I kept lookin ovver me shoulder and then strainin me eyes up ahead, imaginin someone was gonna come suddenly outta the night. I'd got me arm round Arthur, partly cus I couldn't see where I was gan and partly ter give him some of me own warmth.

I'd gan ter London like that, I said ter mesel out loud, and mebbe it was the cider still motorin me head, but I was wonderin why I would think ter gan and Arthur wouldn't. Why would I be wantin outta me room, outta me house, outta the road me house is on, and on, on, outta the town, out from under me mam's feet, and me dad's when he kem in at all hours, outta whatever I'd be doin or mekkin – outta bein a chippy, a plumber, a pipe-fitter or a fuckin road-sweeper, outta bein on the lorries or the taxis, outta packin bickies or bein on the boxes or fillin pies at the pie factory or cuttin carpets till me knees were fucked, outta the dole or fuck-knows-what, and I heard the owl again say *who-who*.

Did yer hear?

Aye, whispered Arthur. One sits on the gatepost ovver from mine. Yer'd think it was stone till it teks off. It teks off right in front us sometimes if I walk by it at night, just falls away, quieter than quiet. Less than a bird, like.

Less than a bird?

Aye. Less of everythin. Less flappin. Less ter say fer itsel. Med fer the night. Left down here, he said, and we headed down another lane, grown ovver I was guessin, cus it felt too narrer fer a tractor. But I didn't know what we were gonna do.

What the fuck're we gonna do? moaned Arthur.

We'll find some light, man, and tek a look at yer hand. Does it hurt?

I can't feel it, Arthur said, and I knew that was worse.

The hedgerows were higher around us, the smell of cow parsley sweet as puke. There were trees up ahead. I could tell by their black solidness and by the wee squeaks and creaks of them movin. Our bare arms were swimmin in the gloom. Me head had the pissedness in it like a weight. There were porch lights and winders, away yonder, and all I wanted then was ter be in the yeller of a kitchen with a kettle on the boil, gettin Arthur's hand looked at and bein told that it wasn't as bad as I was thinkin it was now he couldn't even feel it.

And then we kem outta the lanes under a streetlight in his village. His hands looked wet and orange in the glow, and his T-shirt was hangin off him, wet-lookin in all. The village phonebox was ovver the road, the moths batterin away at it, and the streetlights down the village were mekkin orange tents in the dark. Arthur took us down the road, streetlight ter streetlight and through the dark in between, past hedges of shufflin leaves, all the way ter the closed-up pub with its empty carpark and sign-light off and shutters shut. We crouched round the corner, our backs against the wall.

What're we doin? We can't gan in, I said.

We'll wait, man, said Arthur. See who comes out. There're people still in cus it's Friday. Look! There's light in the cracks. They just pretend ter shut at closin time. Listen ter that.

And sure enough there was a core of light and laffter, behind the porch door, all muffled up inside.

Aye, but who'll be in? We can't just fuckin nab someone and get em ter sort us out, can we?

There'll be someone, said Arthur. Then the porch door was rattled and pulled in so the pub noise was unplugged and spilled out with the light, and a body huge in the doorway roared back inter the pub.

Aye, ta-ra ter yerselves! Ta-ra ter the nee-good bloody lotta yers! And Arthur pulled us back with his good hand, outta the road, as the porch door was chugged shut and the big man struck off across the dark beer garden, settlin his cap on his head, and his boots ringin each step on the pavement.

Not him, said Arthur. We'd get short fuckin shrift from Red Armstrong. He's mad.

Proper mad?

Aye. Proper mad. Kem back from the Falklands with a bullet still in his skull. Never the fuckin same. Lives in a house yer'd think was empty if yer didn't know better. Cobwebs in the winders. I hear him from me bed walkin back from here – steel in his head, steel in his toes, kickin sparks, like. But the farmlads'll be in, said Arthur, and I know one of em – Dan Reid.

I was listenin ter Red Armstrong's boots clatterin and scrapin like horseshoes through the dark.

Dan Reid owes us cus I found his teeth on the road outside our house when he kem off his bike.

Yer what?

His teeth. He went flyin ovver his handlebars and me and me mam were there ter see it. She picked him up and I found his two front teeth and brought em ovver ter him on me palm. They couldn't put his teeth back in, but Dan said he owed us if I ever needed owt, Arthur said as the door rattled and another body appeared, whistlin a tune like a bird from the yeller doorway.

He's away, yelled the figure. The stroppy fucker.

Bry, said Arthur from beside us.

The whistlin had started up again but then suddenly stopped dead. I could mek out the stilled figure peerin inter the dark, the porch-glow snagged in the coils of his hair.

Who's that? Who's there?

Arthur was pushin himsel upright, his hand on me shoulder.

Who is it, Bry? said another voice in the doorway, the two bodies choppin out the light.

It's me, Dan, Arthur said, saunterin twards em, his shadder flung behind him, while I sat shiverin round the corner.

And the voice yelled back inter the pub, Eggy! Come see this. What's the fuckin beef, lad? Yer look dug up.

They don't serve nee one who's dug the fuck up here, said another feller, shovin himsel between the other two and outta the doorway ter stand unsteadily and look Arthur up and down. Then roarin, Haway! the feller reeled off twards the road.

Cmon, Arthur hissed as he passed us, and the shapes of the other lads passed us, and I slipped outta me hidin place and follered.

We trooped along the road and then down a lane, and as we crossed a farmyard a face turned twards us in the dark and said, Am I seein fuckin double or wat? We've gotta another stray ere, lads.

I said nowt and waited fer Arthur ter say summit, but he can't've heard. We were gettin led across the yard ter a door Dan Reid pushed oppen, sayin, Aye, well, get yersels in the bothy and we'll dee a fuckin heid count, and in we went.

They were big lads, different ter us. Their cheeks were sunburned when I saw em in the light, and funny fer bein sunburned there in the middle of the night, as if they didn't belong anywhere but outside in the sun with work ter do. They'd got big cows' heads and Yankee-flag buckles on their belts. They had shirts tucked inter their jeans and cowboy boots on. They looked like they'd just been bathed and dressed up and tucked in tighter than they were used ter. Dan Reid stood and jabbed the air above our heads with a blunt finger, countin us off. There were five of us inside the wee room Dan Reid had called the bothy, five of us includin Dan Reid himsel, whose front teeth Arthur had held on his palm.

Quick as yer like, Eggy had his shirtsleeves rolled up and was stood at the sink, hoddin Arthur's bloody drippin hand in his own. Ovver his shoulder he growled, Where's the juice, Bry? And curly-haired Bry who was whistlin again, lain back propped on his elbers on the narrer scrowed bed, reached under it fer a rusty-coloured bottle without droppin a note. He unscrewed the cap, stood up and headed the light-shade, not bothered when the wee room was thrown high up one wall, and then the other, and all our shadders swung enormously above us.

I hadn't dared ter gan ovver ter the sink, cus I'd've had ter squeeze between the farmlads, so I'd parked mesel with me back ter the bothy door, tryin ter keep outta the way and trade a look with Arthur in the meantime. Clutchin the bottle, Bry shouted, Cups! Cups fer nightcaps! Yous'll be sharin, cus Ah've three fuckin cups in the world. Eggy, pass us them cups, and Eggy turned from Arthur and reached up ter stop the light-shade by clappin his two hands around the yeller paper globe.

In the steadied light, I could see Arthur starin inter his glistenin palm as he flexed the mouth of the cut oppen and shut. Me skin prickled and me gorge rose, but he was smilin.

Then Eggy shoved past us, ducked inter the wee kitchen that was cramped inter the room along with the bed and a wardrobe, and kem out with three mugs hooked through the handles on his big farmer's finger. Just then there was a KNOCK KNOCK KNOCK on the door at me back.

Who's this? Bry hissed, and we were all five of us frozzen. Who did yer ask, Dan?

Nee one, said Dan Reid, and rose up tall off the spindly chair he'd tekkan ter as soon as he'd counted us in and ran his thumbs round his waistband and straightened the bull's head on his belt, palmin flat his copper hair.

Fuckin geddit then, Eggy. Yer nearest. What're they gonna dee, like? said Bry, and Eggy with his frown fulla freckles, as if his face were med of the brown speckled shell of a hen's egg, budged us outta the way and lifted the sneck on the bothy door.

OH FUCKIN HELL, they all roared, IT'S PEEKO! and Eggy dragged the stranger in a headlock inter the light, knucklin the crown of his head as he kem.

I looked sideways twards Arthur, who was windin bogroll round and round his hand, grinnin like the rest of em.

Where yer bin, Peeko? growled Bry.

Eggy had forgotten Arthur and had a mug in one hand and the whisky bottle tilted ter it. Peeko was blinkin in the light, a lad who looked even younger than me and Arthur, his eyes squeezed inter a squashed-lookin face, and his brown hands, chubby as a baby's, stickin outta the sleeves of an oily denim jacket.

Roond aboot, he squeaked, his voice like balloons rubbin together.

Roond aboot, eh? said Eggy.

Sniffin aboot, said Bry.

Sniffin a lady's shoe, said Dan Reid. That'd be right, ey, Peeko? and he slugged from the mug Eggy'd passed him ovver me head, and then pushed it twards me and said, Get that down yer, and I swallered the fumes from the bottom of the mug and couldn't stop me face wringin itsel out.

Aw, he's got smokes! cried Eggy. He's flush. Cmon, Peeko, do the decent and splash em roond. And Peeko threw Eggy a fag from the twenny pack he'd pulled out of his jacket, and then plucked two more and stuck em out twards Dan Reid. Eggy laid a flame ter the one in Peeko's mouth as Dan took one from the two Peeko had stuck out at him and flung it at Bry's feet. Bry got down and ratched fer it and blew the dust from it as he fetched it up off the floor. There was nowt offered ter Arthur and me.

The bothy got bluer and bluer with Regal smoke. So, boys, said Dan Reid, turnin his grey eyes on us, bleak as bad weather. What were yer doin ter come ter this, like?

Dan was doin nowt ter notice Peeko any more than he noticed the draught liftin the rug I was stood on before the bothy door. He waved his fag-tip at Arthur. Him with his hand oppened up an all.

Oh fuck, aye, said Eggy, and he was up ter the sink again, his big raw hand on Arthur's shoulder. Ah'm in the middle of the Red Cross here.

Yer sposed ter be tucked up in bed, said Peeko, two streams of smoke pourin outta his nostrils.

Shut the fuck up, Peeko, or we'll be mekkin yer drink piss again.

Aye, and not yer own this time, hooted Eggy.

Dan Reid nodded at us. Speak up, lad.

We were pissed—

Yer were? Peeko widened his eyes in his puffy face. Big men. But yer look like girls now. Big fuckin girls, he said and then looked round, inter each of the farmlad's faces one affter the other, waitin ter get agreed with.

Eggy stepped back from the sink and said, Peeko, man, Ah've warned yer, like, and smacked the back of Peeko's head so his fag popped outta his mouth and onter the deck.

That's me fuckin floor, Peeko! said Bry, and ground the butt to an ash smear with his boot heel. Look what yer've fuckin done!

Oh, Peeko, yer've done it now, said Eggy softly. Yer fer the chop, and he clipped Peeko another round the head. There was nowt in Peeko's face but stoniness, never mind his fat cheeks, and his eyes lost in the soft meat of em. He was summit stubborn. He was what yer might stub yer toe on, I reckoned from where I was stood, a dumb stony thing, but glintin with meanness.

Cmon, son, Eggy said, with his arm round Peeko.

Aye, added Bry, liftin himsel onter his feet, we'll not be long.

Where we gan? said Peeko.

Just out the door, lad. Nowt ter be worried aboot, said Eggy. Then the big lads were bundlin Peeko inter the fresh air and the dark.

Not you, snapped Dan, and Arthur stopped where he was, halfway ter the door, the twist of a grin left in his face.

Let us look affter that new box of fags, Peeko, while we're at it, like, said Eggy, as he pulled the door shut affter them.

So yous were pissed, said Dan Reid in the sudden smoky quiet.

Aye, said Arthur, an I fell on a brokken bottle.

Dan Reid got up, strode ovver ter Arthur, took his wrapped hand in his own and started ter unwrap it. I could see Arthur colourin at the closeness of Dan Reid, and at Dan's hoddin of Arthur's hand.

It's nowt, said Arthur, shruggin one shoulder.

It's deep, said Dan. Yer not gonna be explainin this away. Eggy's done his best, like, but yer'll want stitched up Ah reckon. Gan on, tek a pew. Arthur sat on the empty narrer bed, re-wrappin his hand.

Dan sat back down in his chair, took up his mug and said, Where're yer gonna gan tonight?

We divn't know.

Yer a bit fucked, then. There was a deeper silence while Dan Reid sucked at the last of his fag and ground it inter a saucer. He was cradlin his mug like a mug of tea.

Aye, said Arthur, as the door fell in again with a rush of cold and the lads trooped in. Eggy took ter his chair, and Bry budged Arthur up on the narrer bed, and held a fag out ter everyone, me and Arthur included. Then he looked fer the bottle, found it and hoddin it up ter the light, sloshed the whisky about inside.

Plenty yet, he said.

Why don't yous kip in the loft? said Dan.

Aye, cus there's nee one kippin here. And that gans fer you lot in all, said Bry, stabbin his finger around the room. He put his forehead in his palm and started ter drag the dark curls in his fringe straight, ovver and ovver again. Ah reckon Ah've had it now lads, he said, blowin out a huge sigh. That's it. Give us me bed back, you. He shooed Arthur up onter his feet and lay down gently, his boots stickin out off the end.

Right, said Dan Reid, and dusted off his hands and stood up, tekkin the mug off Eggy once Eggy'd emptied it inter his gob, then rinsin it in the wee sink. Bry started ter snore. Dan Reid oppened the bothy door and held it oppen. Don't just stand there, he growled at us, cus I was lookin worriedly from the dark doorway ter Arthur's face. He didn't meet me eyes. With a fixed-on cocksure smirk, he ducked through. The sky above the farmyard was purply black. Dan Reid flicked out the weakened yeller bothy light. Yer know where the loft is, he told Arthur.

What der we do with him, Dan? said Eggy, and pointed at a forklift in the corner of the yard with a shape hangin off its lifted prongs. Peeko gev a wee kick of his stubby legs in the air. He had his arms trussed ter his sides, and started ter shout through the rag he had gaggin his mouth.

Ah've got it, said Eggy. Turn the tap, will yer, lad?

I looked about, along the length of the black hose Eggy had picked up, and then trotted ter the pipe stickin up where it was fixed. I turned the tap and heard the watter shootin through the loops where they lay. Eggy pointed the nozzle at Peeko where he swung, shoutin through the gag. The jet fired suddenly, and Peeko was spun this way and that as the watter caught and lost him, and Eggy pointed the nozzle left and right, up and down, inter Peeko's hair so it was furiously blown, and inter his fat face so the force of the watter dented it.

Yer sad wank, said Eggy.

Yer dirty dwarf, said Dan.

Me and Arthur watched as the farmlads called out. Everythin was gan slow. The birds had started up round about us, singin at the wrong speed. I felt like I was gonna puke. The watter dashed off Peeko, onter the concrete yard, and he was humphin and um-ummin through the rag in his gob, and the worst thing was that I wasn't sorry fer him one bit. I hated the little shit, like yer hate bad luck, though there's nowt yer can do about luck – no taps yer can turn ter turn bad luck ter good. Yer just curse it, the way the farmlads were cursin Peeko where he swung. And then in the corner of me eye Arthur moved, and before I could turn he'd slipped around the jet of watter and had kicked the shape, jerkin in the blast, dancin back as the watter slashed and sprayed. Then he was gan in again, hoofin the shape like yer'd try ter kick a door down, Peeko wormin round on his rope, tryin blindly ter wriggle away from the next blow.

Panic shot through us. Before I knew what I was doin, I was twistin the tap closed, and the jet had stopped. The hose died and went limp and dribbly in Eggy's hand. Peeko was twirlin there, drippin, and Arthur was breathin hard in the silence. Eggy threw down the hose, went ovver and climbed the forklift. He slipped a lock-knife from his back pocket, unlocked the blade and sawed at the twine till Peeko dropped with a wet slap ter the concrete. A bag of guts, I thought, as he flopped and struggled ter get up. Then Eggy took him under the arms, as I'd tekkan Arthur earlier, and lifted him up, as if he was nowt but an unstuffed teddy bear, plonked him onter his feet and softly said, We'll get yer yam, ey?

With an arm around him, Eggy started ter walk Peeko ter the gate of the yard, and Dan Reid follered in his boots and checkered shirt and belt with its bull's head buckle, not once lookin back at Arthur and me. I'd gone ovver ter Arthur. Watter was runnin round his feet in dark trails.

Are yer okay? I said. How's the hand?

Numb.

Yer tired?

Aye. We'll hit the hay, said Arthur, and laffed a laff, empty as an old tin. I said nowt, cus I didn't have owt ter say, and we turned fer the hayloft.

Yer'd think a hayloft'd be soft, softer than yer own bed, but it wasn't. The haydust got up our noses, but Arthur and me just clambered up the wall of bales, Arthur pullin himsel up by his good hand. The bales were hard and tied tight around with twine, but when we med it inter the roof-space, where all the heat of the day and the dark was held, we just lay down right at the back, outta sight, where the light was already needlin through the wee piercins in the corrugated roof, and ignorin the sharp straws that poked and scratched, and not carin what might come in the mornin when we saw the cut, we fell asleep.

SIX

Now I'm outta range of me house, I fish me fagbox outta me pocket. Fags hod their position in the box when yer've only smoked one or two, so the pack's still like new – still packed in. But I shek me box and hear em rattlin about in there, tellin us that I'm down ter a measly one or two. There's a trick that I do with mesel every time, which is ter buy a new pack and tell mesel that I'll actually smoke less. I say, Well, I've got em, all ten, so there's no need ter be tappin any from anyone else, and if I've ten, then I can be less greedy, I can keep a neat pack by not smokin many. And buyin a new pack's really better than not, even better for us. But I never trick mesel fer long. Cus what do I do? I smoke em, don't I. It's not as if yer buy a lovely new pack of ten and then keep it new ferever in yer inner pocket, is it? Yer buy a pack and smoke it down ter the lonely last one that yer end up grateful fer findin cus yer thought the box was empty cus the one fag's rattled slantwise in the box and med yer think there was nowt there, and yer smoke that one cus it's a bonus and then yer back to wantin a new box of ten from behind the papershop counter where they're all built so neat inter their wall of boxes and flavours and tens and twenny packs and slabs of two hundreds that the old smokers with their ashy hair and Maggie handbags buy like clockwork.

I tek me second-last fag, slot it between me lips and fire it up with Arthur's Zippo. I let the flame stand fer a few seconds. It's a realer-seemin flame than a flame from a Clipper, mebbe cus yer can smell the petrol and see the wick the flame's fixed ter. I snap it shut, then flip the lid back up, just ter mek sure it's out, then snap it shut again. I tek a big drag.

There're kids playin streets away, but their high voices sound as if they're comin from inside summit. I tek a couple more drags and flick the diff inter the road. It sits on the tarmac, smokin a wisp of smoke that gans straight up, cus there's nee breeze. I wipe me sweaty palms on me jeans, then gan up ter the gate and lean ovver it ter lift the latch and push it oppen. I gan up the front path and knock the knocker above the letterbox. The door oppens.

Yes? says Gillian's mam, dryin her hands on her stripy apron. Her glasses're propped above her forehead, in her hair. She's squintin at us, flour in her eyebrows.

Is Gillian in?

I'll give her a shout. Gill's mam leaves us on the step and gans ter the bottom of the stairs and shouts, Gill! There's someone at the door fer yer! I can see inter the hall, like the hall in me own house, but with sky-blue paper. I wouldn't know, shouts up Gill's mam. She turns and oppens the door wider on us. Who are yer?

Chris, Mrs Ross. We're at school, Gillian and me. She turns inter the hall again and rests her floury hand on the wooden ball on the banister post ter shout.

Gill! It's Chris, ere at the door fer yer! There's a wee pause and I peer in at the mirror on the wall and the knitted straw cross hung beside it. I don't know, she hollers up. She turns ter us and rolls her eyes. Why don't yer come down ere and ask him yerself, and save yer own poor mother her breath? Mrs Ross rubs the back of her neck, where her apron's knotted. Me neck's brekkin ere, Gill, so get down! Or he'll be away!

I can hear the radio from somewhere in the house, carryin on from where I left it with me own mam in her kitchen.

> *We don't have ter tek our* – dum-dum – *clothes off* – dum – *ter have a good time, oh no.*

Soon it'll be the charts, like a ladder countin yer down forty rungs till yer neatly at Monday again. That's how Sundays gan, and all change on Monday, except nowt's changed but the order of the records. I don't do music, me, but I can't get the songs outta me head when I hear em on the school bus, half asleep in the mornin. That's how songs work, I reckon, stickin in yer head till yer might as well give in and buy the record, just so yer not worryin that yer've summit in yer head that yer can't get out again. At least if yer buy the record and play it non-stop then yer've got a reason why the song's rollin round and round in there, and yer don't have ter think it's yer own mind that's tekkan it in and it's hooked there, ingrown and unforgettable. I won't buy em. Not the ones with words in, anyhow. Yer can't imagine yer own pictures ter them, cus there's someone chunterin their own life ovver the tune, and it's never like yer own life, never like the city on a Sunday or like the things I've bin thinkin about in me own room, the black print lurkin in the paper under me bed, and Booby's voice sayin, *Aye man, Arthur and Gill in the cemetery.*

What d'yer want?

Uh.

Did yer want us?

Gill. Yeah. We gan ter the same school. It's Chris.

So?

I just wanted ter talk ter yer. And I do but I've bin caught again, smack in the chops, starin off down the road when I should have bin watchin Gillian Ross come downstairs in her rainbow socks and black leggins.

Well talk, then. Gill crosses her arms and leans against the doorframe. She crosses her legs in all, so one socked foot's up on its toes. Her throat looks long and clean, stretchin out of her pink roll-neck. She's got her eyes narrered at us, like her mam, but her eyebrows're so blonde they're like nowt above her eyes. I see Mrs Ross, ovver Gill's shoulder, checkin on us with a peep outta the kitchen and then pullin her head back in. I can smell a roast dinner roastin.

We gan ter the same school.

Yeah. Yer've said already.

I'm a mate of Arthur's.

Arthur who?

Arthur. Yer know. Arthur.

Say Arthur all yer want but I still wouldn't know who yer were on about.

Arthur Grieve.

Gill puts both her hands on her hips.

Never heard of him. D'yer wanna listen ter last week's charts? I'm mekkin a tape and it's not gettin made while I'm stood here gassin ter you.

No, yer alright thanks.

What else're yer doin?

I dunno.

Come on, then, and she's turned and is away up the stairs, leavin us at the door.

I can't just walk away, can I? But ter walk inter Gillian Ross's house, and then up the stairs ter – ter where? ter Gillian Ross's room? – is madness, like. I look ter me left, at the curve of St John's Close, at the cars sparklin at the kerb, and then look ter me right, up the slope ter the end of the close where the cemetery's set, hidden there behind the hedge. The Black Hole. I'm thinkin there'd be no gettin away from him if he found out I'd bin here. He's two years above us at school affter all, and tomorrer we'll be packed together inter the same narrer place, and there'll be nowt I can do ter save mesel if he thinks I've bin sniffin round his girlfriend.

I tek a step inter the hall and push the front door shut at me back. I heel off me trainers on the mat. A stranger's house puts yer off balance, as if yer in danger every step of brekkin summit. But I'm walkin upstairs now, wonderin if Gill's mam's happy ter have us in Gill's room, me bein a lad an all. So I'm steppin quiet as I can in me socked feet, guilty on every side, and I feel like me head's stickin outta the winder of a train flyin along and there're so many things that might knock it clean off.

At the toppa the stairs there's nee sign of Gill and four closed doors. I'm guessin they're four doors like the four at the toppa the stairs in me own house, a bathroom behind one and bedrooms behind the others. I wouldn't know if there's a Mr Ross, so he could be lyin behind one of these doors, and I've no wish ter walk in on him, in me socked feet, with me stranger's face, gurnin away. I gan ter the first, then the next, puttin me ear each time ter the door, me fingers spidered on the doorframe. I figure that I'll hear the songs that Gill's so keen ter be recordin. But all I can hear is the radio downstairs in Mrs Ross's kitchen. In a stranger's house, yer could walk in on anythin, and be seen yersel, seein it.

What're yer doin?

Gill. I was tryin ter find yer.

Well yer could knock, she says from the doorway opposite, her arms crossed.

I didn't know where yer room was.

But yer looked like yer were listenin in. What were yer listenin fer?

Fer the tape yer mekkin.

Yer weren't gonna hear it with yer ear ter the bathroom door.

I didn't know.

What if I'd bin in there? Were yer tryin ter hear us on the toilet?

No, Gill. Honestly.

What if me mam was in there?

She's in the kitchen, isn't she?

Yer'd've heard me mam on the toilet.

But she's downstairs

Nobody wants ter be heard on the toilet, Christopher. She says this in a louder voice, half-lookin ovver the banister, twards the downstairs.

Shush! I just wanted ter speak ter yer. I didn't wanna hear anyone on the toilet.

I'll let yer listen if yer want, she whispers. I need ter gan right now. And she pushes past so I can smell Gill Ross, a breeze of freshness, shampoo and Lénor Springtime, waftin at us off her jumper. She bangs shut the bathroom door and I hear the lock scrape and snick. I don't wanna be listenin ter Gillian Ross havin a pee, but I reckon Gill's countin on us not listenin. People sometimes say yer can do summit and what they really mean is that yer can't. If Gillian Ross comes out the bathroom ter find us still stood with me ear ter the door, I reckon she'll be none too happy. It's like a dare, her darin us ter be stood here, and she's doin it ter see if I'm alright, ter see that I'm not the kind of lad who stands outside bathrooms while girls pee. I reckon this up pretty quick and head through Gillian Ross's bedroom door.

Here's Gillian Ross's bedroom.

A tightly-tucked-in, narrer flowery bed under the winder.

A wardrobe – shut.

A desk which has bottles and cottonwool balls and suchlike all ovver it, and a mirror fer hoddin Gillian Ross's face as she meks it up.

Me own face slides inter the glass and it's as if the glass itsel doesn't recognise me face and throws it back at us like someone else's. I guess it's cus I've surprised mesel by bein stood where I am.

Tom Cruise gives it some cheese from a poster on the wall above the bed. Music's rushin outta the radio where it sits on the floor, its black flex curled like a tail and plugged in somewhere outta sight. I don't see any photos of the Black Hole.

Yer'd think I'd be feelin the same as if I was in me own sister's room, which would be nowt, cus me sister's room has nowt I've ever bin interested in, just her soft cloth animals, her Care Bear and her clothes, which're nee use ter me and I wouldn't wanna think about. I've never a reason ter be in there, so if I've found mesel in there – ter ratch a pink rubber out of her pencil case or ter tek her a cuppa tea if me dad's med us do it – I hardly look at owt. But in Gillian Ross's room I wanna look hard at everythin. I'm wonderin where ter put mesel in all. The bed's med, so I can't sit there, but ter plonk meself down on the carpet seems stupid. So I'm just stood like a lemon in the middle of Gillian Ross's room, listenin ter the bathroom lock get scraped back and the door oppen with a rush of the toilet's flushin, suddenly louder. And in a rush I'm thinkin that Gillian Ross's fresh smell of shampoo and washin liquid is bound ter be trapped under the rosy duvet on the bed and ter be folded inter whatever clothes there are hangin in the wardrobe and laid in the drawers.

Her bare feet've walked fer sure on the floor where I'm stood.

The whole room's fulla stuff that's bin close ter Gillian Ross's naked body.

The mirror's probly even held that body in it, even though it just stands here, now this minute on Gillian Ross's table, cold and not bothered.

I spose this is what yer do when they go on about yer invadin someone's privacy. Yer do it most of all in yer head, and then how can yer stop it happenin ovver and ovver again? *We don't have ter tek our* – dum-dum – *clothes off* and I'm off, thinkin about Gillian Ross without her clothes on, or of all the clothes that get close ter Gillian Ross, her knickers in all.

Yer didn't listen. I thought yer wanted ter listen ter us, says Gill Ross as she shuts her bedroom door behind her. This is a shock, like. What? she says.

D'yer think yer should shut the door?

Why not?

I know there's not an answer ter this, so I shrug.

Are yer scared ter be shut in with me?

No. I just dunno why yer'd wanna shut it. That's all.

It's my door and I'll shut it when I want. She spins past us where I stand and falls back onter the bed, pulls her legs up so her socked feet are underneath her, and stretches her sweater ovver her knees. Sit down, then. Not there, she says, as I drop ter the floor. Here, and she pats the edge of the bed beside her.

That insecty bitta 'The Sun Always Shines on TV' is on the tape player. There're no insects in it, but it sounds like insects gan mad. Why yer'd want a record of insects gan mad I wouldn't know, and now the chorus is happenin again and the words in it mek no sense in all. In the programmes on telly the sun isn't always shinin, and it sounds like summit yer'd only say if yer were too clever fer yer own good, so clever yer end up sayin nowt. There're already too many things in the world there aren't words fer, but I'm tryin ter think of a word fer what Gill Ross has us caught in. It's not as if I can say no ter sittin beside her on her bed, cus ter say no will look like I think she's gonna kiss us or summit, and ter admit that I'm thinkin that would give her the chance ter tell us that she'd never dream of kissin us and that I fancy meself. But ter sit on Gill Ross's bed, with Gill Ross's crossed leg nearly touchin me own knee, would be ter gan along with summit without even knowin what that summit is. I lift meself up – me ankles click – and perch on the edge of her bed.

Me eyes're on the front of Gill's sweater, and her necklace, which is so skinny it looks like a trickle of silver runnin around her throat and down inside her sweater.

Don't look so worried, she says, and suddenly she's got us grabbed round me neck and me face is pressed right inter her, right against her hot neck. Me own breath comes blowin back ter us warm off Gill's skin. Me head's hurtin now, as if everythin that's tangled up in there has gone hard and scoury.

I'm not worried, I say from in close ter Gill's neck. She swallers and I feel the jerk of it in her throat. I'm lookin hard at Gill's skin and her necklace and at the edge of her sweater, at the wee stitches of pink thread in the pink material, which look enormous from where I'm cuddled. Cus that's where I realise I am, fer sure. I'm gettin cuddled by Gillian Ross. Once I've thought this, I can't get it outta me head. Gill swallers again. Now I can't stop wonderin how far down inside her sweater me own breath might be gan when I breathe out. What if it's gan down inter the gap between her tits, a warm tickle of it, and she can feel it fer sure? If she can feel it and I know she can, but neither of us is sayin so, how can I get her ter admit it? I shift me legs, but not too much, cus I'm worried that me boner'll jab Gill even more obviously if I move. As if I've swooped outta me own body, I see us locked together, Gill in her pink sweater and me leant against her. What if Gill is likin the feel of me breath slippin down inside her sweater and the feel of me boner against her? She might even wanna see it. But she can't just ask us, just like I can't ask her, so we're both locked together, Gill with me warm breath tricklin down inter her bra and me with me boner, which is stuck between us like a hot stick pulled out of a fire that I'm jugglin in me lap cus it's too hot ter be comfortably held.

Well, we can't sit here all day, much as I'd like ter, she says, her voice suddenly loud in me ear and vibratin all through her skin. She strokes the back of me head, just a wee stroke so I reckon I might have imagined it, but a stroke fer sure.

Would yer? I say inter Gill's neck, but I can hardly get any sound out cus me tongue's gone claggy in me gob, like summit dropped on the deck and kicked about in the dust. I'm hopin she's gonna tell us that she can feel me hard-on against her leg and wants ter see it, I'm hopin but I'm nearly sick with the fear of it in all.

What I'd like ter do is ask Gill Ross what we're really doin, me and her. But Gill Ross has told us I could listen ter her as she peed, and I didn't, and now she's got us held against her and me tongue's turned ter scrap. There's nee word fer this kind of move, like, and really people never talk about what's in front of em. So it pops inter me head ter ask Gill Ross straight out.

Did yer shag Arthur in the cemetery?

In a flash, Gill's shoved us away and her legs've straightened out from under her.

Yer what?

I just heard that's what happened. That's why I wanted ter talk ter yer.

Cus yer thought yer'd tek us fer a walk in the cemetery in all?

No.

And who told yer that anyway?

Booby Grove.

Oh, right. She bounces up off the bed and is peerin inter one blue eye, close up, in the mirror. I slide me hands inter me pockets fer somewhere ter put em. Gill's stretchin her face by pullin her top lip under her top teeth and raisin her golden eyebrows. With one finger she pokes the white of each rolled eye, as if each eye's not quite sittin right. She does it just as if she was touchin summit that wasn't herself, like a light-switch or a smear on a winder. I find meself without thinkin puttin me own fingertip ter the curve of me own wet eyeball.

Booby would say that. Just cus I live near the graveyard, they'd all have us carryin on in there at night. They wish, like.

So yer never did?

Do I look like a girl who carries on in graveyards? Gillian Ross says, straightenin up from eyein her own eyes in the mirror and plantin her hands on her hips. I'm reckonin that some people might say yes ter this, but I reckon it would be the wrong answer fer sure.

No yer don't, Gill. But it's just what I'd heard. And I'm lookin fer Arthur. He was in the paper yesterday cus he's gone missin, so I thought I'd ask yer.

Well, there yer have it, Miss Marple. A dead end here, like. Gill falls back onter the bed, bouncin us so hard I grab the edge with both hands. Where d'yer think he is, then, this Arthur feller?

The thing is I've not thought about where he might be. Me sister told us on Friday that someone had called round fer us.

Who?

They didn't say.

Was it Arthur? I said, cus I hadn't sin or heard from him fer nearly a week.

I dunno.

Yer dunno?

Me sister sighed, as if I was the heaviest chore of her whole hot day.

I can't remember what yer *one* friend looks like, can I? She put her hand across her mouth suddenly. He had wellies on, though, she said through her fingers, her eyes laffin at us. I tried ter remember if I'd sin Arthur in wellies, and couldn't.

On Monday I start the Third Year, so I'll be halfway through the years, halfway through school – older now than the whole two years below, but with the Fourth and Fifth Years above. Arthur'll be startin the Third Year in all, when he turns up. Yesterday, when I rang her, Arthur's mam hadn't sin Arthur fer two days, not since Thursday, and now it's

Sunday. Three full days now and nee one's had hide nor hair of him.

When did yer last see him, then? asks Gill, crossin her arms and leanin back on the windersill above her bed.

Last weekend. In town.

Well, was he alright? Did he not say owt?

About you?

No, silly, not about me. I told yer, didn't I? Gill says, swattin us on the thigh. He wouldn't say anythin about me, would he? I'm lookin at her, tryin ter work out if she's askin us a question or not. Arthur didn't say owt about Gillian Ross last weekend, but then I never had a reason ter ask him.

SEVEN

Last Saturday I had a strange feelin, like I didn't know what ter do with me hands, like I was almost feelin sorry ter not be at school. But I wasn't sorry. I knew I couldn't be missin school. Not that. But I couldn't lie with me face in me piller anymore. I had nee patience with bein flat, with me blood roastin me cheek under me face no matter which way I turned, so I had ter sit up.

When I wafted the duvet ter clear out all me banked-away heat from sleepin, me own smell beat us about the face – the smell of me skin and the smell of the places where I was folded and no air had got ter and the fart I'd farted five minutes before that had bin stashed there and rode out fresh on the draught.

Chris, why don't yer do somethin with the day? That's what me mam says, as if she thinks I can roll the day up and tek it somewhere and put it ter some use. The thing is, I reckon she's right, and I often wanna get summit done, but I just forget that I'll feel better if I do, so I lie around imaginin that lyin around is what I wanna be doin. I reckon imaginin is sometimes even riskier than actually knowin. And that was that. I'd suddenly had enough of lyin around. I wanted up and away. I wanted ter do summit with the day.

I pulled on me jeans. I balled me pyjamas up and threw em onter me bed. I ratched a clean pair of socks outta me drawers and podded em out of their knot and yanked em up me ankles. It was nigh on eleven o'clock. I went downstairs and med toast, four slices, with butter. Me mam was out the back, peggin clothes on the clothesline. I stood watchin her from the kitchen winder, her bendin ter the clothes basket and shekkin a shirt out and pinnin it up, reachin fer the pegs down the front of her pinny where she keeps em in a pouch like a kangaroo's. She looked round and up at the sky, a frown scuddin ovver her face. I could see she didn't know I was watchin her, cus her face showed nowt but what she was on with. The whirligig squeaked round. I wondered what she was thinkin on her own out there, without knowin I was watchin – her unwatched thoughts, different ter the ones she'd be thinkin if she saw us at the winder. It med us wanna duck down under the sink so she wouldn't stop thinkin em. So I did. I squatted there a minute till she kem pushin in the back door too soon and I jumped as if I'd bin caught, with a last corner of toast halfway ter me mouth. She jumped in all.

Oh, Chris! What yer doin?

Nothin.

It doesn't look like nothin. Then she said, no kiddin, Why don't yer tek yerself away and do somethin with the day?

Like what?

Oh, I don't know, she said, hoddin the placky clothes basket on her hip. Just get out. While it's nice. Here, she said, budgin the basket onter the worktop and grabbin up her purse from its spot beside the tin of teabags. Me mam's purse is like a brown bread roll, fulla cards and crispy receipts. She popped the popper between the two halves of cracked leather and unzipped the wee pocket of change. With two fingers she fished about and counted us out two pun. Go on. Give yer mother a chance ter get on.

Thanks, I said, surprised like, and headed fer the door. I was thinkin that I'd better get gan before she changed her mind or asked us ter do summit fer the money, like hoover the stairs. I'd stepped onter the back step before I realised I was still in me socked feet. I had ter gan back in fer me trainers and me jacket.

What? said me mam when I pushed back through the back door. What d'yer want now?

Me trainers. I forgot me trainers.

Oh fer God's sake, Chris, she said, as if I'd robbed some-one, as if I'd brokken the law. She was stood at the sink where I'd stood ter watch her hang out the washin, not doin owt that I could see. I wondered then if she was workin out that I'd bin stood watchin her, and I gotta rush of heat ter me gills. Chop chop, me mam said. Yer can go out the front and leave me be. That's all I ask. ALL I ASK.

I couldn't work me mam out. I tried ter as I walked inter town. It was a fair old walk, along stretches of pavement that were fulla the sun, the heat of it comin up through the soles of me trainers. There was nowt special about the pavement that day, just the pavin slabs set together and some of em cracked like eggs and the odd turd laid sweatin on its own flat stone or smeared a distance by a shoe. It wasn't as if I was that much in me mam's way, was it? But mebbe just ter know she was bein watched was enough ter set her off. Mebbe that's enough ter set anybody off.

I walked along. That's what I'd done most days of the holiday – just roved around – but I knew if I went inter town that day I'd see someone, cus town's where everyone gans on a Saturday. The traffic was rollin in the distance. I walked past the houses and the closes. At the corner of Ridley Road and Millholme Avenue I went inter the paper shop and bought ten Regal, a bag of Hula Hoops and a can of Pepsi from the cold cabinet.

The day was so bright it was like gan inter the dark when I went in the ringin door and when I stepped back out it was inter the opposite, and I couldn't see owt fer the glare.

I slotted the Regals inter me inside jacket pocket. I knew they'd sit there while I pretended ter know they weren't there, even while pretendin ter know they weren't there was knowin they were all along. With the Pepsi under me arm I popped the Hula Hoops, then pulled oppen the Pepsi. Smoke smoked a bit from the slot. I could hear the stuff tinglin against the walls of the can.

There's a magic combination ter Pepsi and Hula Hoops when yer mix em together in yer mouth. Yer tek mebbe two hoops and don't crunch em. Yer just let em sit in yer mouth while the salt dissolves on yer tongue. Then yer tek a swig of Pepsi and hod it in yer gob with the hoops, so the Pepsi softens em up. Soon they collapse, the hoops, and yer imagine they're bits of pipe, like the bits of pipe ovver the road on the buildin site, waitin ter be hidden away under the houses, and yer mek em crumble away in yer gob and then wash em away down the tunnels of yer insides.

I walked on, feedin meself hoops like rings off me fingers

and swiggin from the cold can. It's about eight minutes, I reckon, from the paper shop, past the York School playin fields on Boundary Road and the King George, ter the Five Road Ends and ovver St Nicholas Bridge onter Botchergate. I stopped on the bridge ter look ovver at the green stuff growin down below and ter stand me Pepsi can on the pavement, line me foot up and stamp it completely flat.

There're two arcades on Botchergate, a posher one on the corner of William Street called Eldorado, where there's nowt but fruities, and Talky, right beside Danny's Discount Shop. Yer can't see inter either of em, cus the winders're blacked out. I walked inter Talky, cus it's the first one yer get ter if yer walkin up Botch. I was wonderin who was in, but I wanted ter have a gan on 'Grand Prix' in all. The place was fulla old air, as if Friday night was still hangin about, still hidin away in the dim. I went up ter the booth fer change and brok a pun. The lady behind the glass pushed a wee silver tower of ten Ps back ter us through the hatch. Then she reached up with both hands and pulled the topknot of her hair, one clump left and the other right, ter tighten it. She had towers of coppers, fiftys, tens and new yeller pounds, all stacked up in front of her. She didn't say owt. The coins smelled like a rusty city stream.

I strolled round the machines, the fruities with their ladders of lights and wheels all flashin, and listened ter the arcade's blips and tootles, the chatter of machines, all tryin ter speak ter us, all with summit important ter say. There was the *chugger-chugger-chugger* of a bandit payin out. There were lads I didn't know, two of em in one corner, the one with his arm ovver the top of a cabinet, peerin, while the other stood like a gunslinger pushin the buttons. Another lad was gan from machine ter machine down the rows, palmin the coin trays and pokin inter the wee coin traps with their swingin metal doors, checkin for forgotten coins. There's no law against that, I was thinkin, and I've checked the trays meself. But I knew right then he'd be trouble, so I took mesel out inter the sun on Botchergate, cus I wasn't gonna hang about anymore in Talky, what with that lad lurkin about in there like a veiny old leaf trodden in off the street, there ter mek me skin shrink tighter ter us. I thought about gan ter the flicks ter get inter the quiet and the dark, but I'd seen *Teen Wolf*, about the lad who's a werewolf, and didn't fancy it much a second time round.

So I went up the road, catchin me own reflection in the winders as I passed, gan around a girl with a pushchair, carrier bags hangin off either handle, and between big geezers, their arms swingin out and their chests packed tight inter their T-shirts. Me reflection slid with us, ovver the winder of the baker's where the gingerbread men lay in trays, and I caught a glimpse of the baker spinnin a loaf in a paper bag by the ears and passin it ovver the counter.

It was when I pushed in the door of Eldorado that I found Arthur. I stood blinkin fer a minute in the doorway, while me eyes did their adjustin again, and as the place hatched outta the dark I spotted him at a machine, the only person in the place and a relief ter see. I sloped straight ovver.

Alright, Mister Grieve!

Arthur gev a wee start.

Oh man. Yer nearly med us hit the roof! I'm jumpin outta me fuckin skin here.

What yer doin? I asked him, cus I was pleased ter see him, pleased ter be out of Talky, pleased enough ter forget the mornin and start the day ovver on a firmer footin, with me mate beside us.

Nowt, he said, and sure enough there was no money in the machine and it looked as if he'd just bin stood watchin the lights snake ovver the face of it. The feller behind the glass in the change booth had his socked feet up on the counter and his hands behind his head, just his socked feet and elbers pokin up above the high wooden counter.

Shall we mek a move, then?

Mek a move?

Aye. Get outta here. Yer not playin, are yer? Let's gan ter the park, I said, only findin I wanted ter gan ter the park when the words were outta me mouth.

The park? said Arthur.

Aye. Bitts Park. Let's gan down and see what's what. Arthur gev us one of his long greasy looks, his gob hangin oppen, playin dumb just so I seemed the dumber. I wouldn't be put off, though. Cmon, I said.

Nah. I can't be arsed.

There's nowt doin here, is there? Yer've no money. I bet yer, I said. Arthur rolled the lit end of his sucked-flat fag in the battered silver fag tray next ter the machine, kinda sharpenin up the tip of it before he levered it up ter his lips and took another draw. His eyes looked red raw. He was squintin ovver me shoulder at the door.

There's nowt down there.

Aye, I know that, I said, but summit was already naggin faintly in me head, the way a moon's sometimes there all day in the blue sky, but turned out. Let's just gan and see who's on the swings, I said, and winked at him, and he wobbled his eyebrows at us, cus seein who was on the swings was really seein if the skirts of any lasses on the swings were gonna get whipped up as they swung, and cus they'd be hoddin onter the chains of the swings, they'd be helpless ter wrestle their skirts back down. Me and Arthur had sat on the roundabout opposite the swings in Bitts Park before and watched fer the different colours of knickers.

Not today, ey.

Just fer summit ter do, Art, that's all, I said, and I was mebbe bouncin on me heels, cus I was happy ter find Arthur, and Saturday was suddenly pannin out better than it had bin and I couldn't keep hod of any one way ter feel anyhow. So I was bouncin like me mam says, bright as a button. Mebbe Arthur wasn't lookin so keen, but I don't reckon I noticed, fer all me bouncin. I remember the feller behind the change counter had a hole in his sock where his yeller big toe poked out.

But when yer think back, yer never remember what yer need ter remember very clearly. Arthur was Arthur, and I was naggin him ter come with us ter the park, and some ghost of an idea was just gettin snagged like fluff onter the inside of me head.

Why d'yer wanna gan, though?

I dunno, I said vaguely, bouncin on me heels, cus me and

Arthur never normally needed a reason between us ter do owt. I stopped bouncin. It hasn't rained fer ages. It'll be dead dry fer sittin out, I said. Cmon, Art. I med me thumbs hook inter imaginary braces and flapped me elbers and mebbe I even did a wee dance on the fag butt he'd thrown down at last.

Gotta fag?

Yer've just had one, I said, but I brok one out fer him, out of me fresh packet, and he lit it himsel with a silver Zippo from his jeans. I could smell the petrol off the Zippo's wick as he lit mine in all and then snapped the lid ovver the lazy flame and stowed it back in his pocket.

When did yer get that bitta kit? I asked, and sucked on me fag and felt the ball of smoke in me gob before I took it down inter us.

What? he said, lookin at the door.

The Zippo.

Oh aye, he said, and patted his jeans pocket and didn't look at us. D'yer like it? he said.

He kept on starin away at the door as he dropped the silver Zippo inter me hand.

It's a fair old weight, I said as I hefted the thing. Feels nice, like.

Oh, aye. A nice bitta bullion.

I flipped the lid and thumbed the big wheel, the sparks flashin from it with a gratin of the metal on the flint, and the wick hoddin a steady flame tall all of a sudden. Then I snapped the flame back inter the heavy silver case. The case was smooth, not a mark on it, a slab of silver with me face showin shrunk there when I peered down inter it.

How d'yer know it's not alight when yer shut it?

What yer on about?

When yer shut it up. How d'yer know the wick's not still alight, like?

Yer a one, you are, a worrier and no mistake. He was lookin at us now, with a smile on his narrer face. Yer think they mek it so it stays alight in yer pocket, yer rivet?

It's not so stupid, like.

Oh no, it's not so stupid, he said, and laffed, his whole face drawn wicked and long with the lafter. Stick it away in yer pocket. I med ter hand it back ter him. No. In yer pocket. Keep it. Just mek sure yer pocket's not afire.

He laffed again and I said, I can't tek it, Arthur.

Course yer can. Get it in there, he said, and flapped oppen me bomber jacket and slipped the Zippo down inter me inside pocket, next ter me fags, and zipped us up so the collar was up too high around me chin and I had ter unzip it straightaway, like I had ter do when me mam still zipped us up ter gan out inter the cold.

I can't, I said, and stuck me hand down inter me pocket and closed it round the Zippo. I'm not tekkin it.

Yer are. Arthur put his hands up and backed away so as not ter tek it off us when I held it out ter him. I tried ter lunge at him and stick it in one of his jacket pockets, but he shoved his hands in and tightened his coat around himsel and kept just steppin away from us, as if I had the lurgy.

I'll just put it here then, I said, and reached up ter leave the Zippo on toppa the cabinet of the bandit. Someone'll have it if yer don't tek it back.

Yer havin it, Chris. Stop fuckin about, he said, but I was at the door with me fingers in the wire mesh ovver the winder, ready ter leave him and the Zippo there.

I'll tek it if yer'll come ter the park with us, I said, feelin the cleverest by far. That's the deal, like. Fair's fair.

Arthur stood lookin at us, then reached up fer the Zippo and tossed it to us where I stood. I caught it and stowed it in me jacket. Cmon then, I said, and pulled the door in so the bright day fell through it and I blinked, and together we headed out.

EIGHT

It took us ten minutes ter get ter Bitts Park. We carried on up Botchergate, then ovver the road and through the sandstone city gate past the courts, through the middle of town, past the Civic Centre, a proper skyscraper with its winders snap-pin away in the sunlight, and down the subway where our footsteps suddenly echoed with us as we walked, inter the sunken middle of Hardwick Circus, where there's a fountain that never spurts in a blue fountain bed. Sure enough the grey watter was oozin thickly out, as if the fountain-head was blocked, inter the basin that turns it a false bright blue only cus the tiles're blue, and Arthur scooped a palmful of the watter at us from the basin as we took the first subway of three subways that each led somewhere different, and it seemed our footsteps caught us up again and walked a step behind us down the tunnel with the leafy green light in its mouth that led us down and inter Bitts Park.

Arthur dragged his heels, but I ran straightaway down the slope, off the cinder path, cus there's nowt like bein run faster than yer can run by the steepness of a soft grassy slope, yer teeth gettin chattered in yer head by the unwillin speed of yer legs, and then the flat ground comin up ter meet yer again and yer findin yer breath and yer legs again under the great rhododendron at the bottom.

There's a queer difference between Bitts Park and the

Arches. There's a statue of Queen Victoria fer starters, med of black metal, stood on her own set of stone steps. There're flowers in flowerbeds and the grass is neater than grass elsewhere. Cus the park's sunk in a bowl below the traffic, which all goes high ovver the river on the Eden Bridge, there's a quiet ter the place that's like the quiet yer get in graveyards. But yer never think yer walkin ovver anyone in Bitts Park. Me and Arthur wandered about, ovver the grass and up the slope on the other side and under the corridor of trees that hung ovver the path beside the river.

Yer never far from a river round here, or just a wee stream, but some bitta watter anyhow that's pushin somewhere, even if I wouldn't know where it was pushin ter. The watter in the River Eden stirred thickly as it ran on, as if summit under the surface was shoulderin through every once in a while but never comin up fer air. And there was muddy hair at the edge, clarty and fulla twigs and tins and yeller foam. I was stridin, watchin the yeller foam wobble in the shallers, when I realised Arthur wasn't follerin us. He'd gone the opposite way, and then I heard him yellin from through the trees.

CHRI-IS! CHRI-IS!

The sun was mekkin the path scaly with light as it got tipped and canted about among the leaves above me head. I jogged back down the corridor of trees and across the soft grass. Arthur was on Victoria's steps.

There yer are, he said, even though he'd bin the one who'd gone walkabout. Show us again, will yer?

Come on, Art. I've shown yer a hundred times.

Well, just show us once more.

It's easy.

Aye. So yer say. So it's easy fer yer ter show us again. He was marchin round and round underneath Victoria, who was stood high up in her folds of metal, hoddin a big metal stick with a cross on and a metal ball with a wee angel balanced right on it, with black metal wing-feathers in all. The queen's black face was lookin sad and armoured smooth, and cus I was right underneath, I could see right up the sockets of her nose. She was like an engine when I looked at her and med mesel forget she was a queen – a perfect engine stalled right there, med of parts and nee oil ter get her parts movin again.

Is it here? Arthur asked, from off ter one side of her, his hand shadin his eyes.

Nah.

Here, then.

Nah.

Here?

Nah. It's here, I said, tekkin pity on him. Yer stand here, I said, sayin the words like a joke or a magic spell, and yer can see Queen Victoria's big old bell-end.

Arthur shouldered us outta the way and squinted himsel. He stood fer a long moment so I took a look round, across the lawns at the red castle on its hill and at the plank benches sat sittin one affter the other beside the path, and the trees with a current in their top branches like the river's current, though I could hardly feel any breath of a breeze on me own face.

Ha! Yer fuckin right.

Aye, course I am.

Yer spot on. Look! She's got a cock, a proper cock.

I know, I said, scuffin the edge of the step with me trainer sole. Arthur was lookin fixedly at Victoria, as if this was mekkin his day, mekkin his week even. He was flittin from angle ter angle, lookin at her again from the front, the big stick with a cross on top cradled in her one arm, the ball gettin trod by the angel in the other, and the stick stickin out, if yer looked at her from the side, right where yer'd expect it to if she had a cock and it was hangin out.

They must have known. How could they not know? It's a cock with a proper cock-tip and everythin. And it's there, right where it should be, said Arthur. Yer can't tell me they never knew.

It's true. Yer can gan and have a look yerself. If yer were drawin a cartoon cock it would look the same as hers does, but Arthur'd seen it plenty of times.

Yer think it's revenge? he asked.

Revenge? Revenge fer what?

Yer know what revenge is, yer dipshit, he said, and I snapped me face twards him, cus his voice had a sharper edge than it should've had. But he just went on.

When yer born, like, yer don't have any choice in it, do yer? And yer get whatever's left fer yer by everyone else who's already bin and gone. Revenge is what old people have on young people. That's revenge in the long term, like.

He banged one of the metal plates set in each of the four faces of Victoria's column with the flat of his hand, COMMERCE it said, with a few lads frozen there in Roman clothes, and it med a hollowish *bong*.

This has ter be revenge in all, Arthur said. There yer are, some bod who meks statues, havin ter turn out another statue of the fuckin queen, and yer've sin yersel who gets put up, haven't yer?

Who gets put up?

Aye. Who gets ter stand with a face like fat fer years in a park. It's always the same lot, the queens and the fellers with moustaches who spend their time up there lookin out ovver the rest of us. Well, yer'd do it, wouldn't yer? Yer'd get yer own back. Yer'd let us all see that when yer stand in a certain spot they're all the fuckin same as us. That's revenge on anyone who tries ter say otherwise.

Cmon, Art. Yer sound like a teacher, like fuckin Cannon-ball-nostrils in History.

Aye, but yer'd never know from Cannonball that they all had arses and wiped em. Arthur stood with his hands on his hips, starin up. He didn't look like he was gonna move an inch. He looked like he was hoddin onter Victoria fer dear life with his eyes.

Aye, but what if it's just us? I said.

Yer what?

What if it's just us that can see it? Whoever med it might never have seen that she'd have a cock, might they? It might be just us, just our minds.

Oh, cmon, man!

Well, it's true, isn't it? Yer dunno what they were or weren't thinkin.

Yer as bad as the rest of em. They gev her a fuckin cock and that's the end of it. We see it. They would've. That's that.

There's not much arguin with Arthur, not fer me anyhow. Some people yer just don't argue with, d'yer? Mebbe cus there's summit more important than bein right or wrong, which is just ter be knockin about. And I figured that if I argued with him we wouldn't end up doin what I wanted ter be doin, which was findin where that tramp had just got burnt.

NINE

I led the way, away from Victoria, back along the corridor of trees, and the sun went in as we walked so the light wasn't gettin coined on the path by the leaves anymore.

Where're yer tekkin us? said Arthur, catchin us up.

We're gonna find where that tramp got burnt.

Yer what?

Yeah. Yer know. Last week, affter yer got back off yer holidays, that tramp that got burnt down here. We're gonna find the spot, cus it must be still here, musn't it? It's bin on the news and everythin.

No, said Arthur, and stopped.

Yer what? I said, stoppin in all.

I mean yer can't, can yer?

Why not?

There'll be nowt ter see.

Aye there will. Just like affter Bonfire Night. There'll be the patch, won't there?

Cmon, Chris. Don't be a reckoner, like, pretendin yer gonna get close ter a thing, just cus yer scuff a bitta black earth with yer toe.

I'm not, am I? I just wanna see what's left ovver. There's no reckonin to it, and I dunno why yer mekkin out there is, I said, cus I didn't know. As far as I was concerned, I just wanted ter check the place, cus yer hear about plenty of stuff gan on, don't yer, but how d'yer know it really gans on if yer haven't seen the spot fer yersel if yer can? It'd bin on the boards outside the paper shops and all ovver *Border News.* I'd wondered ter mesel if I'd ever seen the feller, cus *he was well known in the Carlisle area* they'd said on telly, which meant he was a regular nutter.

Arthur jumped up ter grab a leaf hangin off an ovver-hangin branch. He started ter tear it inter pieces along its folds.

Are yer comin, then, or what?

Aye, whatever, Arthur said, and dawdled affter us. Then he stopped ter point out a splash in the river that might've bin a fish jumpin. Then he tried ter get us talkin about the arcades, as if I might forget what we were on with and just drift outta Bitts Park and up inter town again. Then he dawdled a bit more. But I was led by summit strange in us and we found it, a patch of black ground like the mark of a campfire, but bigger.

It was off the path and ovver squidgey ground that our feet sunk inter as we got closer ter the river. Big leaves like rhubarb leaves flapped at our knees, them leaves that hod perfect drops of watter, like blobs of glass in their creases, even if it hasn't rained, blobs that yer brek when yer brushin through em so they gan ter liquid again and run away off the leaves' edges and soak yer kegs. I was thinkin that I'd hear the river in all as we got down ter it. But yer don't hear a river if there're nee rocks fer it ter run ovver or get squeezed between, and the river was just hissin along with nowt in its way, fast and quiet and brown. The Eden Bridge was high up ter the right of us, so the cars and lorries were gan rumblin ovver above us, and the arches of the bridge were above us in all, the bricks all damp green and hidden from whoever it was who was gan ovver the bridge. One minute Arthur was complainin about the wetness soakin inter his trainers and the next we were both stopped dead by the sight of the blackenin, there in a clearin where all the leaves and stalks had bin trampled down and a bitta yeller tape was flappin from a tree trunk.

D'yer reckon that's it?

I dunno, says Arthur.

I looked at him and he was rubbin his left arm with his right hand, up and down, up and down, as if he'd got a dead arm and was rubbin the life back inter it.

I told yer we'd find it.

Aye, well, yer've found it now, so we can gan.

Hod on, I said, and I remember feelin giddy, as if I was close ter the heat itsel, even though there was no heat left and nowt ter say what kinda heat it had bin. I stepped up close to the ring of black, so I was right on the edge where some leaves were lyin, half of them burnt away and half of em still brown and mulchy.

Chris, said Arthur, cmon.

What? I stopped and looked at him. He hadn't moved and kept flickin his face left and right, throwin the odd look ovver his shoulder. D'yer think it looks like the shape of a body?

I don't fuckin know, he said.

We're not doin owt, are we? I said, ter reassure him. I

grabbed a leaf-stalk and stripped away the big leaf so it was just a green stick in me hand. Then I poked inter the cinders with it. I heard Arthur suck air through his teeth. I poked through bitsa burnt wood and scorched green glass lyin there.

I'm gonna have a whiff, I said then, and dropped down onter me haunches. Me ankles clicked.

Chris, said Arthur, louder then, with a crack in his voice that med us look round at him again.

What?

Fuckin leave it, will yer?

I mebbe just grinned at him. That's mebbe what got him mad. I grinned at him cus I was enjoyin havin him try ter stop us. It'd bin the other way round often enough, and I was likin the feelin that I was gonna do summit that Arthur was scared ter do, cus that was how he looked – white and knotty and scared in the face.

I turned back, leant me palms outside the patch and lowered me face right down ter an inch above the scorchedness, and sniffed.

I could mostly smell the greenery, a layer of it close ter the ground, from the leaves and the river, which was there in the earth. But I could smell ashes in all, the smell of summit burnt, but burnt out and wet, like a coal in the rain. And I was thinkin all the while that someone had died on that spot, that I was close ter summit. Then suddenly I felt a hand on the back of me head and me face went right inter the ground, right inter the soot and ashes, and got held there as I twisted.

Me eyes wobbled, I don't mind tellin yer, as if they were

gonna dish big tears. I knuckled em clear as I stumbled back along the bank, batterin through the leaves, them leaves each hoardin their own drop of glass, with the sound of Arthur trampin behind. Back along the path I nashed, under the trees and down the tunnel of the subway ter the fountain, where I stuck me face in the blue watter and shook it about, then swished it back out and felt me cheeks and forehead and nose with me fingers, felt em fer the bitsa green glass I thought were stuck in em. Then I spat at the thought that the ash had got onter me lips and inter me mouth, that I'd swallered a bitta the burntness that was a bitta the tramp's fuckin skin or beard or burnt-up hair.

Arthur kem through the tunnel as I was wipin me hands on me jeans.

Well yer said yer wanted ter find it.

What d'yer do that fer? I shouted at him, shoutin partly cus I was so mad ter have nearly balled.

Yer wanted ter get up close, Arthur said. He'd stopped a good few feet away from us.

Yer fucker! I shouted.

Less of that language, young man, said a voice, and there was a woman just poppin outta the tunnel that led off the Eden Bridge. She was draggin a wheely case behind her as she marched up ter us. What would your mother say? She was shekkin a short, rolled-up umbrella. Me and Arthur just gawped at her. Well? she said as she got right up ter us. I'm waiting for an answer from you. She glared at the both of us, but mainly at me, from under her see-through placky bonnet.

What? I said, stupidly.

What do you mean what? You open your mouth and filth falls out of it. She shook her brolly a bit more. Don't you dare walk away from me, she shrieked, cus Arthur had just turned and started ter walk inter the subway mouth.

Cmon, he called ter us. I looked at the biddy, who was just darin us ter do the same.

What's she gonna do? Arthur called from in the echoey tunnel.

Sorry, I said ter her, sorry mostly cus it was difficult fer us ter edge along the rim of the fountain and leave her stood there, difficult ter ease mesel out from under her look and away from her brolly. Hod on, I called out ter Arthur's back. I could hear the biddy shoutin, Young man! Young man! till the traffic round the roundabout above us swallered the wobbly sound of her all up. I spat again as I caught Arthur up cus the thought of the blackness in me mouth had come swingin back through me mind.

Yer fucker, I said.

Aye, well, what's she gonna do?

No! Fer shovin me face in the fire.

Arthur just shrugged and kept on walkin, up past the Civic Centre with all its cloudy winders, up Scotch Street where there were people facin us as we went, and on through the middle of town onter English Street, where the smell of coffee from Watt's scarved around under me nose and I was grateful fer its spicyness as we passed the turn onter Bank Street. I was sure I had a different look from everyone else, that me face was sooty fer a start, and that what I'd had me face close ter was showin through fer everyone ter see and know. But I looked at Arthur as we went and he just looked at us and said, What? so I figured me face wasn't lettin owt on ter anyone else.

We crossed the road at Woolies and went through the wee door on Devonshire Street, then climbed the stairs ter the top floor and pushed through the door ter the snooker club. Arthur went up ter the counter and bought us each a can of Coke. Then me and him crossed the wide wooden floor, cus there're only two snooker tables in the snooker club and an echoey wooden emptiness ter the rest of the hall. We took a pew under one of the tall blacked-out winders. In the quiet of us havin stopped walkin ovver the boards I could hear the clack of the balls and then the balls swishin and bumpin along the cushions, cus there was a game on, but hardly anyone in the place, just like always. Me and Arthur pulled the tabs on our cans, and Arthur took a long pull on his. I could hear the stuff gan sizzlin down his throat. Then he blew out, then breathed in again, then burped and right on the end of the burp said, Sorry.

I sniggered with me mouth fulla Coke so it fizzed right down the inside of me nose, then we watched some feller in the shadders round the table lean inter the light ter cue.

I'm gan ter the bog.

Arthur got up and stalked off across the boards, and I sat there under the winder where here and there the black paint had bin scraped off the panes and cracks of daylight were burnin. Not cracks I could've put me eye ter and sin out of, but fierce scratchins and splintery bits of light. I was desperate fer a piss in all, but I couldn't gan till Arthur had got back. I took a sip of me Coke but it tasted rusty, like a nose-bleed.

The town winds down when there's still plentya light. That's what I like about the summer. Me and Arthur knocked about in the gloom of the snooker hall till the late affternoon. Arthur went out and got us chips and gravy when we got starvin, and then we kem down the stairs and inter the sun at closin time. The light was a shock and there were a few people about on the way ter the bus station, kinda dawdlin cus the sun was still hittin the shop winders and the sky was blue, but lasses with handbags and coats were comin outta shop doors, and whoever it was who had ter lock up was lockin up behind em and turnin off the lights. There was a hollerness ter the town that was like the hollerness of the snooker hall, med bigger. A feller was whistlin from round a corner and down a street, way off, but his whistle was easy ter hear, and the city felt like it was breathin easy, with a good bitta heat left in the pavements and the bricks and a few hours ter waste, all locked up. We sat on a bench in the bus station, waitin fer Arthur's bus. There were pigeons like fat soldiers wobblin up and down on the pavement, even one old pigeon with a limp. They weren't bothered about the people stood about at the stops, or about me and Arthur perched there.

Yer won't tell anyone, will yer?

Tell em what?

Tell em what I did ter yer?

I scuffed me foot on the tarmac, which had a coat of dust mekkin it faded-lookin and worn on its crackled top.

Why would I?

I dunno. Yer'll do owt, you.

It fuckin hurt in all.

Yer should've sin the look on yer face when that biddy was ravin.

Yer shouldn't've done it, should yer?

Yer shouldn't've bin lookin fer it.

Here's yer bus.

Arthur got up so his shadder fell ovver us.

See yer.

Aye. See yer, I said.

Then Arthur went ovver ter the bus where it was parked and I stood up as he went. Yer can't wash it off either, he called out from behind the wee line of people climbin up inter the bus, then he took a step himsel up inter the cab, then popped his head back out and beckoned us ovver. Yer won't tell, will yer?

No, I told him, and watched as he paid and piled down inside the bus, and the bus shuddered inter gear and began ter slide out backwards. I nodded ter Arthur in the winder, cus if I'd have waved I'd've had someone else on the bus thinkin I was wavin at them and mebbe even wavin back, and Arthur nodded ter us and then looked forward as the bus started forward and swung outta the station and was gone down the road, swingin round the corner and away.

And that's it. I went home and had some tea. I mebbe

didn't gan straight home, like. I mebbe had a mooch about till the town started on with its Saturday night, when the same lot that had bin workin or shoppin in the town all day rolled back inter different parts of town, past all the parts that were locked up, ter parts that'd only just oppened up. I mebbe did that, sat havin a fag on the war memorial, flippin the lid of Arthur's Zippo and watchin the people as they started ter come back in. I mebbe waited in town ter see if I heard sirens firin up. I mebbe took a wander back down ter the mouth of the subway, but nee further, just ter see if there was owt gan on down there in the dark. But there wasn't, and that was the last time I saw Arthur.

TEN

D'yer wanna cuppa tea? Gill says.

Have yer got coffee?

Might have, she says, and bounces up from the mirror and out of her bedroom door and I hear her gan gallumpin downstairs. I get up on the bed and plant meself unsteadily on me knees at the windersill. I look down at the Ross's drive and the rest of the close. There's a funny, flattened quiet ter the road and dusty hedges. A trail of sudsy dark's gan down the road beside the kerb ter the drain, and I put me face right against the chilly winder and squint up the road ter see some feller tossin a bucket of watter ovver the roof of his car and the watter explodin in a feathery sparkle. The radio's just buzzin like it's got flies trapped behind the speaker's silver mesh, cus Gill turned it right down ter listen ter us, and I only remember it's on now there's nowt else ter hear and me mind's hoverin here in Gill Ross's house.

Last Saturday I saw Arthur, and sniffed the black patch. Yesterday Arthur was in the paper. If Arthur's bin three nights away from his own bed, then where's he bin sleepin? He'd have ter have money in all, fer food, and he'd be wantin ter change his clothes, or at least change his socks if he'd bin on the go. Me feet're jigglin with the thought of it, cus I'm thinkin about summit that I can hardly put me mind ter, cus me mind's hoverin so light. But me feet're jigglin alright and the feller up the road's tekkin a rag ter the long bonnet and bodywork of his green Capri, buffin away. Yer'll rub it out, I whisper to mesel as I lean me forehead on the cold winder glass and see the Black Hole walkin up the close, on this side of the road, the zips on his jacket sleeves glintin, his hair bleached up in frosted spikes.

He's throwin a look up ter Gill Ross's winder where me face must be moonin out and mouthin away at him, and he just looks and keeps walkin till he's past, and I'm not hoverin anymore. I'm rooted right inter me body which is wound tight around us, stuck here in the winder, me body like a tree and all me muscles turned ter ivy.

D'yer want sugar? I've given yer two anyways. And I was thinkin that he must've gone somewhere he knows, musn't he?

Yer what?

Yer mate. Arthur, says Gill, pushin the door to again with her foot. He won't've gone somewhere he doesn't know, will he? Yer wouldn't, would yer? Yer'd be hidin away somewhere yer'd already checked out. He wouldn't've just gone on the wander without knowin where he was gan. Ere. Well tek it, then. Don't just be gawpin out there. Gill's stood, stickin the mug of coffee twards us.

I've just seen fuckin Carl, haven't I.

Carl who?

Carl yer boyfriend.

Did he see yer?

He looked straight up here.

Well yer had yer face there, full in me winder, so he

must've seen it, yer jowie, and he's not me boyfriend, Gill says.

He would've seen us, then?

Oh, shut it, will yer.

I thought yer were his girlfriend.

That's what he says, and there's nowt much I can do about what he says, is there?

Gill tilts her face and bats her eyes at us, darin us ter answer.

Yer can't just say yer someone's boyfriend. He just says he's yer boyfriend and that meks it true? It seems so silly and so simple at the same time that I nearly laff as I say it.

Well, it's not true, is it? Cus he isn't.

It's just about true. Everyone gans about as if it is true, so it mostly is, I reckon. If it's just you who says it isn't, yer about the only one.

Just cus everyone says it, doesn't mek it true.

Carl must reckon it is, and I'm not arguin with him, like. Except he's just fuckin seen us here, I say, realisin it all ovver again with a rush of the heebies across me ribs. So I'm gonna be arguin it out with him tomorrer most likely, when I don't have any fuckin choice.

Keep yer voice down. If me mam hears yer swearin she'll have yer out faster than yer can think. And that'll be so much faster than you can think, yer cabbage. And yer helpin us with me History if she asks.

I'm shit at History.

She doesn't know that. Drink yer coffee and then we'll gan.

Gan where?

Out, she says, and teks a sip from her mug. Shall I get yer a bicky? We've got a whole bag of misshapes downstairs. All sorts.

I'm alright, I say, and I tek a sip of me coffee, and see me own half-crossed eyes reflected in the brown surface. It steams inter me face, and I get reminded that I'm alive. I'm alive but the Black Hole's gonna kill us, whether Gill Ross thinks she gans out with him or not, and there're parts of me own body I know nowt about, mostly the bits inside that I'll never see, and me body's fulla nerves like lightnin, strikin from me fingers back down me arms and inter me guts, ovver and ovver again. Mebbe this is what gans on in yer head when yer've eaten the ash of a burnt-up body.

Gill's balanced with her tea held in one hand while she bends down ter pull first one heel then the other inter each of her black plimsols. Yer not thinkin about Carl are yer? Cus he's not me boyfriend.

No, I say.

But I am. I'm thinkin about the Black Hole and the tramp both. I'm thinkin that I feel different since Arthur ground me face inter that black patch. Me skin's tighter, as if everythin inside us is closer ter the surface and threatenin ter spread out of us, like ketchup from one of them wee plastic packets yer get with yer chips. As if I'm not movin but smearin about the place. Even a cup feels different in me hands. I'm hoddin the mug out, as if I'm silently askin Gill ter top it up, but I'm just lookin at me hands as if they're not mine and I wanna see me own look pass ovver Gill's face, and then be certain we're seein the world the same way.

As if she can read me mind, Gill rolls her eyes at us and says, Oh, don't mek out yer anythin special, Christopher. She crouches again ter peer inter the mirror. She pulls at her jumper where it's gripped ter her shoulders and lifts her chin ter stretch her neck and looks at hersel as if she's just caught hersel lookin and turns her full self side-on. She's so busy doin this, me heat-filled face has time ter cool down again.

Right-o, Gill says, and pulls a wee handbag from the bottom of her wardrobe and slings it ovver her shoulder. I'm ready.

I foller Gill Ross downstairs and she calls, See yer later! And her mam shouts from the kitchen, Don't forget yer babysittin! as Gill shoves us outta the front door.

Who yer babysittin fer? I ask as Gill stands and unsnaps her wee bag and looks down inter it, then snaps it shut again, as if whatever should be there is there.

Me big sister and Mal Sharkey, her cruddy boyfriend. They've got a kid, so I'm an auntie, if yer must know, she says as she leads us out the gate and left up the close. There's a helicopter choppin the air some way away, but it fades ter where I can't be sure if I can still hear it, or if I can just remember what it sounded like, and then it's gone. We gan past the gleamy washed Capri stood in its patch of hosed dark tarmac, and I step off the kerb and fall in beside Gill.

We're not gan affter Carl, are we? I mean we're not. We're definitely not. Yer can forget it.

Gill sighs. Where d'yer wanna go? If yer could gan anywhere at all.

Cus this is the way he kem, Gill, I say, but Gill's snickin oppen the gate ter an earthy path at the end of the close that's leadin away left between a high wooden fence with leafy branches pushin through it and a hedge that's growin ovver from the other side, so it's like a shady corridor and smells clammy, with just a hinta dogshit.

If it was anywhere at all, it'd have ter be hot. With a beach. Like Spain, but not Spain, cus I've bin there. Have yer bin? she asks and turns ter us, and the shadiness is slidin ovver her angly face and I catch her silver necklace glint before she turns back ter the path again, which has led us up ter another gate. Through this one there's a great lumpy stretch of grassy dry wasteland with the behinds of the houses just ovver ter our left and the ovverhead lines of the railway loopin away ter our right.

I've bin and it was fulla fat men from ovver here and wimmin with their bits out. Yer'd probly love it. If yer like yer knockers ter the knees. D'yer? I bet yer wouldn't be able ter keep yer eyes in yer head, yer little perv. Gill shifts the strap of her handbag up her shoulder, just the same way I've seen me own mam do it, then snicks oppen this next gate. Yer know what they call these, don't yer? she says, hangin onter the gate so it's shut on us and she's lookin ovver the rusty top bar of it straight inter me face. It's a kissin gate.

Oh. Right.

Yer supposed ter give us a kiss ter come through, like yer supposed ter mek a wish on a star.

I don't think it is one, I say. It's metal fer a start. All the proper ones are wooden, aren't they?

What difference does that mek?

It's not old enough ter be a proper one. It'd have ter be old and in the country or somewhere, but not here, like.

Your loss. I wouldn't have said it'd mek much difference, but yer obviously an expert, she says, and rolls her lips in thin and then out again, looks at her nails, and then turns and sets off across the grass leavin us ter push through the gate and let it *gong* behind us. It's queer how yer get out from under the roof of a house and stuff changes. I spose it just does, doesn't it? There's nee one ter ovverhear her so Gill's mebbe just a bit more of what she was in her own house. But I'm not trustin her one bit, fer all her witter about kissin gates.

Come on, slow coach, she says.

I'm tekkin a good look round fer any sign of Carl, aren't I?

He won't do owt ter yer, yer know, not if I'm with yer.

I say nowt and keep walkin, the smell of hot grass, seeds and dust in me nostrils. I kick the head off a hairy old nettle. We gan down close ter the railway tracks and I knock a bumblebee away from me head so Gill grabs us squealin and starts ter stamp and hoy her arms about like a proper girl. The tracks're shiverin in the heat, wriggly as summit silver and alive.

Oh no.

What? I say, cus I was miles away, gan north on a train, before Gill's voice brought us back onter me tiptoes, ready ter do a runner, cus there's a figure that I'd not spotted mekkin his way twards us across the grass, determined-like.

Don't say owt ter him.

Ter who? Who is it?

Let me do the talkin, says Gill, and puts her hand fer a second on me shoulder.

And don't whatever yer do ask him about his sword. She turns and starts ter mek her way across ter meet em, whoever they are. I tek one more look round, twards the gate and the earthy path that I can't see anymore cus the ground's hummocked. I look at the backs of the houses and at the ovverhead lines that I can hear purrin away, then I pitch affter Gill, cus if it's Carl, I'm thinkin, it'll only be puttin off what's surely gonna come on the morrow.

ELEVEN

I see pretty quick that it's not the Black Hole cus this feller's wearin a white get-up that's fairly blindin in the sun. Gill's got ter him and is chattin away when I catch up.

This is Michael, she says ter us. She's got her arm stuck through his. He nods at us, very serious, like, with his mouth turned down. He's wearin a padded white pyjama jacket tied at his waist with string. Michael's trainin out here, aren't yer Michael?

Trainin fer what? I ask neither of em in particular. Under me jacket, I can feel me T-shirt stickin ter me shoulderblades in a map of sweat.

Just trainin, says Michael, and crosses his arms, never mind Gill's arm, which gets trapped against his chest. Then I see the handle of the sword at his waist, and it's a fuckin samurai sword, the handle braided with strips of some leathery stuff and the scabbard hangin there off the string tied round his pyjama jacket. He's wearin slippers in all, just slippers like yer get at Marks and Sparks with an oldie pattern on em. I look Gill in the face and she flashes us a wee grin as if ter say, *Yeah – what of it?*

I look back at Michael. Nice sword, I say. Give us a look. Gill's frownin now and rolls her eyes at us. Michael plants his feet apart and drops his left hand ter rest on the hilt of the sword. Gill gets her arm back and stands with her hands on her hips, shekkin her head. I see the back of Michael's hand is all cracked and rough-lookin, the knuckles crazed with white, unhealed splits.

It must draw blood if it's drawn, he says.

Yer what?

I must honour the blade if I'm ter tek it out of its scabbard. Yer should never tek it out fer no reason. It's dishonourable ter draw it fer nowt. So I'd have ter cut yer with it.

Michael stares at us with his mouth turned down again. I realise that he's just keepin his mouth turned down cus he reckons it meks him look like Bruce Lee, or Grasshopper off *Kung Fu*.

I could just hod it as it is.

Yer could, says Michael, and his eyes shift about sideyways as he thinks about it. Then he reaches right around himsel and drops on one knee with the sword held out flat ter us with his head bowed. There's a tassle swingin off the handle. The scabbard's glossy, polished like the leg of an old wooden chair. I reach out and tek it with both hands, the handle in one and the scabbard in the other. It's heavier than I think it's gonna be as I turn it about, and it nearly hums, the way the ovverhead line above the railway track hums, cus there's summit dangerous runnin through em both.

I thought it was fake, I say, and I gan ter oppen it by pullin the scabbard away from the metal guard, but Michael steps forward and clamps his hand around the gap that's oppened up, where I can just see the glint of the blade, and I have ter let go.

It's not fake, he says. Look at the skin on the tsuka. It's stingray. He hods the handle out fer us ter look at the criss-cross leathery stuff.

Stingray? says Gill, peerin hersel at the handle. Yer tellin me it's a fish's skin? Michael just looks at her with his most serious ninja look.

That's a blade tested on dead bodies, he says. On dead bodies or criminals. I give a wee shudder at this and hope he doesn't notice. They'd cut em up bit by bit ter mek sure the blade wouldn't brek. So this has cut through real bodies, and through livin people in all.

Yer can cut me with it, says Gill suddenly.

Me and Michael look at her.

Yer said yer couldn't get it out unless yer cut someone with it. Well, yer can cut me. So come on. Get it out. Gill's lookin straight at me.

Are yer sure?

Yes, Michael. Or I wouldn't have said it, would I?

I look at Gill's face. She's stickin her chin out and there's a dare in her unblinkin eyes. I'm thinkin about Gill tellin us I could listen ter her pee and whether she meant that or not. Mebbe she would have said Michael could cut her even if she didn't mean it, or mebbe she really does mean everythin she says. But who ever means everythin they say?

Okay, Michael mutters, and whips the sword outta the scabbard with a sound that's half a swish and half a kind of ringin. Then we three just stand lookin at the blade.

It's not silver. It's got a silver edge, but the body of the blade's dark and swirly, as if there's blown smoke caught in it. I reach out ter it. Don't! Michael snaps. It's really sharp. He puts out his white-sleeved arm and lays the curve of the blade on it. I step up close and look down inter the metal.

Tempered steel. Japanese steel, mind, the real stuff. There's a soul there in the metal, says Michael quietly.

I peer at the pattern runnin along the edge, a pattern like ripples in oil that sparkles starrily, sparkles the way a pencil lead would if yer had yer eye right up close ter a newly sharpened one. They call that the hamon, he says. The metal was folded and folded, ovver and ovver again, and hammered out. That med it perfect. But it was too perfect, so the swordmaker had ter melt in old nails or buckles ter tek it back ter just less than perfect.

It looks like space, I say.

Well, it's carbon, isn't it? It's what we're med of, he says like a smartarse.

What d'yer mean there's a soul in it? Gill asks.

A samurai's soul'd be his sword, so he'd do owt ter get it back if he lost it. Otherwise he'd have nee soul.

So yer soul's in this one, then? I say. Michael acts as if he hasn't heard us, his mouth turned down. Come on. If yer a samurai then yer soul's in this one, isn't it? Yer may as well say if yer think it is.

Leave him alone.

Yer the one who's gettin cut.

Yer are, says Michael ter Gill. I've got it out now and yer said yer'd tek the cut.

I want him ter do it, says Gill, noddin her head at us. No

offence, Michael, but yer've got the eczema, haven't yer, and I don't want yer ter touch us. So give him the sword.

He's not gonna touch yer, Gill. He's just gonna cut yer with the sword. He doesn't have ter touch yer.

Still, she says. I want *you* ter do it. Give him the sword, Michael.

I'm realisin suddenly that I wanna see Gill get cut and I want Michael ter do it, cus it'd serve the two of em right, Michael fer tryin ter be summit he's not and Gill fer tryin ter have control ovver everythin. I wanna mek her tell us if she's shagged Arthur, and she hasn't told us, and now Michael's got the sword on his shoulder, like a soldier on parade with his rifle, the silver tip flashin in the sun. I cast about the place, seein the washin on a distant line flutterin brightly ovver the back fence of one house in the row and the trees packed greenly round the cemetery and the long, tinselly grass, so tired and dried-out now it's bin gettin long fer the whole summer. I'm not wantin anyone ter come ovver the grass and find us with a fuckin sword. Yer hear about it, don't yer? Yer hear about deadly weapons and I'm pretty sure it counts as a deadly weapon.

I don't have ter do it, says Michael. Yer don't have ter get cut, he tells Gill.

But I thought yer said it had ter be done? Yer said so, I say, half-desperate. Gill's mouthin summit at us, her mouth shocked oppen.

It doesn't have ter be Gill's blood, does it? I can find a cat or summit.

Yer've gotta be jokin! says Gill. I'm not lettin yer kill a cat, yer dirty bastard. Just give him the sword.

Michael teks the sword off his shoulder and stabs the point of it in the ground between us so it's stuck there, upright and wobblin, the tassle flickin about the handle.

If he wants ter, then he can, says Michael, and crosses his arms and stands there in his slippers.

Come on, then, Christopher. Where're yer gonna cut us?

I'm not gonna cut yer, Gill. It meks nee difference ter me if his sword's not happy, does it?

Yer the one who wanted ter see it, so it's only fair that yer do what yer sposed ter do. Isn't that right, Michael?

Michael says nowt.

Alright, I say, and I tek the sword by the handle and tug the blade outta the ground. I feel the grit in the earth skid against the blade, though it comes friskin out so easily, and I've got it, me two hands round the handle, heftin the weight of it. As Michael and Gill both step away, I sweep it through the air, turnin the blade so the edge of it is cuttin through, first ter me left and then ter me right. The air's like watter, I'm thinkin, and I can almost see the shapes of the slices I'm tekkin through it, the blade blurrin and the air swirlin away in perfect halves. I've got it gripped so tightly I can feel the singin of the blade through the handle. I swish it low through the stringy grass and the grass hardly catches the blade ter hod it back. Then I stop. I'm outta breath. I lean on the sword like a walkin stick. Where's it ter be, then, Gill? I gasp.

I think it should be yer arm. Just here, says Michael, pattin his forearm.

Shut yer mouth, you, she says. I want yer ter do it here.

Gill shrugs off her handbag, so it thuds inter the grass, and lifts her pink sweater up and points at her belly. Then she sits hersel down in the grass. I'll lie back and yer can pinch a bitta skin from me belly and just give it a little nick. She stretches hersel out with her arms coverin her face and her sweater pulled up ter her ribs so the white edge of her bra's showin. Come on, she says. Get on with it.

Gan on then, says Michael.

Still leanin on the sword, I squat down in the grass ovver Gill. Her belly's gan up and down as she breathes. I tek the sword and lay it ovver me thighs and look at the blade again with me own shadder thrown ovver it, at the wicked edge of it and the smoky metal that looks like it doesn't even need the light ter sparkle, as if it's an underground thing that would sparkle anyhow, even in the pitch dark. I pick off the bitsa earth left on the end of it with me thumbnail, keepin me thumb away from the cuttin edge. Then I put me hand ovver Gill's belly and I reckon I can feel a heat comin off her that's even hotter than the affternoon's heat. I look at the waistband of Gill's black leggins, where it's bitin inter the skin below her belly button, her skin that looks soft, as if it doesn't see the daylight much, and disappears inter her leggins, inter her knickers, and is all hers and a mystery that meks us look as if lookin can solve it. As I'm lookin she rubs her thighs together, up and down. I put me thumb ter the cuttin edge of the sword and draw it down the blade and feel nowt, even once I lift me thumb ter me eyes and there's a wee pause, as if the blood's mekkin its way there, before the cut grins oppen and blood starts ter pump out and run down me wrist and drip on Gill's bare stomach.

Oh! she screams, and twists hersel up so she's sittin and her arms're thrown out and her shoulders're thrown back, as if she's tryin ter be as far away from the splashes of blood there, bright on her skin. Oh! Oh! she says, hoddin the hem of her sweater up ter her chin. What d'yer do that for, yer fuckin gowk!

I didn't cut yer, I say, fallin back on me arse in the grass and hoddin me left thumb in me other hand and watchin the blood pump out. The sword slides off me knees inter the grass.

Are yer alright?

Aye, I'm alright, I tell Michael, still hypnotized almost by the sight of me own blood, which is so red, like red laquer, and comin out of us still, a surprise though I knew me blood was in us, a surprise cus of its redness and the amount that's slipped down between the fingers of me right hand and is even now tricklin down me left wrist ter drip onter a grass blade where it clings in a bead of darker and oilier red. I'm alive, I say ter meself.

I can see yer alive, says Michael, but are yer alright?

Never mind him! squeals Gill. Give us a tissue or summit, will yer? I've got his blood on us. Oh! Oh! she gans.

What? What? says Michael, still weighted ter the spot and rubbin his cracked knuckles, gentle-like.

It's gonna go in me belly button! she howls, and she's tearin up handfuls of grass and madly rubbin her belly with em. This seems ter uproot Michael and he drags a blue hankie out of his white kegs and squats ovver Gill. She snatches it away from him and mops her own belly with it. Me thumb begins ter hurt, the kind of stingin hurt that comes with a clean cut and is sure ter get worse. It's silly, but all of a sudden I wanna see me thumb with a hat on, a clean hat of white cloth that'll stop it bleedin and stop us havin ter sit hoddin onter it while the blood gans tacky between me fingers.

Michael steps ovver ter us, but it's just ter reach down and tek the sword outta the grass and guide it back inter its scabbard, which is a tricky operation by the look of it. He stands with the sword and the scabbard at arm's length from each other till he gets the tip lodged in the mouth of the scabbard and then hisses the whole length of the sword away, his hands meetin and the hilt lockin in with a *snick*. He hangs the sword back on his belt of string.

I'd wrap that in a dock leaf if I was you, he says ter us as he turns away.

Where yer gan? I say.

I'm gan home. Yer can keep the hankie, he tells Gill. I wouldn't wannit back anyhow, he says ovver his shoulder as he strides off across the grass.

I fuckin told yer, didn't I? What did I say?

How d'yer know him anyway?

I told yer not ter ask him about the sword, but what d'yer go and ask him about, straight off? Here, says Gill, on her feet. She tosses Michael's blue hankie ter flutter down inter me lap.

Ta, I say, and unstick me hand from the other, the blood

startin ter clot and gan claggy. I tek the hankie and bind it round me thumb.

I want a shower now, don't I?

D'yer?

I can still feel yer blood on us. Ugh! she says, and shivers and wipes her hands ovver her belly through her sweater and scoops up her handbag and fixes it again ter her shoulder like a big padlock. What d'yer go and do that for?

I wasn't gonna cut yer, was I?

Why not? I said yer could. But I didn't say yer could bleed all ovver us.

I say nowt and wipe the blood off me hands on the grass either side of us. I re-knot the hankie around me left thumb and clamber up ter me feet.

Look at yer. Yer look a right state. God knows what I must look like, Gill says, and runs the palm of her hand ovver her forehead and smooths back her hair. Cmon.

Where to?

Ter get yer cleaned up, yer dummy.

At yours?

Yer kiddin, aren't yer? If I dragged you home lookin like that me mam's eyes'd pop.

I'm not a dummy, yer know. I'm not and yer can stop tellin us I am, I say, and straightaway wish I hadn't, cus Gill just grabs us and settles her arm around me shoulders.

Yer not gonna bleed on us, are yer? she says, lettin go of us.

No, I say, and she grabs us again.

Poor Christopher. Yer not a dummy, but yer supposed ter tell us I look alright, aren't yer?

Am I?

Aye, course yer are. If I start gan on about how bad I'm lookin, yer sposed ter tek the hint and tell us I look like the best thing on two legs. That's all, she says, and gives us a squeeze.

Oh. Right. I look at me thumb and shrug a bit, and I feel Gill's arm drop away.

Oh fine, she says, and swats us across me back and strides off the same way Michael went, so I'm left ter jog affter her across the lumped and tufted grass, wonderin where we're gan and what I'm sposed ter do ter keep Gill Ross just halfway happy.

TWELVE

There's an expectedness ter the day now the sunlight's gettin feebler. Me and Gill skirt the garden fences that back onter the waste, steppin ovver a placky toy tractor and paint tins dribbled down with dry crusty colours and a burst black sack, all scobbed ovver the fence here and there. We gan inter the shadder of the fence, a shadder that seems ter swoop like a wing stretchin out ter chill us as I foller Gill's swingin pony-tail. The day'll end, that's what's so expected. The day'll end, then night'll come, and then tomorrer'll break fer sure. I can hear voices from behind the fences, the grizzlin of a babby, some woman sayin, If yer tek a piece by there that's it, some feller's voice drillin through the fence with an, Upupup yer silly! and a *crack* like the flat of summit plankish hittin a cement deck. We're like spies, the two of us, and the knot-holes in the wooden slats of the fence are starin at us from the shade in all. I'm thinkin about what yer never notice, like them in their backyards never noticin me and Gill, though we're sneakin along just a coupla feet away. I wanna shout, Look what can be runnin right past yer without yer even knowin! But I don't.

The fences curve round and me and Gill come under the cool of a few flaky city trees, their trunks grey, and hearts and cocks and names carved inter em, and a few yeller leaves ter crunch already under our feet. I squeeze the blue hankie round me thumb, and me thumb throbs, enormous and hidden. Where we gan, Gill? Gill turns ter look us up and down, then skidders down the ramp of earth where the tree roots are clutched like bare black knuckles. She comes out below us on the pavement again, stampin the earth off her plimsolls.

We're gan ter sort everythin out, aren't we, so we can start tomorrer nice and new and easier in ourselves. Cmon.

She sets off down the crescent. I've got me hand on the scarred bark of one of the trees, nowt but uneasy in meself, it has ter be said. A breeze gans through the toppa the tree and I feel the branches shift. I'm expectin the whole sad thing ter sway, but it's a solid pillar under me palm, rock solid. I clatter down the bank then, and comin out from under the trees and onter the pavement is like comin back ter where I'm always expected ter be, with the winders of the houses all gleggin at us and the pavement, where I'm always sposed ter be walkin, right under me feet. I can't help it, like, can't help kickin the pavement where it's laid so certainly, and feelin that I'm always better off when I'm walkin outta the way, somespot where I'm not expected ter be. Gill! Hod on, I holler, and I'm affter her, affter her pink jumper and her black legs.

She's at the end of the road already, the end of a close like St John's Close, and she stops at the kerb where I catch her up and we wait fer a car ter gan by, then trot ovver the road. We say nowt. The sky's lowerin above the locked-up pub, which is plonked on its own bitta pavement on the corner, and I get me bearins again as we start down Kirklands Road.

I'm wonderin what time Gill's babysittin and whether she has ter gan back home first fer her dinner. I reckon I'm hungry as we cross Scalegate Road, me own road, and start down Mount Pleasant. Another car gans past, this one with its exhaust pipe hangin off and clatterin on the road. I'm fiddlin with a corner of Michael's hankie, windin and unwindin it from round the end of me thumb where me heart's beatin hardest it seems, right there in me thumb's meat. I can see me blood seepin through it.

Where are we gan?

Yer'll see.

Yer never said yes or no, I say as we gan past the low hedges and the housefronts. Two young lasses, one sittin on a bike with stabilisers, watch us as we gan past, their thumbs in their mouths.

Ter what?

Yer never said if yer knew Arthur or not.

Here we are, says Gill, and turns left inter a yard through an oppen gate and gans up the path ter the door. She's pushin the doorbell as I stand beside her on the step, twistin the hankie and wonderin who's gonna answer. There's nothin in the bare concrete yard, nee grass or nothin. Gill's pullin the hem of her jumper straight and scrunchin her hair tight when the door oppens, but just a crack cus it's on a chain. I can't see inter the dark.

Hullo, Gran, says Gill loudly. It's me, and I've brought a friend.

Gill's gran puts half her face ter the crack in the door and one eye blinks at us.

Who's that? Is that you, Gill?

It's me, Gran.

And who's this with yer? she says, and Gill's gran tries ter look at us through the crack. Her eye's bright blue, like Gill's eyes, but her hair's wispy and white. Her old fingers're there on the edge of the door, fingers like me own fingers if me own fingers had bin in the dark fer ages, growin rooty.

It's a friend, Gran – Christopher. Say hullo, she says ter me.

Hullo, I say.

Gill's gran kinda hurrumphs and her face disappears inter the dark and the crack in the door closes up and me and Gill're left stood on the step.

It's alright, says Gill. She's just careful.

I can hear the rattlin of the chain behind the door. Me stomach gurgles. Then the door oppens and Gill's leadin the way inter her gran's hall, and her gran's mekkin us tek off me jacket and hang it on the post at the bottom of the stairs, and I'm taller than her now I'm stood beside her, lookin through the wispiness of her hair as it stands out from her head, and smellin her house. Fags and polish and Glacier Mints. It's nearly always what yer can smell in old people's houses. I'm smellin it and imaginin drawers fulla old stuff, folded up. I reckon there'll be old air – the air everyone's breathin in old photos – folded inter old coats and blankets and licked inter brown envelopes. A cat's suddenly slippin around me ankles, purrin.

She likes yer, whispers Gill from beside us.

Does she?

Aye. The cat does.

Gill's gran leads us down the hall. She kinda rolls, as if one hip's bad. The cat slips through me legs as I gan. I can hardly risk puttin one foot in front of the other, in case I step on it, but the cat's like watter flowin around us and never gettin snagged. In the kitchen there's a table I stand at till Gill tells us ter pull up a chair. I do and sit down as her gran fills an old-style whistlin kettle and plonks it on the hob.

Gran, have yer got any plasters?

Medicine box in the bathroom. Why? What's up with yer?

It's Christopher. He's cut himself. Gill looks at us and I hod up me hand with the hankie tied round me thumb.

Oh! says Gill's gran, and rolls ovver ter us as Gill gets up and disappears outta the kitchen. Let's have a look, then, little man, she says, and grabs me hand and starts ter unwrap me thumb with her knotty brown hands. I'm wonderin if gettin older is just gettin tangled inter yersel, as if yer eventually see so much that everythin stops feedin inter yer eyes smoothly and starts ter get nested up and muddled, and all that muddlin's happenin under yer skin. Oh my, says Gill's gran. Me hand's patched with brown dried blood. The cut runs lengthways along me thumb and its edges've gone white and bloodless. I'm suddenly shit-scared that I've cut me own thumb ter the bone.

How'd yer manage that? says Gill's gran, peerin at it.

On a fence, I say, quick as owt, just as the kettle starts ter whistle.

Hod it right there, she says to us, arrangin me hand so it's stickin out ovver the table and then turnin ter lift the kettle off the gas.

I try ter squint round me thumb without movin it from the position Gill's gran's left it in, but then I don't wanna see inter the cut, ter the white bone all of a sudden, so I look at the snowy houses on the biscuit tin on the table instead.

Gill's gran's mekkin tea with tea-leaves in a pot. She pulls a knitted cosy, like a woolly hat, ovver the pot, then she bends double and I watch her fetch up plates from a cupboard under the sink. Gill slips back inter the kitchen with a green plastic box in both her hands.

We'll get yer cleaned up, says Gill's gran, settin the cosied teapot on the table. Gill grins at us ovver the propped-oppen lid of the medicine box. Her gran puts plates and cups on the table in all. Right-o, she says, and scoots the medicine box around and away from Gill and starts ter ratch about inside it. She sets out a tin dish, a roll of bandages, a box of Elastoplasts, a pair of wee silver scissors and a bottle of TCP. Then she turns ter lift the kettle off the hob, and pours steamin watter inter the tin dish.

Her gran teks me hand in her hands and turns it ovver, peerin at it some more. Hod it there, she says, and teks the bandage-roll and the scissors, unwinds a length of pure white cloth and snips it off. Then she teks me hand again, none too gently, dips the bandage inter the tin dish and starts ter mop around the cut. She dips the bandage, squeezes it out in the dish and mops again.

Are yer gonna use TCP? says Gill.

You pour the tea and look affter yerself, says her gran, but she unscrews the TCP and glugs a splash of it inter the dish. I getta horrible sweet whiff of it.

This'll hurt, says Gill, liftin the teapot.

It might sting a wee bit, says her gran, more ter Gill than ter me. I look at the pink watter in the tin dish. I mek me face as stony as it'll gan, but then Gill's gran just sticks the wet bandage right onter me cut.

It stings like fuck.

It stings so much I might've sucked air in through me teeth when she did it. But now Gill's gran's dippin and squeezin, and sticks it on again, and I kick back in me chair and stamp me foot, and feel a softness under it just before there's a *meowl!* and a blur shoots from under the table and outta the kitchen. Gill's stopped halfway through pourin the tea, so there's just steam puffin outta the spout. Gill's gran's still got me hand in her hands, and the bandage held ter me stingin cut, but her old face is yanked twards the doorway the cat's torn through. Me thumb's stingin like fuck, and I'm kinda twistin in meself cus of the pain, but tryin not ter move, as if by doin this I can tek back the fact that I've stamped on the cat.

Chistopher! says Gill. Yer stamped on the cat!

I didn't mean ter.

It doesn't matter whether yer meant ter, does it?

Oh, she's an old ratbag who's sin worse.

She means the cat, says Gill, crookin her neck and givin us a hard look sideways.

Yis, I meant the cat. He knew that, didn't yer, lad?

Aye, I say through me teeth, cus Gill's gran's still got the

TCP bandage held against me cut, which feels massive now, like a cut I could fall inter. Can I use the bathroom? I say.

We'll get a plaster on this quick as yer like, she says, and at last teks away the stingin bandage. I breathe out as she snips a length of plaster from the skin-coloured roll of Elastoplast she's ratched from the box.

Keep still, she says, and hovers the plaster in front of me thumb while she aims the pad of it at me cut, then sticks it suddenly ovver it and wraps the two ends tightly. The cut kills. Me thumb's throbbin fatly. Up the stairs, she says, packin everythin back in the medicine box and snappin the lid shut. Yer could mek friends with Genie while yer up there. She's probly under the bed.

I slip off me chair and I'm down the hall and up the first two stairs before Gill's gran shouts from the kitchen doorway, Bring us a new box of twenny, will yer, lad? They're in the spare room, on the side.

Okay, I call back ovver the banister.

I look at the stuff hung on the wall up the stairs as I climb. A photo of a grey soldier, a bunch of flowers med of china, a long wooden face with holes where its eyes should be. I hear Gill's gran cacklin at summit Gill must've said below us. The toppa the stairs is gloomy, as if the whole house is leanin in around us, tired of bein the house it is and has bin.

The bathroom's green. I shut the door and turn the cold tap on at the green sink. In the cabinet mirror, I look inter me own eyes until me own eyes could be someone else's and me face could be a wooden one. The bog seat's gotta cosy on it, like the teapot downstairs. I lift it up and drill a slash inter the green bowl. Even the bog watter looks old, as if it's stood fer a long time in this house, like a rock-pool the sea hasn't reached fer ages. There's a chain ter pull ter flush it. I don't pull it. I put me right hand under the tap and watch the dried blood on it start ter flake away. I do me other hand in all, tryin ter keep me plaster from gettin wet. There's a pink towel hung on the back of the door. As I dry me hands, I hod it away from mesel, so I don't getta whiff of it.

I leave the tap runnin and pull the green door oppen. I can hear the murmurs of talk from downstairs. Around the gloomy L-shaped landin all the doors ter the rooms are half oppen. The first one I gan ter is Gill's gran's bedroom, me thumb beatin in its plaster.

Here kitty, here kitty, I say as I gan in, mostly so that if anyone's watchin us it'll look as if I'm lookin fer the cat, and not just nebbin. The first thing I notice is that the bed's got a pink skirt. I gan down onter me hands and knees and lift it up ter look under the bed. Here kitty, ch-ch-ch, I say as I peer under. In the catty dark there're suitcases and boxes. I drop the skirt and stand up. Here kitty. I sweep a look round the room, which is busy with stuff – bottled stuff and ornaments on a dressin table, clothes hangin, even on the outside of the wardrobe – then I gan out.

Gill's gran's fags are in a brick of two hundred on a table in the next room, which is emptier and feels spare, as if there's nee use fer it ever. She smokes a fag I've never seen before, not even on an advert. I tek a red and gold box from the brick, mekkin a quick count of the number of boxes before I do, just ter see if there're enough gone, but not as many as would mek it obvious. But I reckon the box I've tekkan is only the second, mekkin it too easy fer Gill's gran ter know if I nicked a box. The bed in this room's tucked as tight as the plaster's wound round me thumb, as if the blood ter yer head'd be cut off at the neck if yer slept in it. The curtains're drawn at the winder.

Ch-ch-ch, I gan as I back outta the room and mek me way ter the next, hoverin mid-step in the hall while I mek sure there's still cosy talk murmurin up from the kitchen. Here kitty, I say as I push inter the last room, and stop dead, even as the door's still creakin oppen on its own weight. I snatch a look at the head of the stairs. Here kitty, I'm sayin as I pile in ter look at the walls and the cabinets, at the medals and silver and the old gun on its side on purple cloth under glass, and at the bayonet and the photos of soldiers and horses and soldiers sittin up straight on horses and not smilin, and at the cap with a badge pinned ter it.

It's a war room, is what it is, and I wanna dawdle round everythin, starin. But I can't, cus I'm thinkin about the time I've bin up here and how it'll only be so much longer before Gill and her gran are wonderin where I've got ter. So I hurry round, starin down inter the cabinets and runnin me eyes ovver the shelves, tryin ter tek everythin in, and even though I wanna stare at the glum-faced medals till I can read what's written on em, I mek me eyes gobble em up, along with the ribbons, and the dull blade of the bayonet, which I don't even inch me eyes ovver, lookin fer stains.

I can feel the time fingerin me neck and I'd swat it away if I could. I'm even ratchin vexedly at me neck, at the collar of me T-shirt, as I gleg round the room, but there's a yeller ivory elephant I've spotted on a shelf, and before I've even picked it up and felt its chilly smoothness, I know that I'm gonna tek it and I hardly look at it, cus I'm gonna have the time ter look at it later. I push it, careful like, inter me pocket. I check ter mek sure it doesn't bulge too obviously through me jeans, then I gan outta the room, pullin the door to.

I catch me breath, not realisin till now that I needed ter breathe, and slip back down the hall ter the green bathroom where the cold tap's still runnin, like a clock, at the sink. I pull the chain, ter let on ter them downstairs that I've only just finished. The watter falls away and as it does the cold tap nearly stops runnin, as if there's only so much watter ter be had in Gill's gran's house. I twist the tap off, scoot outta the bathroom and start down the stairs, the box of fags in me hand and the elephant rubbin me leg through me pocket as I gan.

Gill's munchin a bicky and points ter the biscuit box as I tek me chair in the kitchen again. Go on then, she says, swallerin. We couldn't wait fer yer.

Here yer are, I say, handin the fags ovver.

Ta, lad, says Gill's gran, and starts ter fiddle fer the tab of cellophane that'll get her in. Her hands seem too big fer the box, and much too big fer the fiddly cellophane. I fumble a shortbread outta the tin and Gill pushes a cuppa tea twards us. I lift the cup awkwardly and tek a sip. The tea's tea and I wish it was coffee. I bite inter me shortbread and me stomach remembers how holler it is.

How's the thumb, little man?

Alright, ta.

Don't talk with yer mouth full, says Gill.

Leave him be, yer madam you, says Gill's gran, and kisses her lips around a fag. Her lips are so crumply it looks as if they might crack and fall off her face. She strikes a match and sucks the flame inter the fag end, then sheks the match out. The blue matchsmoke drifts. I get a sudden yawnin in me stomach that isn't bein hungry, but a cold flush as I feel the tusky elephant in me pocket. Not that I've forgotten the thing, but as if I'm sure of it in an extra-chilly rush. I suck the butter outta the shortbread. Me gob's dry. Gill's lookin at us big-eyed ovver the rim of her cup as she sips. Gill's gran's leanin against the table, the fag slotted between the fingers of the leant-on hand and her mouth workin on summit. I look from one ter the other in the quiet of us sippin tea, Gill sayin nowt, cus I reckon she's mekkin silence fer us ter squirm in, waitin ter see if I'll risk sayin owt, and her gran chewin ovver summit, and now liftin her hand and tekkin a drag that her whole face puckers around. I sip me tea. I tek another munch of shortbread. I'm chewin and wonderin if I could swing it so I could get back upstairs and put the elephant back. But ter gan upstairs again'd look too suspicious. I could somehow let on that I'd picked it up by mistake. But I can't see this in me head – me hand gan ter me pocket and me pretendin, Oh, what's this? It's probly nowt anyhow – just a toy elephant. It's probly nowt and I have ter act normal, which is mostly just convincin mesel that it won't even be missed and that I've done nowt wrong, which means I'm shiftin on me chair and havin me biscuit gan ter brickdust in me gob fer nowt. I chomp and then try ter swaller the ticklin dry ball.

What's up with yer?

Slap him on the back. Gan on, lass, hard.

Gill's bangin us on the back. I'm coughin madly.

Yer scoffed that down too quick, didn't yer, Christopher?

Fetch him a glass of watter, says Gill's gran. Cmon, lad, yer alright, she says, her knotty old hand on me jerkin shoulder. Gill's up ter the sink, and then plonkin down a glass of watter in front of us. I grab it up and tek a long pull, then watch a drip slip down the outside of the glass and the specks like dust still swirlin in the watter.

That better? says Gill's gran.

Yeah, I say, still puffin. Thanks.

Right, says Gill, clappin her hands. That's us. Thanks fer the tea, Gran.

Goin already?

Yep. Cmon, Christopher, she says, shooin us around her gran and outta the kitchen inter the hall.

Thanks fer the tea and the plaster.

He's got manners this one, hasn't he? says Gill's gran, rollin down the hall affter us. The elephant in me pocket rubs horribly.

Don't look so sad, says Gill, and hooks me jacket off the post at the bottom of the stairs and shoves it inter me arms. Yer look like a duck's arse, she hisses at us under her breath as she turns ter oppen the door.

You come back, says Gill's gran, the tip of her fag glowin from her fingers in the hall.

I will, says Gill, as she pushes us out inter the day, then swings out affter us. Ta ra, Gran.

THIRTEEN

There yer are, says Gill as we gan bundlin outta the gate, all patched up. I look at her, and then at me bandaged thumb as I push me arm through the arm of me jacket. I just nod. Don't thank us, then, she snaps, and trounces off down the road.

Hod on, I say affter her, but I don't move. I look right, up the way we kem, and left, the way Gill's gone. She's not even lookin ovver her shoulder. I put me hand on the elephant lump in me pocket. If I gan home, that'll be me – stuck at home till tomorrer, nee answer from Gill and all me worry about Arthur lurkin there, under me bed. But if I foller Gill, there's more and more chance that she'll find out what I've nicked from her own gran, and I won't even be able ter tell her why I've done it. I'm weighin these things up in me head, but me mind's like the dark space under me bed, fulla clutter and fluff, and me thoughts're just gropin blindly about in there. So I start off affter Gill, cus not ter gan affter her would be ter snap summit between me and her that's almost like a spidery thread now I've called at her house and she's tekkan us ter her gran's and I've nicked summit that's tied ter her in all.

I brush the glossy leaves of the low hedge as I scuff affter her. I bring me thumb up ter me nose and sniff the sweet medical smell of the plaster. I'm not lookin ahead, cus I'm pretendin ter ignore Gill rushin ahead of us, as if I'm not bothered how far on she is or even if she loses us round a corner. But I half know how far ahead she is, and I clock her turnin left at the end of the road. I start ter walk faster and slip me hand inter me jeans and finger the pointy bitsa the elephant, its trunk mebbe, or its needly tusks. The shelly smooth of an ear. I tek me hand back out with the elephant in it and look down at it as the pavement flows away under me feet. It's even got carved ivory toenails. I quickly pocket the thing as I get ter the end of the road and swing a left.

Front yards. Houses follerin the up-and-down of the road. Cars parked on that road, and me shadder in front of us suddenly, runnin up the bricks of the wall I'm walkin beside and gettin pulled like a sheet ovver tiny pebbles on the pavement, which is funny ter think of, cus I reckon I'm pushin me shadder.

I jump when Gill steps out, her hands on her hips. Me shadder's run halfway up her legs.

Did yer see him?

Who?

Never mind, she says, turnin back ter gan up the road. Yer should keep up, Christopher, or yer'll get left behind. Cmon.

See who, Gill? I chuck a look ovver me shoulder. I scan the other side of the street. Me belly unzips suddenly, cus I'm wonderin if it's Carl who's sin us tek the elephant outta me pocket. If he has, then the Black Hole's got summit ter hod against us, even if he doesn't know he has. I'm rememberin the weight of Booby's hand on me shoulder yesterday on the Arches. I hunch inter me jacket. I touch the numb-feelin rough plaster with the pad of me forefinger and find meself trailin affter Gill, just the way I didn't wanna be.

What's wrong with yer anyway? she says.

What d'yer mean?

Yer look like the back end of a bus.

What d'yer think's wrong? Me mate's gone missin.

There's nowt yer can do about it. Pullin faces isn't gonna change it.

I'm not pullin faces.

Well yer look like yer are.

I say nowt. I'm watchin me and Gill's shadders thrown together on the pavement in front of us. Even though we're nearly joggin along, past the wing mirrors of parked cars and the front yards, our shadders are kinda fixed. I lift me foot as we trot along and tek an extra big stride. I do it again.

What yer doin? says Gill.

I'm tryin ter stamp on me shadder.

Gill looks down at her feet in all. She teks a stride twards her shadder, but it slips away ahead of her. She teks another stride, hangin onter me arm as she does. I tek a stride. Then we both tek big strides at the same time.

Gill lets out a little yelp. It's so annoyin! she says. I wanna trample all ovver it, but it won't let us. And now I can't forget it, it's gonna keep annoyin us, Christopher. She teks another enormous step.

Yer'll forget it when the sun gans in.

I wannit behind us, she says, and she spins as she walks and starts ter walk backwards.

I laff. It is behind yer! Gill grins at us, her pink tongue, small as a cat's, nipped between her neat little teeth. We're side by side and face ter face, me and her, with Gill walkin backwards and both of us nearly at the end of the street. I thought it'd be in front of yer, I say, cus I had thought, just fer a second, that Gill's shadder'd spin with her so she'd be facin it.

Course it's behind us, she says. Yer a funny one, you are. Yer turn up at me house, yer bleed on us.

We've stopped at the end of the street. Gill's still facin the wrong way. I wait, but she doesn't say owt else.

Which way, then?

Whichever way it is, mine's not your way, Christopher. I look across the street. We're at the edge of Carlisle where the houses stop and the green country starts. There's a cut ovver the road that I know we could gan down and then cross a scribbled and sprayed bridge ovver another railway line, and then cross the river Caldew and be beside the empty red-brick mills. The weir'll be gan, the watter white as it steps down, and then calmed back ter brown as it pushes smoothly on its way. And even though me and Gill aren't there ter see it, I reckon the weir'll be gan.

If yer go left and I gan left, we'll both gan different ways.

Aye, I knew what yer meant, I say.

Don't be a grump.

I'm not bein a grump. I'm just sayin that I knew what yer meant. I put me hand ter me head and scratch back against me hair's direction. The sun gans in. The pavement flattens sadly, as if it's givin summit up. The lump in me pocket's even shitter ter us all of a sudden than it was. I put me hand in me jeans and touch the elephant.

Cmon, says Gill, and turns ter face the way I'm facin, and puts her left arm through me right arm. I snatch me hand outta me pocket.

Gill locks her arm properly in mine as we walk. The sun slides out, as if a lid's bin lifted off it, and heat sits on me head. Our shadders run out of us again like watter, darkenin the low wall ter our left now.

I say nowt. I reach me left hand inter me jacket carefully, cus of me plastered thumb, and fumble me fagbox out. I pop the top oppen and put the box ter me mouth and shek me last fag round till I can bite it and drag it out. I crumple the box and shove it inter a hedge as we gan past.

Diffs on that, says Gill.

I just nod with the fag clamped between me lips, cus I'm mostly just sparkin it up so I've time ter think of summit ter say. I fish the Zippo outta me jeans. I hod it away from me face and snap it oppen. Then I realise I won't be able ter thumb it alight, cus of me plaster. Before I can get it inter me right hand, Gill grabs the Zippo.

Here, she says, but she just hods the Zippo fer a second and looks at it. We've stopped walkin. Here, she says again, and we close together, still arm in arm, like a hinge, and Gill thumbs the wheel and the flame leaps up first time and I push me face near it till the fag-end's just blackenin in the fire and I suck. Gill snaps the Zippo shut and I tek it off her and pocket it and breathe out smoke, and we're walkin again up Lund Crescent.

Did yer hear about that tramp?

Me throat tightens up and I nearly cough smoke. What tramp? I say.

The tramp who got killed.

Oh aye, him. What about it?

I'm just mekkin chat, Christopher, aren't I? Till yer've smoked half that fag. And don't smoke any more than half, cus I don't wanna be left suckin the filter. They reckon he was a rich man. They reckon he had all this money, but he wouldn't touch it and lived on scraps and leftovvers cus summit had happened ter him that touched him in the head. Wouldn't yer love ter know what it was?

What what was?

What it was that happened ter him, stupid.

I know what happened ter him. He got burnt.

Yer really funny, says Gill, meanin I'm not funny at all, and cus she's got her arm through mine, I feel even worse about not bein funny. I say nowt. I tek another drag and then look at the tip of the fag where the fire's pulsin under the grey ash.

If we knew what had happened ter him ter mek him a tramp, we might have an idea of where all his money was, mightn't we?

Watch the glass, I say, and me and Gill step around a smashed green bottle sparklin on the pavement.

Cus they reckon his money's hid somewhere, says Gill.

Who reckons?

I dunno, says Gill. Just people. Just talk. Yer hear it, don't yer, and then yer tell what yer've heard, like I'm tellin you. Does it matter, like? And give us that, yer hog. Gill snatches the fag from between me fingers and sucks at it. We've nearly walked all the way up the crescent now.

Not ter me it doesn't.

Well, then, she says, tekkin another suck of smoke. If yer were a tramp, where would yer stash yer money? Where d'yer keep yours?

In me pockets, I say, and regret it, cus I get a sudden idea that Gill's gonna shove her hands inter me pockets. But she doesn't.

Right, she says. So yer'd keep yer money on yer, cus yer wouldn't stick it in the bank if yer were a tramp. On yer would be where yer'd be able ter feel it, nice and safe and next ter yer skin. But I never heard that any money got burnt.

Nobody'd burn money.

Exactly, Christopher, which meks yer wonder, she says, drawin eights in the air with her two fingers, the fag between em.

Meks yer wonder what?

Meks yer wonder where the money is if it didn't get burnt. Meks yer wonder how yer mek someone tell yer summit if they don't wanna tell yer, Gill says, and flicks the fag inter the road.

I say nowt. I can feel me forehead, furrowed up. I can smell the smells of people's dinners, and under that, the black smell of the scorched patch in Bitts Park that's in the back of me nose now and won't be blown out.

I've gotta babysit, says Gill suddenly, and stops. I keep walkin fer half a stride, and have ter pull mesel back, cus Gill's arm's still through mine. What're you gonna do?

I dunno, I say, and look up and down the road. Aren't yer too young ter babysit?

Gill pulls her arm out from mine and pushes the strap of her handbag back up her shoulder. I've got an older head on than you have, Christopher.

Oh, right, I say. I look again up the road, and then back at Gill, who hasn't moved.

Well? she says, and folds her arms.

Thanks.

Thanks fer what?

I dunno.

Don't thank us fer nowt, Christopher. It meks yer sound desperate. And why wouldn't yer wanna come and babysit with us?

FOURTEEN

Gill had knocked on the door and Mal Sharkey had oppened it and bundled me and her inter the house. Gill's big sister was out, but Mal med us both fall inter the sofa and then talked madly at us, grinnin like a lantern, a rat-black hook of dead hair danglin ovver his flickerin eyes. Little Liz was crawlin across the floor, her nappy bulgin through her red baby boilersuit. While Mal was jabberin, Gill had grabbed Liz up off the floor and started ter joggle her on her knee. Mal asked Gill how her mam was. Little Liz had hoddin onter Gill's thumbs, one in each fist. Mal didn't wait fer Gill ter answer before he was tellin us how he'd driven ter Southend and back last week, all in one day, and hadn't slept since, cus of the drugs.

Magic powder, that speed, said Mal. Wanna drive all night? Yer just get yersel some magic powder. He laffed at this till he cried, proper streamin tears, then told me as he wiped his eyes that I should sit on me hands.

Gan on. Get sat on em. Keep them hands outta trouble. I can see trouble. Can't I, Gill? he said, hoppin from one foot ter the other in front of us. Can't I see he's trouble? Mister Trouble.

Oh, Mal, he's not trouble, said Gill as she joggled little Liz. He's just Chris. But he'll sit on them, if that's what yer want. Won't yer? she said ter us, and looked at us with summit seeded in her eyes that was fer me alone and not fer Mal Sharkey.

Aye, I said, and slid me hands under me legs.

Mal tapped the side of his nose and winked at us.

Now I've bin here sittin on me hands fer so long while they talk in the kitchen that I've got pins and needles in me left arm. Little Liz sits on the carpet, chewin the corner off a wooden block. I look again at the hatch in the livin-room wall. Mal's got a breakfast bar built so stuff can get slid outta the kitchen through the hatch and inter the livin room, and there're a coupla leggy stools ter be sat on. Me left arm's like somebody else's arm, or just like the gap where me own arm used ter be. I wiggle the fingers on me numb left hand. I wouldn't've bin sittin on me hands just cus Mal told us to sit on em if it wasn't fer them black seeds in Gill's eyes. They were the black seeds of summit serious, more serious than Mal Sharkey not bein able ter hod still and stop jabberin.

I can hear her now, not really talkin ter Mal. She's sayin words but they're just the noises someone meks when they're stuck listenin. Oh, I know, yeah, yeah, I know, says Gill, and then the talk stops. Both me and little Liz are lookin at the hatch when the hatch slams oppen.

Hey, hey, says Mal, as he sticks his head through. Listen, when the phone rings, yer can get off yer hands and pick it up, yeah?

I look at his face, yeller as an old potato, and nod. He pulls his head back through the hatch and starts ter slide it shut.

Hey, hey, he says, and slides it oppen again and sticks his head back through. When yer pick it up say, Hello, Mister Trouble here. Yeah yeah, do that, he says, his head shekkin so much with laffter that the hook of hair falls down ovver his eyes and he starts tryin ter blow it off his forehead. This sets him laffin even harder, so he can't even draw breath ter blow, his mouth stretched wide, but not a sound comin out. I can see his tongue squirmin in there, like summit caught in a trap. Liz is sat, givin it frog kicks as she watches him, still grinnin. Hello, Mister Trouble here. Say it like that, just like that, he says at last, pullin his gigglin skull back through the hatch.

I hear Gill say, Oh, Mal, behind the slammed hatch, and more of his muffled gigglin.

I pull me numb hand out from under me leg where I'd quickly stuffed it and look at it. I mek a fist and then oppen it, mek a fist then oppen it. Me hand slowly comes back ter us. I figure that I can stop sittin on me hands if I'm sposed ter pick up the phone, so I pull the other hand out in all. I look at the stuff scattered about the livin room as I hod both hands out and squeeze em in and outta fists. I snatch a look at the hatch, but I can still hear Mal's voice chuggin away through there, so I lean down off the sofa and start rummagin about. I stop dead when I see the edge of yesterday's paper. Not till right now had I thought of all the papers besides me dad's that woulda got delivered yesterday.

Abba abba, says little Liz, pushin herself up, arse first, and then totterin back ter gum the damp patch on the cushion edge. I rake the paper out from under the bike mags and start smoothin it out beside us on the sofa. I rattle oppen the first page and there's Arthur's name in stark black print again.

I whip the paper shut and shove it back under the sofa, whumpin back inter the sofa cushions and wedgin me hands under me thighs. Liz is bouncin again, only stoppin ter peer down at her own legs and then grin back at us, as if I should be amazed in all that she's stood. The elephant's stickin inter me leg through me pocket linin. I slip one hand out and hod it close ter Liz, but I don't dare touch her head where her hair's all newly wisped. She's spankin the sofa happily, with nowt hidden about her, and cus of all that's hidden about me, I snatch me hand back. I'm scared ter touch her hair or have her grab one of me fingers.

We've gotta get outta here, whispers Gill, and I've bin listenin so hard ter the roar in me own head that I never noticed the kitchen gan quiet. I scrabble round onter me knees so I can peer ovver the back of the sofa at her, set on her tiptoes in the doorway.

Pass us that poor mite, she says, startin twards us.

I turn ter look at Liz.

Abba abba, she says.

Oh, she loves that Abba, says Gill. Cmon, Christopher, get her hoisted ovver here, cus he is fuckin off his head, she whispers. I didn't realise till we got in, but now he won't let us gan. He only let us outta there when I said I had ter pee.

I start ter speak and reach fer the paper, ter show Gill, but she jabs her finger ter her lips and meks her eyes wide, so I suddenly tek hod of little Liz under her arms and lift the warm, red-wrapped, kickin weight of her up ovver the back of the sofa and inter Gill's hands. As she teks her, Gill's hissin, This is what we're gonna do, but before she can tell us what we're gonna do, the phone gans, I jump and Gill spins through the door with Liz gurglin on her hip, the two of em vanishin up the stairs.

Mal's shoutin from the kitchen, Get that! I've bin waitin fer that! Mister Trouble, don't forget!

It's on the fourth ring, affter I've bounced off the sofa and skidded about on the shiny mags and scattered buildin blocks, that I find the phone on the windersill, behind the net curtain. It's a green, old-style rattlin phone. I watch it ring a fifth time and then I pick up the handle, mostly just so it'll stop ringin. And now I dunno what else ter do with it, so I put it ter me ear.

Mal, lad, says a voice I recognise, deep as a barrel and clear as yesterday on the Arches. At the same time I hear the hatch oppen. Elberin aside the net curtain I've got mesel wrapped up in, I see Mal's grinnin head stickin through the hatch. He's noddin at us madly, mouthin, Gan on, gan on.

I reckon I've stopped breathin, so I mek meself tek a big breath ter speak with.

Hello, I say ter Booby Grove, Mister Trouble here.

There's nowt but a long quiet on the other end of the phone. I've got me eyes fixed on Mal's yeller face. He's laffin so hard I reckon he can hardly stand up. His head's lollin ovver the lower edge of the hatch. The quiet in me ear crackles.

Mister Trouble, Booby's voice says carefully, is Mister Wall there?

Mal's still cracked up. I look at the empty doorway Gill went through.

No, I say, tryin ter sound as little like meself as I can.

Is it him? hisses Mal, workin the fingers of one hand through the narrer space at his ear and then tryin ter use them fingers ter wipe the tears off his cheek.

Is Missus Wall there? says Booby.

No, I say.

It's not him? hisses Mal, who's got his head crooked as he works his other hand through the hatch. As I watch, his whole arm pops through the hatch and he rests it on the breakfast bar. Then he sets ter workin his whole other arm through. I shek me head at him and shrug me shoulders, meanin that I dunno who he means.

Are there any Walls there? says Booby in me ear.

No, I say.

WELL IF THERE'S NO WALLS, roars Booby, THEN WHAT'S HODDIN YER FUCKIN HOUSE UP? His voice is so loud I have ter tek the phone away from me ear.

Oh fuck, says Mal.

When I put the phone back ter me ear, Booby's sayin, Mal. Yer there, Mal lad? I put me hand ovver the mouthpiece.

What shall I tell him?

I'm stuck, says Mal.

I tek me hand off the mouthpiece.

He's stuck, I say, in the deepest voice I can.

No! says Mal from the hatch. I'm fuckin stuck. I'm stuck here. I can't get out!

What yer on about? says Booby down the line. Who the fuck is this?

I'm stood with the phone on me sweatin ear, watchin Mal. His head and shoulders're jammed through the hatch and his arms're stretched out ovver his head. His knuckles are rappin on the breakfast bar as he twists and squirms.

Ey. Is that you? says Booby. It is, isn't it? I know it is. Yer've got some fuckin cheek, doin a runner, but yer won't get far. I'm on me way, yer gobby little cunt, he says. I slam the phone down and stand lookin at it.

Yer have ter give us a hand, says Mal. Come round and pull us out, he whines. The phone starts ringin again.

I lift the handle and put it down.

Cmon, lad, Mal says. Stop fuckin about and help us out.

But I just stand, wrapped in the net, watchin the phone. Sure enough it starts ter ring again.

Six times it rings, then stops. I look at the green shell of it fer long enough ter clock the last ring still tremblin through it, then I move, swattin me way outta the curtain and zippin ovver the livin room and behind the sofa, me eyes dartin away from Mal's eyes, which're glarin at us through his ratty fringe. He's breathin hard, his elbers restin on the breakfast bar. He tries ter force his head round ter watch us as I nip through the doorway, inter the hall. At the bottom of the stairs I shout, Gill! then I stand and listen, me foot on the first step.

Mal's cursin comes streamin outta the livin room. From upstairs, there's nee sound. I turn on me heel and head fer the front door, Mal's voice behind us. I put me hand ter the handle, turn it and pull. The knocker knocks with a jolt. I stick me head out.

Outside's a pure relief. I step down onter the front step. The streetlamps've lit, but they're just wee slipsa light in their cases. I tek a breath with wet gardens on it. Then I'm back inter the house and slammin the door on the sight of Booby Grove ovver the hedge, strollin down the road. Mal's shoutin, but not proper words anymore.

I race ter the bottom of the stairs and shout, Gill! Where-ayer! Then I'm chargin up four steps and twistin me neck ter look up inter the upstairs.

Nowt.

He wasn't in a hurry. He was just strollin hugely along, like he owned the joint. I nip back through the doorway, across the livin room and inter the kitchen.

Hey, that's the ticket, says Mal from through the wall. His legs and half his body're stickin outta the hatch. Just grab this one, he says, and his left leg wobbles up and down, a black slip-on shoe on the end of it. But I'm already tryin the handle of the back door with both hands, tuggin at it.

Don't be shy, lad, says Mal muffledly as I start huntin the kitchen surfaces fer the key. Lad? Chris – that's yer name, isn't it? Chris, just help a feller out, ey? I've got me little girl ter think of.

I pull oppen one drawer, fulla knives and spoons, then the next, fulla curtain hooks. I don't bother pushin em shut. There's a mug tree stood on the counter and I check it fer hangin keyrings. Nowt.

Ey. Ey, stop that. Get outta there, yer little sod. Yer tek owt and I'll fuckin skin yer.

Mal's legs're really kickin now. He looks like a man who's woke up built inter a wall. He kicks the slip-on off, ovver the kitchen and straight inter the sink, but I'm suddenly listenin ter the air gan in and outta me nose. Stop and think, I say ter meself, stop and think stop and think, but I can't stop or think, so I gan chasin round the kitchen again, lookin at the walls fer hooks and keys. Nowt.

I can't breathe, says Mal. D'yer hear? On yer head be it when they find us here blue. Lad?

I'm right behind Mal's legs and his legs've gone still and bent at the knees, as if he's tekkin the weight off. There's quiet fer us both ter hear KNOCK KNOCK KNOCK on the front door. Mal's legs straighten up in a hurry.

Hey! he shouts, as I stuff me good hand inter the pocket of his jeans. He bucks and squirms, but me hand's lodged there and he's too stuck ter shek us off. I'm keepin mesel ter his side where he can't kick us. I don't wanna touch Mal's tackle, but me fingers close on small change, a screwed-up bitta paper. I rip it all out and let it fall, the coins ter get scuffed about at Mal's feet, and then I tek a wide berth round ter Mal's other side. I jam me hand in his other pocket and me fingers grabble straightaway on a buncha keys. Hey! he's shoutin, his voice raw from so much shoutin. HEEEAY!

Ovver Mal hollerin, I can hear the front door gettin barged, and I'm glad, cus if Booby's bargin the front door, then he hasn't thought ter come round the side, and I'm slottin the longest key of the bunch inter the slot and turnin it and the door's squeakin as I tug it away from its frame.

I fall inter the backyard. A saggy washin line, a motorbike without wheels, grass and dry dirt the grass has bin rubbed away from. Fences either side. I pull the back door affter us. I'm keepin hod of the handle while I scrabble ter get the key in the outside lock. The key chatters on the plate around the keyhole. I'm tryin not ter look through the cobbled glass at the shadder of Mal's legs, the blurry angles of the kitchen, a hugely loomin shape there suddenly. Then the key gans in. I turn it, yank it out and let the whole bunch drop. The *chink* of em on the cement backstep rings in the gloom.

YOU! roars the voice of Booby Grove, and a baby's cryin starts up behind the winders and walls. I hear it in the past already, from ovver the yard where I'm jumpin the bike frame, me mouth fulla the acid taste of me own insides, and then I'm at the bottom of the yard, at the fence. I'm gan ovver it at the place where Mal's shed's rammed against it, mekkin a corner I can jam me trainer in ter grip and push. I'm strainin ter hear brekkin glass, any shoutin or feet shekkin the ground behind us, but the alley I'm runnin down only gives us back the bright *whack-whack-whack* of me trainers, and me breath's gan as if there's a hood ovver me head, keepin me panic right in me ears.

I slow down and me legs wobble now they're not fired with pure fear. I stop, cus I can't gan on. Me lungs're aflame. I'm leanin with me hands on me thighs, spittin down onter the pavement. I stare at the white froth and glinty wetness.

I squeeze me eyes shut, breathe and oppen me eyes again. I start walkin cus I daren't stop.

I've done a loop, follerin the alley behind Mal Sharkey's till it pitched us out on Durdar Road. Then I've gone down Durdar Road till I could brek left and run up the way me and Gill had come, and then I'd tekkan a right that's led us round ter me own road again. Through a winder, I catch a room's two walls meetin in a corner where a telly flickers. It's burnt inter me head, this room fulla light. House affter house I've passed where people were slowly gan upstairs, or just wanderin from one lit room ter another.

The sweat's cold on me neck and me back. I lift me shoulders so me jacket settles around us more cosily. The streetlamps're gettin their strength up. I can feel town gettin scrunched by the dark, cus the night's drawin in and it's the night that's mekkin the houses tek a step closer together and the alleys get narrer. I duck down behind a parked car as another gans past, its long-fingered headlights feelin the road. I'm wonderin where Gill and little Liz are at and what's gan on back at Mal Sharkey's house.

I cut right down Scalegate Road, me hand orange with streetlight when I tek it outta me pocket ter zip me jacket up ter me throat. I gan tense at a draggin, scratchin sound I don't recognise, till with a sudden flush of relief I see in me head dead leaves gettin pushed along the pavement by the wind. Booby's mebbe squeezin down a cut this minute, his man's face white as lard and the town like a toy town he can kick ovver ter find us. But I turn inter me yard and gan up ter the back door. I have ter wait on me own back step while I slow meself down. I breathe, cus I know I can't bring the outside in. I can't let me mam and dad and sister see us gan at full tilt and blurry while they're all parked solid inside. I breathe in. I breathe out. I empty me face. I put me hand ter the door handle and breathe in again. I push in the door.

FIFTEEN

Christopher, me mam calls from the livin room. Is that you?

There's summit in her voice that grabs me throat and squeezes it even tighter shut than it was. I push the back door closed behind us. I'm roastin in me sweat now I'm in and stood still. I pinch me T-shirt off me neck and shek it so air gans down me front.

Come through here, love, she calls, so nice and polite that I know. I heel one trainer off, me feet shekkin from the run, and then I heel off the other. The kitchen's too bright. There's no telly on, but I reckon every light in the house is. Stood on the side are two tins of hotdogs. What I know by her voice is that me mam's bein ovverheard by someone else, by someone waitin with her in the livin room. As I gan ovver the kitchen I look at the winder above the sink, but I just see the kitchen and meself in it, lookin back from the dark. I cross from the kitchen inter the hall. I stop at the side of the livin-room door ter swaller. I have ter show nowt in me face, so I bend double and peer at the pattern of threads in the carpet. I'm thinkin about what's gan on down there where me feet're plonked. I put me mind down there, outta the way with the threads and the dust, while I pull me socks up me legs ter hod up havin ter gan through the livin-room door. I dry me palms on me jeans. I've got nowt left ter do now but gan through.

Me mam's on her feet, as if she's just jumped up, but me eyes're mainly on the pair whose faces're turned twards us from the sofa where they've obviously bin waitin.

Christopher? says the straightfaced woman, and I know fer sure they've bin waitin fer me.

Yeah.

I'm DC Hughes and this is Detective Inspector Harrison. Why don't you sit down?

Hornies. Me heart loops and drops through us, like a wonky paper plane.

She points ter the dinner chair that's sat in the middle of the floor, the chair me mam probly jumped up off, specially brought in ter the livin room.

I gan ovver ter it, the heat of their eyes on us so I can fairly hear the sweat sizzlin out of me skin. I keep me hands at me sides, hidin me pocket where the nicked elephant's stashed. I don't look at me mam, but plonk meself onter the chair and hook me socked feet round the cool wooden legs.

Do you know why we're here?

No, I say, cus it's best ter admit ter nowt, I reckon.

No idea at all? she says.

No. I chance a look at me mam. She's stood hoddin her elber with one hand and gnawin on the knuckles of the other. I switch back ter the pair. They've not got uniforms on, which is summit I reckon, cus they'd have em on, wouldn't they, if they were here ter haul us away? They're as neat as neat, the two of em, the woman's white hands in her lap and the cuffs of her dark jacket ruled across each of her wrists.

You're a friend of Arthur's, aren't you? Arthur Grieve?

Aye. Yes, I say, cus in front of me mam it'd be stupid ter say otherwise. The feller beside her, Harrison, whose name I'm rememberin cus it's *harry son, harry son*, is just watchin, his steady eyes, green as ignition lights, pouched in dark folds.

Have you seen him? says PC Hughes. Arthur?

I say nowt. They wait, watchin us say nowt. I slide me hands under me tacky legs.

No? she says.

I shek me head.

When did you last see him?

A while ago.

Today?

No. A while ago.

Did you see him at the weekend?

This weekend?

Yes, she says.

No.

The weekend before, then?

Aye. I saw him on the Saturday. I watch Harrison scribblin with a wee pencil in a black book that he's smoothly reached inter his jacket fer and flipped oppen on his knee.

Saturday the twenty-third?

Aye, if that was the twenty-third. The Saturday before the Saturday just gone.

Where did you see him?

In town.

In Carlisle?

Yeah.

And what did you do, the two of you, when you saw him?

I dunno, I say, and then I think that she knows fer sure that I do know. We were in the arcade, I say, then we played pool.

Which arcade?

Eldorado.

Harrison's scribblin still. It's funny ter have me own voice pushin his pencil along, and me own silence mekkin it hover – like magic.

Eldorado on Botchergate, she says, hardly ter me, but as if she's wantin her voice ter be written down in all. What time were you there, Christopher? Is it Christopher, or d'you prefer Chris?

I'm not bothered.

And the time you saw Arthur in Eldorado?

I dunno. Before dinnertime.

You mean midday? Or teatime?

Before midday, in the mornin, but not that early.

Saturday's for lying in, ey? Did you have a lie-in, Christopher?

I budge uncomfortably on the hard seat.

You remember, don't yer, love? says me mam.

Aye, I say, but I'm thinkin of PC Hughes pokin around me bedroom, me bedroom from last Saturday, where I was lyin sweatin under me duvet. Not fer long though, I say, and wish I hadn't.

And then you played pool. In Eldorado?

No. Yer can't there. It was in the snooker club ovver Woolworths.

So you went there after Eldorado?

Yeah. I try ter hod her level look with me own eyes but me eyes flitter down ter the black shine on her snub-nosed shoes.

You were in Eldorado then the two of you went to the snooker club. Is that right?

Yeah.

Did you spend the whole day with Arthur?

Yeah. Then he got the bus home. Ter his.

Which bus? What time?

About six or seven o'clock, I reckon. Harrison's pencil keeps gan. His neck's blue like me dad's with under-the-skin stubble.

The whole day, then. That's a long day, she says, leavin it hangin, kinda with a question mark, and kinda not. I squirm the tiniest squirm on the chair, left and then right. Me mind's the black scorchmark in Bitts Park, and I know how wrong it is ter have gone lookin fer it, and how much worse it was ter sniff it, ter have got down onter me knees and put me own face ter the last of someone.

Was it wrong, I say, ter be there fer so long?

Do you think it was?

I dunno. No.

Is that all you did on that Saturday?

I say nowt, then I think that sayin nowt is sayin more than if I just say anythin at all. We mosied about a bit. About town.

How was Arthur?

He was just Arthur.

What did you talk about?

Er. About the machines, and then about playin pool.

Did he say anything unusual? Anything that you thought was out of the ordinary?

He didn't say anythin unusual.

But he did something unusual?

Nothin unusual. But he was. Er.

Harrison and Hughes keep their faces totally flat and still, like masks of their own faces turned twards us. They say nowt and wait.

He was lookin. He was on the lookout, I reckon.

Did he tell you what he was looking out for?

Nah. He just looked a lot.

Was he frightened, Christopher? Is that how he seemed?

Mebbe. He didn't say.

Did you ask him?

No.

Why didn't you ask him?

Yer just don't, d'yer? Should I have done?

Do you think you should have done?

Is Arthur in trouble?

With us?

Yeah. With you.

No, not at all.

So why're yer here, talkin ter me?

We're wondering where Arthur is, says Harrison, suddenly enough ter mek us twitch on me chair, and his voice is different ter the way I thought it would be from the look of him. It's got a crackle at the back of it, like a voice comin through a badly tuned radio.

His mum and dad are wondering where he is, and now they've asked us to help. To look for him.

Harrison gives a pebbly cough inter his fist and then clears the static from his throat. The sound meks us think of seaweed, wheezin dry on estuary mud.

So where is he?

We don't know, Christopher. That's why we've come to you, says Hughes.

I dunno where he is.

No. We didn't expect you to. But you're one of the people who saw him last. Do you understand?

Yeah. I saw him on Saturday. Who else saw him, then?

That's part of what we want to find out.

Okay, says Harrison, and clears his throat inter his fist again. Summit in the air of the livin room gans slack, and I know I can tek a deep breath, though I daren't do it yet. PC Hughes looks ovver at me mam. I look in all, and she drops her knuckles from her mouth. Then Hughes and Harrison are both standin up off the sofa.

I stand up in all, pinchin me kegs off the back of me sticky legs.

Harrison's slottin his pad away under his jacket.

Mrs Hearsey, he says, and me mam starts outta the livin room and they wait ter foller her.

If you remember anything else, Christopher, anything at all, says PC Hughes, your mam knows where we are.

Aye, okay, I say, and then I'm on me own in the livin room, stood lookin at the cold grey stone of the turned-out TV as I listen ter the three of em gan ter the front door.

Okay, I hear me mam say from the hall.

Okay, says Harrison, and there's some murmurin, and a scatter of words in the oppen air, flutterin in, and then the door's shut and the house is sealed.

Hotdogs fer tea. Hotdogs in proper white hotdog buns, with tomato sauce and slippery fried onions ter gan on the dog and get squidged out when yer shut the bun and squeeze it together. Me mam's waitin ter fish the hotdogs outta the pan with a spoon shot fulla holes. Meantime, we're all stood pressed inter the kitchen, waitin with her, me with me hands washed and me fringe still wet where I've splashed me face in the bathroom, and me sister balanced on one foot with her ankles crossed, lookin so neat and proper that me dad says ter me, Stop slouchin, cus I've got me chin in me hands and me elbers on the counter with me empty plate between em, waitin. Me mam's face is shiny. She's sawin oppen the buns and liftin the lid now and then ter peep inter the saucepan, and then stirrin the onions in the fyin pan where they've bin meltin down, fillin the kitchen with oniony smoke. We're all watchin her, the three of us, and she's shiny with bein watched, is what I reckon, cus she hods the holey spoon and she'll know when the hotdogs are hot enough and this is what we're all really waitin fer. Fer her.

Are they ready?

Nearly, Chris, not long, she says, as she puts the plate of sawn-oppen buns in front of us on the counter. Why don't you butter them fer us while yer wait? Good lad. Then she lifts the pan lid again so the let-out steam barrels up in a cloud ter the ceilin where it spreads and flattens and disappears in the kitchen spots. I tek up a knife and start ter scrape marge from the tub and onter each half of bun. The buns aren't cut all the way through. Each has a hinge of bread left so the hotdogs'll nestle in em. Good lad, she says again, and I know she hasn't told me dad yet.

Are yer okay? me mam asked when she kem back inter the livin room affter seein out the coppers.

Yeah, I said.

Put that chair back, ey.

I'd done it, and then gone straight up the stairs ter me bedroom. I'd imagined me mam stood in the livin room below us, her knuckles gan back ter her mouth ter get gnawed. I'd tekkan the ivory elephant outta me pocket and turned it ovver in me hand. There was still light faintly enough outside me bedroom winder so I didn't have ter turn me lamp on.

I'd stood the elephant on the shelf beside me bed while I ratched out a clean T-shirt. I'd looked the elephant in the eye where it stood, liftin its foot. Then I'd snatched it up and stashed it under me bed with me coffee mug from this mornin, and me dad's nicked newspaper.

Then I'd gone ter the bathroom and unwrapped the plaster. The skin around the cut looked yeller from the TCP. The cut itsel was white-edged. I could see the deep red meat of me thumb, but no bone. I stuck the plaster back down again.

Now me thumb feels big and clumsy as I try ter hide it on the handle of the knife while I spread the marge. Right, here we go, me mam says, and we're all watchin her lift the lid off the pan and lay it steamin on the side.

They're brilliant hotdogs. I bite inter mine, inter the soft white bread and then through the hot tube of meat, then I chew, the onions greasy on me tongue, and smoky at the same time. I'm starvin. Me sister's got tomato sauce smeared round her mouth, but I don't tell her. I just let her keep munchin, sittin watchin telly. No one's asked us about me thumb, but me mam keeps givin us gentle looks with her sad face, cus between me and her there's the cops callin ter speak ter us, and Arthur's disappearance, and it feels like relief, this secret spread between us. It's relief but I can't feel its edges, ter know how far it's spread and how long it might tek ter spread ter me dad. He's wipin his sticky fingers with kitchen roll, the same way I've seen him wipin engine oil off em with a paper towel. I can see the claw marks the comb's left set in his raked-back, shiny black hair. I know outside is there – loomin – but I've got away from it, inter me own bright livin room where the telly's babblin away and there's nee answer ter give. The whole house feels fitted around us.

Are yer all ready fer tomorrer? says me dad. It sounds like a question he's tried out before askin it, but it still hasn't kem out right.

Yeah, I reckon, I say, which is a surprise, cus I didn't think I was ready.

Where yer been all day?

He's been out in the fresh air, says me mam. Haven't yer, Chris? Me mam smiles at us, and I smile back at her. Me sister's dabbin her mouth with the soft inside of one wrist.

Yeah, just out, I say, and smile, and I reckon everyone smiles back at us.

Set ter be nice again tomorrer, me mam says, cus she always knows what the weather's gonna do.

It's a lovely tea, mam, me sister pipes up, isn't it, Chris?

Yeah. It's great. Thanks.

You two sound like yer can manage another.

I can, I say, and me mam starts ter get up, but I say, I'll get it, and me dad wants another in all, so I get up with me plate, and tek his plate off him and gan through ter the kitchen. I put the plates on the counter and then I tek the holey spoon and fish us out a hotdog each from the warm pan. I snuggle each dog inter its bun, shovel on some onions, then trail a slow line of tomato sauce along each one, and then close em up.

I'm practisin smilin as I do it. I wanna check me smile, so I peer inter the silver metal strip of the oven handle, at me face stretched there. I practise smilin and feelin snug and fulla light. Then I pick up me and me dad's plates and gan back through ter the livin room and smile at me dad when I hand ovver his plate with his hotdog built.

Good man, he says, then, Look at him go! I turn ter look at the screen where a big, low-slung Buick Riviera's liftin off the road as it flies ovver a hill, bottomin out with a fan of sparks as it motors down a street steeper than any street round here.

I sit on the floor with me plate on me knees and me back against the sofa. I'm tekkin a giant bite outta me second hot-dog when three solid knocks sound on the door.

Who's this? says me dad.

We've all stopped chewin. I'm watchin telly. The picture's movin but me eyes aren't movin with it. I try ter swaller me mouthful but it won't gan down.

Yer not expectin anyone, are yer? me mam says brightly ter me dad.

No, he says.

Maybe it's fer one of you.

I'll see, says me dad.

No, I'll go, says me mam, and she's sprung up before me dad can lift himsel outta his chair. I try ter get me jaw workin on me mouthful again. I'm strainin ter hear me mam gan down the hall, but she must already be at the door cus I hear it gettin pulled oppen. I hear a man's voice from outside, and then me mam's voice sayin summit back, and then the voice again.

It could be the milkman, come fer the milk money, or Mrs Banks from next door wantin ter borrow a cuppa milk. And then, madly, all I can think of is milk, cus Booby's roarin, *Yer gobby little cunt*, *Yer gobby little cunt*, ovver and ovver, deep in me ear, just as he was on the phone at Mal's. I hear the front door gettin shut and feel the house gan airtight.

Who was it? says me dad as soon as me mam steps back inter the livin room. We're all three of us lookin at her, waitin ter know.

It was fer Chris, says me mam, smilin at us, but I told his friend we were all havin tea.

Me mam's tekkin me dad's plate, and then me sister's. She meks me sister stack her plate on toppa me dad's so she can hod em both, then she bends down ter mek me stack mine in all. Me plate clanks. There're onion bits leftovver on me sister's plate that I know'll be squidged between her plate and the bottom of me own. I've waited with me second hotdog sittin in us like chewed wood, but it's as if me mam won't say who it was at the door.

Yer not goin out again tonight, says me dad, raisin his hand ter push his fingers through his hair.

I never said I was, I snap back at him, mostly cus I'm still waitin.

Dan, he said his name was, me mam says quickly ovver me and me dad. He said he'd come back.

Not tonight he won't, says me dad, who musta remembered his hair's just combed and is lettin his hand just softly pat it in place.

It's not that late, says me mam.

They have to be up in the mornin, says me dad, as if me and me sister aren't sittin right here, listenin.

You'll be up no problem, won't yer Chris?

Yeah, I say, and nod, still thinkin, Dan, Dan, Dan. Did he say anythin else?

No, just that, says me mam. It's mebbe just those welly boots, but he's a tall lad, isn't he?

Dan.

I suddenly see Dan Reid in me head, a bull's head buckle on his belt, Dan Reid on me doorstep, knockin on me door – me sister oppenin it on Friday and me mam just now – Dan Reid askin fer us and both times gettin turned away.

I'm stood in me bedroom with the light off, lookin at the street outside, at the buildin site abandoned and the street-light with its head hangin and orange light drapin down ter the pavement. I've reckoned it all up. Arthur'd be the only one who might've told Dan Reid where I lived, and sent him.

When I hear me dad downstairs in the hall, pullin his jacket on, I scrape the change off me bedside table. I'm at the toppa the stairs when me mam calls, Newcastle Brown, love! Me dad grunts and pulls the front door shut affter him. I gan down. I can hear the cab start up through the door as I'm pushin me feet inter me trainers.

Chris? me mam calls from the livin room.

I'm just goin ter use the phone, I say as I pull oppen the door and put it on the latch.

At this time? she says, but then she changes her mind, and says, Okay. Don't be long, ey?

Okay, I say and step out and pull the door to affter us.

I stand on the doorstep in the chilly gloom. I can hear next door's telly, laffin through their wall. The night smells damp, as if someone's dug a fresh hole. I gan down the path and trek down the street ter the phonebox, past me dad's empty parkin place.

I pull the phonebox door oppen with a *screak*. It flexes shut slowly on its muscle once I'm in. I unhook the phone. I feel as if I'm on show in this box of light, ter whoever gans past or happens ter be lookin. I can hear the tone really loud, before I've even got the phone close ter me ear. I hod it till I hear the tiny voice say, The number you have dialled has not been recognised please hang up and try again the number you have dialled has not been recognised please before I *clicker-clicker* the cradle and hear the far-off machinery cuttin out and re-connectin, and then the tone startin up again.

I crook the handle in me neck between me chin and shoulder, so I can sift me change in me palm. I feed the slot me fifty-pence piece. Then I wedge meself so me back's ter the houses, and give the front of the phone a bang with the side of me fist. The bang's so loud I cringe, tryin ter keep the noise close ter me body and not have it roll out and around the streets. Me coin rattles inter the tray. I feed it in, listen ter the coin settle inter the insides, then bang it through again. I start ter dial Arthur's number.

There's a silence affter the clack of each number. I'm imaginin somespot far off, where the numbers get typed out, cus that's the sound in me ear, of the number typed with one finger and kept somespot, on a secret slip of paper. I shift me feet and me backbone against the edges of the winderframes. Down the line, the phone starts ter ring. I breathe inter the black mouthpiece, the placky startin ter warm and ter stink the faint old stink of other breaths.

Hello?

His mam's voice has come all of a sudden again, ragged as this mornin when I said nowt ter her.

Hello. Is Arthur there? I say, as polite as I can. Silence fer long seconds, so long I say, Hello. Hello.

Who is this?

It's Chris. Mrs Grieve?

Is it you – you who's been ringing? I'm warning you. We won't have this, not now, she says.

It's me, Mrs Grieve – Chris.

I hear a scrunchin in me ear, and I guess she's puttin her hand ovver the mouthpiece, then muffled voices.

Hello? I say.

No more, says a man's raised voice. Do you hear me?

Hello. Mr Grieve? It's Chris, Arthur's mate. Is he there?

Chris who? The police are involved, you know. If this is more funny business—

It's Chris Hearsey.

Do we know you?

Yeah yer know me, I say. I've stayed at your house.

Do you know where he is? Is he with you?

No. That's why I'm ringin. Is he not back?

Back from where? says Arthur's dad quickly.

I dunno. That's why I was ringin. There's more scrunchin in me ear. Muffled voices. I'm waitin fer the pips ter tell us I'm runnin outta money. I swap the phone round. The earpiece is warm on me cold other ear.

You were with him when he cut his hand.

A bolt gans through us. I say nowt.

You know I had to take him to hospital, to get it stitched up?

He's not back, then? I say.

What's your address? Where are you?

I have ter go.

I'll find out. You know I will, says Arthur's dad, his voice scrabblin fer us down the line.

Bye, I say, and cut him off. I stand hoddin the phone a little way from me ear, listenin ter the tone. I'm wonderin how much me own dad'd know about me if one day I never kem home, how much me mam'd have ter fill him in. I hang the phone handle ovver me shoulder by its thick silver cord and stick me palms inter me eye sockets, pressin slow fireworks onter the blackness that's there all the time – me own blackness stored behind me eyelids, the way the tone's stored in the handle of the phone and'll be there, even affter I've put the phone down and gone.

The winders're misty with me talk. I squeak a cold squiggle in one winder with me fingertip. I wonder what it'd tek ter turn the mist back inter me words again. I'm watchin the headlights of me dad's cab swing round the corner and point right at us as he pulls inter his space. They're flicked out. He climbs onter the pavement, an offy carrier bag hangin from his hand, slams the door, and strides up ter the house.

I push oppen the phonebox, lettin the night in and me out. I tek a big breath. The pavin stones're sparklin the way they do when the dark gets hod of em and shows em off. All up and down the road the streetlights've got fuzzy haloes, each stood, just mindin its own bitta pavement. From some backyard I can hear a dog whimperin ter get inside. If I was a dog I reckon I'd be doin the same. I look at me hands and I can see the whiteness of em just leakin out inter the dark. I squeeze the plaster round me light-filled thumb and head fer the front door me dad's already through.

SIXTEEN

I draw me curtains. I'm tryin not ter think of me school clothes hangin in me wardrobe. I get on me hands and knees and reach and grab the ivory elephant out from under me bed. I stand it on me bedside table while I get inter me pyjamas. I climb inter bed and lie on me side, leanin on me elber, me chin in me hand, and stare at it.

I thought I said yer weren't to go out! yelled me dad when I stuck me head inter the livin room, just like I'd expected him ter.

He just nipped out ter the phone, me mam said, her nervy hand gan ter me dad's arm where it rested briefly as a bird.

Shoes off! he shouted.

I heeled me trainers off where I stood.

In the hall. Go on.

I bent down and clamped me two trainers in me left hand, so I wasn't usin me thumb, and took em back ter the hall where I lined em up.

Don't just stand there, me dad said, cus when I kem back I just stood in the livin-room doorway.

Are yer okay, Chris? Me mam was turned with her glass fulla brown ter look at us. Yer look white as a sheet.

I didn't know what I was gonna say but I was ready ter

say summit. I was ready ter ask em if they thought Arthur'd get found. I was gonna tell me dad I'd tekkan his newspaper, and then tell me mam ter tell him about the cops, cus then I could have a good enough reason fer hidin the paper, which'd be me own worry, backed up by the knuckle-gnawin worry of me own mam.

I started ter speak.

Mam, Dad—

Why don't you get an early night? said me mam. Go on, love, she said and nodded us gently away.

So I didn't say what I was gonna say. I turned and started upstairs. I heard me dad mutter summit, then say, Stupid boy, and me mam's voice tricklin like watter ovver stones.

Just as I got ter the toppa the stairs she whispered from the bottom.

Yer okay, aren't yer, love?

I stuck me face ter the bars of the banisters and peered down. She was stood, her hands knotted in front of her and her face lifted twards us, fulla fret. I knew then I had ter smooth out some of them frets, cus it was just her and me who knew and could share the knowin silently, face ter face. Yeah, I said.

You were a long time on the phone.

Yeah, but I'm fine, I said. Night.

Chris?

Yeah? I slotted me face back between the banisters.

She was smilin hopefully up at us. See you in the mornin?

Yeah. See yer in the mornin, Mam.
Don't wake yer sister.

I tek the elephant and put it under me piller, then I knock off me lamp. I watch the crack of light around me bedroom doorframe in the dark. I turn ovver ter face the wall. I'm thinkin about dyin, which is not wakin up ferever. At least then I wouldn't have ter get up and gan ter school, where Carl'll be waitin in the cloakroom, sat tucked in among the furry-hooded coats. And I'm thinkin about that time Booby bought us the booze, when Arthur wanted ter try gettin pissed so badly that he med an enemy fer life of Carl Hole.

Booby'll get it fer us, I'd told Arthur as we searched the avenues.

Aye, said Arthur, but what'll he want?

Nowt. Mebbe some extra cash, but he'll just get it, I said. It's no big deal.

And then we'll gan out ter mine.

Then we'll gan out ter yours and yer'll tell yer mam we're stayin at mine.

Aye, said Arthur, and yer've told yer mam that yer at mine.

Aye, I said, but I was peerin ahead. It's the Black Hole, I said.

We saw him as we got closer – Carl and who-knows-who-all-else, just stood about in a front yard. They were watchin Booby, who had a broom balanced on the palm of one hand and was starin up at the head of the broom in the air.

We could gan, I said.

The Black Hole's lookin right at us, said Arthur. If we bottle it they'll fuckin start affter us, won't they? Cus we'll look flairt.

I shrugged and led us on, Arthur laggin behind. I spat inter the gutter, half expectin the spit ter be red with the taste of me own batterin heart. Booby had started ter gan round and round on the spot, turnin on his heel, his face starin up at the head of the broom, big Booby spinnin round and round, and light on his toes fer the size of him. He went wobblin round in a circle less and less true as he turned till suddenly I heard em all shout SWEEP! and Booby let the broom fall inter a sweepin position and tried ter push it across the grass. But he couldn't push it straight and he staggered under the sheer weight of himsel and went ovver and onter his back, where he lay with his arms out and his shirt whipped up ovver his wobblin white gut.

WHOAH! they all shouted, hootin with laffter. Carl stepped down inter the front yard and reached down fer the broom. From ovver the road I watched him crouch at Booby's head and say summit ter Booby. Then he stood and handed the broom ovver ter a long streak of a gadgee who raised it upright on his palm and began the same routine as Booby. Booby meantime was rollin himsel onter his elbow and heftin himsel onter his feet, one hand grabbin at the air ter steady himsel, the knuckles of his other hand across his eyes. From where me and Arthur were I could still see the stagger gan through the trunks of his legs.

Once we got almost level with the crew, their eyes started

flickin from the streaky feller with the broom ter us and back again. I reckon I was ready ter gan straight past, ter forget our big plan, but Arthur started veerin ter the right. Before I knew what was what, he was crossin the road. Come on, he said ovver his shoulder. Yer wanna get pissed in all, don't yer?

SWEEP! they all shouted, and in Arthur went, up the path ter the front of the house the lads were stood against, watchin the skinny feller fall ovver the broom, giddy with gan round and round, and ovver the road I follered, and started up the path.

WHOAH! they all shouted cus the streaky feller had staggered inter the low front wall and tumbled right ovver it and onter the pavement. Booby strode ovver and scooped the broom up off the grass. He'd got his balance back. The broom looked half-size in his hand.

Chris lad!

Booby.

Where yer bin?

Oh, yer know.

I'm sure yer'll do better than Gogs there, he said, swingin the broom handle twards the feller still flat on his back on the pavement. Here, and he tossed the broom at us lengthways and I fumbled it, the shaft of it nearly crackin us under the chin.

Middle of the grass, broom in the air and ten times round, said Booby. Keep yer eyes on it. We'll all count.

Booby strode back ter where Arthur had med space fer himself beside Carl in front of the house. The Black Hole's eyes were on us, unmovin, even as he leant in ter hear whatever Arthur was whisperin. Booby took his place beside em, bendin one huge leg ter rest his footsole against the wall at his back. There was him and then Carl and then Arthur. There was another gadgee stood on the other side of Arthur. He had a flick of brown hair and a T-shirt with RELAX written across it. The skinny feller, Gogs, was still pullin himsel up off the pavement. Carl was leanin twards Booby, passin him, I reckoned, whatever it was Arthur had asked. I took all this in and then I stepped inter the middle of the yard and swung the brush up inter the air, keepin the handle balanced on the palm of me left hand and hoddin it steady with me right. I squinted up at the brush swayin against the sky. It was cuttin out the sun, then lettin it blare through again. I brought me trainers together and started ter shuffle round, me ankles locked stiff.

One! yelled Booby.

Two! yelled Booby and another.

Three! yelled Arthur's voice fer sure amongst em.

Four!

Gan on, lad, someone hollered. Faster.

Five! they all yelled. I felt the house come back round but didn't see it, cus the head of the broom was movin with us so it seemed I'd not even moved.

Six! they yelled, and me ankles had unlocked and I was pushin mesel round faster and faster on one heel.

Seven! I heard, and I chanced a look down from the brush ter the ground, but only the yellin of their voices was givin us any direction.

Eight! I heard, their voices gettin dragged so I couldn't place em certainly as I turned, and I was startin ter get dragged in me mind the opposite way ter the way I knew I was really turnin.

Nine!

Comin up ter ten, lad, then yer sweep.

SWEEP! they all shouted, and I struggled ter bring meself ter a stop, then I let the broom fall like an axe ter the grass and pushed. The broom handle went bendy. I staggered as if I was gettin barged invisibly from one side ter the other and none of me weight would be budged ter get us back straight. The ground was sawin and gan round. When I gev inter it, it was as if I was givin inter meself, and I pitched with a grunt inter the smell of the grass and the hard dirt the grass was stragglin outta. The dirt was colder underneath us than I thought it was gonna be, and the ground was still tippin one way, then the other, like a plate I was gettin served up on on me belly. Me eyes were gan round in me head. I tried ter focus on one blade of brown grass close up, but that single blade was bendin and tiltin madly too.

WHOAH! they all shouted, hootin and sniggerin. I concentrated on the dirt packed underneath us. I was tryin ter keep me eyes still by starin down a set of passages and archways runnin through the blades of grass.

Don't mek yerself too comfortable.

The head against the sky above us had sunlight dazzlin around it when I twisted round and blinked up.

Booby says he'll get us it, said Arthur, his face loomin ovver us, his hand reachin down so I could grab it and haul meself up. I stepped two steps ter me right, cus me legs wouldn't keep us in one spot. I tried ter look up at the row of them all stood against the house, but their faces kept slippin and slidin out from under me eyes.

When? I said, as I started ter foller Arthur unsteadily up ter the front of the house.

Soon as we're done here, Arthur whispered, cus Carl had kicked off the wall and was steppin down ter meet us on the path. His bleached hair was sweated inter dark spikes. I could see beads pricklin outta his forehead. He snatched the broom outta Arthur's hand.

Are yer gonna puke, Chris lad? he growled.

He's not gonna puke, Booby shouted down. Yer med of pipe-cleaners, aren't yer, Chris lad? But I know yer a different story, Carl. You watch, he said quietly ter me and Arthur as we kem up ter the wee strip of concrete in front of the house. I was still swayin. I didn't dare try ter mek space fer meself against the house itsel. I looked where everyone else was lookin, at Carl stood on the patch of yard grass with the broom already up on the palm of his hand.

Yer ready? called Booby.

Aye. Yer'll give us fifteen, eh? said Carl.

Oh ho ho! Booby bellowed, and elbered Gogs next ter him and the RELAX lad on his other side. Oh aye, Carl, fifteen, then yer can tek me fuckin appendix out. Gogs'll get the bread knife ready.

Gogs nodded, deadly serious. Carl said nowt, but looked up ter the sky, deadly serious in all.

Cmon, Chris lad, said Booby. Get a perch here with the rest

of us. He squidged ovver and Gogs budged too, and Booby slapped the wall where I was sposed ter gan and stand. I wobbled up and stood against it, Booby on one side of us, Gogs on the other, and Arthur left ter gan ter the end of the line and tek his place beside the RELAX lad with the flick, who crooked his face round ter look square at us and stuck two fingers ter his lips and raised his eyebrows, meanin, *Have yer gotta fag?* I turned me palms up and shrugged. He just shrugged in all and turned back ter watch. Carl began, slow and certain, ter gan round. Twice he'd bin round when Booby growled, Faster! but nee one was countin out loud. I was countin under me breath. I heard the rest of em count *Five* ter themselves.

How many? said Carl, his voice like a ribbon, like a black ribbon I reckoned, comin outta his mouth and wrappin itsel around him as he turned.

Yer'll know, said Booby. Don't yer worry.

Nine times round I'd counted, and Carl was turnin on the dead same spot, unwobbly.

Off school now, ey? Gogs muttered from beside us.

Aye.

Long summer holidays, ey?

I said nowt.

SWEEP! shouted Booby and Arthur and RELAX lad.

Carl stopped gan round, but did it as if he'd hardly moved. He just stepped outta his spin, easy as yer like. He let the broom chop down and took up his position behind it, then he pushed it straight across the grass. He even gev it a short double brushstroke, like yer do when yer come ter the end of sweepin a straight line, then he turned and swept back the way he'd kem.

OH HO! bellowed Booby.

Arthur was clappin.

You watch, Gogs muttered ter me.

Get that fuckin bread knife! Booby shouted. It's brain-surgery time! He turned ter his left and put his paws around Gogs's head, tiny between em, and held it while Gogs stamped and clawed at Booby's fingers. Then Booby let him gan as quick and Gogs stood red-faced, mussin his hair and scowlin.

You watchin? Booby said from close ter me ear. You watch. His breath smelled raw, like mince, the words warm in me ear. I watched as Carl propped the broom carefully against the coal bunker at the edge of the yard. He put his hands on his hips and stood. Then in one quick move he leant ovver behind the bunker and puked. He stayed leant ovver and we heard him barkin, bringin nowt up, then he kem upright, wiped his mouth with the back of his hand and snarled a crooked smile.

Foul, said Gogs, his arms crossed, shekkin his head.

Yer've nowt left, have yer, Carl? said Booby.

What yer on about? Carl snapped back, his top lip hooked back off his teeth.

Nowt left ter get dizzy. That's how yer do it, isnit? The rest of us, like the lad Chris here, he said, his heavy hand comin down on me shoulder, we've gotta wee bit left rattlin about. Enough brain ter let us know where we're at, like.

Him! shouted Carl, and he flung his arm twards us.

Booby's hand was heavier still on me shoulder. What yer sayin, eh? That he's got summit I fuckin haven't?

Me guts jumped, the sourness of em at the back of me throat, and Carl was stumpin across the yard, his white fists at his sides and the strings in his neck yanked tight.

Ignore him, lad, said Booby ter me. Yer just havin a wobbly, aren't yer, Carl? But yer'll not be gettin too fired up, will yer? Booby's hand was still pressin down on me shoulder. I could feel the weight of him in the muscles in me thighs as he turned his whole body twards Carl, and Carl stopped stumpin and just stood, his chest heavin.

Yer should say sorry ter the lad. Sorry fer bein a radge. Don't yous two think so? Booby said, lookin from Arthur ter Gogs. They both nodded. I could feel a trickle of sweat runnin down inter the crack of me arse. Me fingers were pushin inter the wall at me back, as if the wall and me could get squeezed together inter summit unbreakable. I didn't dare move.

Fuck off, Booby, said Carl.

Oooo! said RELAX lad. From beside us, Gogs let a hiss of air out from between his teeth.

Now now, said Booby. If yer not gonna be good, we'll have ter set the dogs on yer. Chris here's done nowt, has he? So say yer fuckin sorry.

I was wonderin where the dogs were. I was also wonderin how long it'd tek ter get ter the off-licence and have Booby buy the booze, like Booby had said he was gonna, and then fer me and Arthur ter get oursels out on the bus ter Arthur's house.

Come on, Carl, said Gogs, fair's fair.

Fuck you.

I'm still waitin, said Booby ter Carl.

Kiss me arse, yer fucker.

Oh, Carl, said Booby, swingin his big head sadly. What're we gonna do with yer?

Booby turned his wide white face from Carl ter me, then back ter Carl again. He looked down and brushed summit invisible off the denim strainin around his propped-up leg. I tried ter mek meself relax, cus I realised me arms were locked behind us as I pushed me fingertips even harder inter the wall.

It's dead simple, Carl, said Booby. Yer just say sorry fer the bother yer causin. It's not askin much, is it? Yer mek up with the lad here. Otherwise. Well. Booby looked from Gogs ter RELAX lad. Gogs shook his head. RELAX lad med a face that meant *Oh well* and shrugged. Carl's chest was heavin up and down. I snatched a quick look at Arthur. He'd got a grin hoverin on his face as he watched Carl. I quickly looked away.

I'm sayin nowt, said Carl.

Fair enough. If that's the way yer wannit, say nowt, and as he said this, Booby pushed himsel off the front of the house and stepped down, calm and easy, off the strip of concrete, onter the yard grass. Sayin nowt is certainly yer best option, he said as he stepped up ter Carl.

Fuck off, Booby, said Carl, but the words were hardly outta his mouth before, quicker than yer'd think he could move, Booby had barged right inter Carl, his belly bouncin Carl off his feet and onter his back with an Omph! on the grass. From beside us, Gogs had slid away from the front of the house, and him and RELAX lad were onter the grass and droppin ter their knees on Carl as he tried ter get up, kickin and strugglin, fuckin this and fuckin that, but mostly screamin that Booby was a fuck. I hadn't moved. Suddenly Carl's arm lashed free and RELAX lad got a smack in the side of the head. The sound was solid, like a bat on a ball, but only seemed ter mek the lad more determined ter hod Carl down.

Beside us, Arthur had bin twitchin, his hands at his sides, flexin, as if he was mebbe gonna gan down there affter Gogs and the other lad, but he was shocked ter a stop by the solid sound of the smack.

Shall we scarper? I whispered ter him. He looked at us, frownin.

Yer kiddin, aren't yer? This is fuckin priceless, this like. He turned back ter watch.

I was still clutchin at the wall. Gogs and RELAX lad had bundled the Black Hole ovver onter his front, pinnin his arms behind him, and then they hauled him upright, his feet kickin. I could tell they'd got Carl's whole weight held between em, cus when he kicked both feet out at the same time he stayed held up. His face was twisted purple. Booby was stood, watchin, his arms at his sides. I noticed how short his arms looked, with his sides bulgin out so far. Carl was kickin like mad and, as I watched, one foot caught Booby right in the bollocks. Booby didn't so much as flicker, even though everyone – even Carl – paused affter the kick ter see what Booby would do.

Carl shouldn't have stopped strugglin, cus Booby just stepped twards him and with both hands yanked his jeans down around his ankles. Either Carl was snake-thin, or Booby was so strong, that Booby didn't have ter undo em, and Carl's skinny white legs were trapped together then in his pulled-down kegs, his brick-red undies out fer the world ter see.

I was findin meself steppin forward then, ter getta closer look at the Black Hole, ter see him as I didn't think I'd ever see him – at someone else's mercy.

We're all behind yer, Carl, said Booby, and the two of them hoddin Carl sniggered. Carl thrashed. The other two tightened their grip. But when I ask yer – when I tell yer – ter say yer sorry, said Booby, who'd reached behind him inter his back pocket and pulled summit out, I'm hopin yer hearin me. He shook his fist beside Carl's twistin head. I was near enough ter hear the matches rattle in the box. The Black Hole was tryin ter bite Booby's wrist, like a dog on a short leash, but Gogs had forced Carl's wrist up ter his shoulderblade so he couldn't twist his head far enough round.

Fuckers, he was spittin all the while, yer fuckers.

Aye, I know, said Booby. Fuckers.

He'd pushed oppen the matchbox, tiny in his hands, and had a match in his finger and thumb.

Hod him still, will yer, lads? he said, and the lads braced emselves and hoisted Carl so he was held tighter and stiller. Then Booby raised his foot and stamped down on Carl's jeans, hoddin Carl's tied-together legs ter the deck so only his white knees were buckin. The lads were whoopin and cacklin. Booby clamped the matchbox in his mouth, hooked oppen the front of Carl's undies with one finger, struck the match in his other hand on the matchbox, as if he was strikin it on his own teeth, and then dropped the match as it flared inter the Black Hole's undies. Then he let the elastic snap.

Carl screamed.

I looked guiltily ter me left and right, knowin suddenly there were houses up and down the street. I was wonderin how long it'd tek someone ter come and see what was happenin if they'd heard screamin. I reckoned I was gonna do summit, but I didn't know what it was. It might've bin ter just run. But Booby was strikin another match. Carl was thrashin. Gogs was sayin summit in the Black Hole's ear, though the Black Hole was roarin and his head was twistin about. Booby's match had gone out, so he took the box out of his gob and ratched out another, his big foot all the while stamped on Carl's yanked-down jeans. Then, with the matchbox back in his gob, Booby turned ter me. He beckoned us with a jerk of his big head. I shook me head. He shrugged. I turned twards Arthur, cus he'd tekkan a step down off the concrete strip. Booby had hooked oppen the front of Carl's undies again, but he'd paused and turned twards Arthur. He spat the matchbox out.

Yer want yer booze?

Aye, said Arthur.

Yer want us ter stop fuckin about here so yous can away and get some pop inter yer?

Aye, said Arthur.

But yer'd pick up me matchbox if I asked yer? said Booby.

I watched as Arthur stepped down inter the front yard and bent ter grab the matchbox outta the grass. Booby was beamin at him.

Fish us a match outta there in all, lad, and strike it while yer at it.

Arthur pushed the box oppen and nipped out a match carefully, struck it on the sandpaper and cupped it lit in his hand. I was imaginin the cracklin stink of the Black Hole's pubes. Booby nodded down at Carl's hooked-oppen undies.

Gan on, lad.

Carl screamed.

SEVENTEEN

Suddenly I'm woken in the black dark by the front door shuttin and me dad's steps scuffin down the path outside. It must be near ten at night if me dad's gan out ter work, and I musta dropped off, thinkin about Carl and Booby, and Arthur scratchin a match alight. I slip me hand under me piller and close me fingers around the elephant. I squeeze it till its little points start stabbin inter me palm. Me dad oppens the cab door, slams it, then fires up the engine and pulls away. I shut me eyes. I shut me eyes, but me eyelids snap back oppen, like suitcase catches, and I can't get em ter stay clicked-shut ovver me eyes.

Then I'm jerkin me face up, cus I'm sure I just heard summit.

I knock the covers down from around me ears, so there's no crumplin of me pillercase or close-in scratchin of the covers, just plenty of empty air fer me ears ter flap about in. I'm strainin, but all I'm hearin is the car that's gan past outside, its headlights rakin ovver us and me whole room stretchin in a yawn of light that's closin as quickly again inter blackness. I'm listenin, not breathin, but there's nowt ter hear now the car's gone by but the zizzin of the night which is always there, and might even be the sound of me own neck muscles strainin. I let me head sink back inter me piller.

dink

I'm up, sittin properly upright with me eyes wide. I kick off the covers, swing me legs out and plant me bare feet on the floor. I'm like the steel scaffoldin ovver the road when a scobbed stone's rung against a tube of it, cus I'm ringin with the shock, me hands clamped ter the edge of me mattress. And there fer sure's the sound of another hard summit missin me winder and bouncin off the outside of the house. I'm seein Booby under me winder as I'm rigidly sat, his fat face stained with streetlight, Booby who's mebbe watched and waited all this time fer me dad ter gan out.

dink

Another un, solid on the glass, and mekkin us stand up, half with the shock of it, me legs wobblin. I move, cus I have ter move, and as I move I decide. I decide I'll peep through me curtains, and if it's Booby, I'll wake me mam fer sure. I'll peep through me curtains and if I don't twitch em, then Booby won't know fer certain that I'm up here, and he might just gan away. But if he doesn't gan away, I'll wake me mam and tell her everythin, cus me mam had looked up at us from the bottom of the stairs and her fretted face had bin askin us ter reassure her, ter let her know that whatever was spread between me and her wasn't bigger than I'd med her think it was.

I start ter creep ter the left edge of the winder, the chill of the dark chillier on the parts of us that were cosy under me duvet but are leakin their cosiness now. I watch me shufflin feet gleam. Now they've crossed inter the orange bar of streetlight let onter the carpet under the winder. I crook me head sideways, hod me breath and slowly peer inbetween the wall and the hangin curtain edge.

Cus me bedroom's dark I can see outside inter the night easily enough, down ter the road and me grey front path and ovver ter the scaffolds of blacker shadder across the road. The curtain's waftin under me nose and me angle's only good ter see everythin ter the right, so I'm on me tiptoes, tryin ter getta look at the places Booby might be standin, when me eyes catch a flicker ter the left and I jump back from the winder, me heart like a rocket screamin up inside us, cus the *crack* against the glass felt aimed right at us.Before she can throw another even heavier coddy, I'm clawin me way through the curtains and unhitchin the winder ter let cool night come breezin in.

Fuckin hell, Gill!

Get down here, she hisses up at us.

I'm stood with me bare feet on me bedroom carpet and me bare face in the night, the cold slippin onter me skin down the front of me pyjamas.

Why?

Just get down here.

I watch her as she darts back around the house and outta sight. I can hear the city rumblin, and it feels like only the loosest, thinnest layer now between the wide-awake, chancy city and me skin.

I shiver as I pull the winder to and ease the catch on, quiet as I can. Me brain's like a nest of ants, seethin in me skull. I draw the curtains. I gan softly ovver the floor and feel fer the handles of me top drawer. I slide it oppen and ratch in the gloom fer me darkest clothes. I pull em on ovver me pyjamas, pull on me socks, then head fer me bedroom door. At the last second I gan back ter me bed and feel me own warmth still beltin outta the thrown-back covers as I slip me hand under the piller. I pocket the elephant. Then I hump the covers up ter look slept-in and gan fer the landin.

The light on downstairs is mekkin the stairway glowy and the banisters nowt but black bars. I tek me first steps on the landin like moon steps, so slow that I figure it'll tek us hours ter get ter the toppa the stairs. I stop steppin. I stand and listen. I can hear nowt but the house doin what it does while we're all asleep – the immersion heater hummin, the walls and floors tickin now and then as they brace emselves against the night that's suckin at the winders. I start steppin, quiet but surer – quicker. I'm hoddin me mind on the creaky third stair, and havin ter avoid it, and just as I get ter the toppa the stairs me sister's door cracks oppen. I freeze.

She looks out, rubbin one eye with her fist, her other eye blinkin at us, her face all crumpled and white. I getta flash of what she's seein, me own shape frozzen in the glow at the head of the stairs, where I'm not sposed ter be, in dark clothes I'm not sposed ter have on, with a look of pure fear on me face. I stare at her and she stares back at us, neither of us movin a millimetre. The air between us is bristlin. The whole house is ready ter choke on us, is ready ter cough us up in a blaze of lights and what're-yer-doins. But me sister pushes her door shut. Without a word or a sound her face disappears behind it inter the dark. I wait. I hear the mattress janglin as she climbs back inter bed. I wait and the quiet starts ter trickle and fill up the seconds.

I tek the first step downstairs.

I wait.

And now I tek the second, movin like a deep-sea diver. I can feel on me skin that I'm so far down in the quiet that there's nowt of mesel that could snag on me mam's ears ter pull her up and awake. Down I gan, and now I'm off the bottom stair and grabbin me trainers up so carefully from the mat.

The lamp's on in the hall. The only hint of us as I gan is the swingin of the tassels hangin off the shade.

I can mek out the taps glimmerin in the kitchen as I creep, me trainers in me hand. At the back door, I stand and listen once more. But there's nowt ter hear but a blood-beat – me own sound – and it can't keep us still, so I turn the key and push the back door handle down, as if it's a ton ter push. Nowt's clicked or sprung ter brek the silence, and suddenly I'm easin oppen the door and slidin meself out inter the airy dark.

What took yer? she says, before I've even had a chance ter pull the door shut behind us.

Shush, I hiss, cus I'm doin the shuttin in slow motion. I kem as fast as I could.

Well, hurry it up, she whispers, lockin the dark lump of her handbag onter her shoulder.

I feel the door meet the frame and I let the handle off

slowly. I push the door's edge with me fingertips, ter mek sure the latch has caught and the door's solid, and then I sit on the step ter pull on me trainers. The cold in the stone creeps straight through the meat of me arse and inter me arse-bone. Gill's stood ovver us. I can hear her breathin fast. I snatch a look up from knottin me laces but I can't see owt in her face fer the dark. I get ter me feet, tryin not ter shift me soles and scrape the grit, cus the dark's like an unbaffled exhaust pipe, with nowt ter stop every gritty crunch and whisper roarin out, full bore.

Cmon, hisses Gill, and I foller affter her, past the cut-out of the back wall and under the back wall's straight-cut shadder, laid exactly on the ground. The gable of the house next door's pasted up like a billboard flat against the night, and the scuffin of our steps on the path shrivels us inter mesel. I've crept out, I'm away, and me teeth're chatterin, even though the night's not cold. Gill's crouchin ovver ahead of us, and I'm crouchin the same, as if there're gun-sights on us. She gans left outta me front gate and I foller, duckin with her inter the cut. It hods us like a tunnel, and our footsteps're brittle-soundin in the deeper shelterin dark. Gill sticks her palm out, turnin a pale look twards us, and I stop where I am and stand, lookin from one end of the cut ter the other while she nashes down ter check there's nee one comin. I listen ter the soft *slap-slap* of her plimsolls dyin down the cut. Me hands're pale too when I look at em, dipped in the dark, and I'm imaginin me own face as Gill slips back again, runnin on tiptoe along the fence, the shadders dragged ovver her. Suddenly her face is so close I can feel heat fizzin off her cheeks and smell apple shampoo.

Listen, yer in big trouble, the two of yer—

Trouble?

I heard—

Where did yer gan?

Let us speak, fer Christ sake, Gill snaps. Booby thinks yer know where Arthur is and he's mad.

Suddenly I'm aware of all the words I wanna say backed up in me throat.

I tried ter show yer the paper, I say. The cops kem and asked us—

But Gill's grabbed me arm. Just shush and listen ter what I'm tellin yer, Chris. Arthur knows it was them. That's why they're tryin ter find him, and when Booby spoke ter yer on the phone at Mal's house—

What yer on about? I'm gan from foot ter foot as we whisper.

Ow!

Listen, hisses Gill, and her nippin fingers loosen off me wrist. Yer have ter get it inter yer head.

Okay, okay. What?

They're the ones who did that tramp.

In the silence I hear Gill swaller. I'm totally still. Her fingers're locked onter me wrist.

Booby and them did him, she says, her voice fulla husk. Chris?

Aye, I whisper, I know who yer meant.

I couldn't not tell yer, but I saw them two hornies with yer mam when I kem before, so I didn't knock at yer door. I heard em say it, Chris, at Mal's house. I heard Booby say it.

I lift me arms and shek Gill's grip off me wrist. I put the heels of me hands ter me eyes. There's grit behind em when I rub, like the sugary dust yer get leftovver in a bag of cola-cubes. I oppen me eyes and blink the blotchy floaters out of em. The dark's just the same, with the streetlight spillin in at the end of the cut and Gill stood so close ter us. But everythin's tilted, like it was affter the broom game, and Gill's tilted it.

So Arthur knows it was them, I whisper.

That's what I'm tellin yer. He knows it was them and they're affter him, which means they're affter you in all.

How'd yer get outta Mal's house?

The front door. Booby smashed it in and out I snuck with Liz while they were in the middle of rowin. Mal's there shoutin ter get pulled outta the hatch and Booby's shoutin, Where is the cunt, and they're shoutin ovver each other, and I heard Arthur's name, didn't I? Mal's askin Booby if he's sin the fuckin paper and Booby's roarin about you, tellin Mal he shoulda grabbed yer when he had the chance. And that's when he said about the tramp.

Gill stops and looks away from us inter the gloom.

Said what? I say.

He'll have us all up fer the murder. That's what Booby said, and it shut Mal right up, and then Booby asks Mal did he not know you were Arthur's mate, and that cus Arthur's run off and drawn so much attention he's sure ter get found sooner or later—

When the police'll be askin him what med him run away.

Exactly, says Gill, foldin her arms.

We stand in the dark, neither of us sayin owt. I'm pantin like I've run a race, and now I realise Gill is too, and I can't stop mesel hearin both our breathin startin ter saw in and out at the same time. I hod me breath, ter brek the pattern, and concentrate past Gill, on the sound of cars in the distance, their engine noises risin and fallin away. A dog's gan off half the city away, just the flimsiest ghost of its barkin floatin up and ovver the roofs from some strange, unfriendly spot. Above us I reckon I can hear the wires hummin as they feed lecky inter the houses. Gill's started ter scuff her foot back and forth, the sound echoin in the cut.

Suddenly Gill stops scuffin.

Chris?

Yeah?

I never told yer.

Never told us what?

If I tell yer—

Never told us what? What else, Gill? I say, louder than I mean ter, me heart boxin behind me ribs.

It was Carl I saw today.

I told yer. I saw him at yours, out yer winder, I say, me face pulled inter a frown I know she can't see in the gloom.

Not then, says Gill. We kem outta me gran's and when yer caught us up I asked if yer'd seen someone. It was him.

Oh, says Gill, through her fingers, cus her hands've gone up ter cover her mouth. I reckon he was follerin us today and I never said. If I'd known, Chris – if I'd known what they'd done.

It's alright, I say, but I hear me voice come out as flat and cold as a field in the rain.

What're yer gonna do? she says, and I'm suddenly certain, stood here in the dark, breathin fresh night air and knowin Gill owes us summit fer not tellin about the Black Hole.

We're gonna go and see Dan Reid.

Who's he? What's he gotta do with anythin? And what's this we? says Gill, lettin her voice gan shootin high off the end of the last word.

Yer comin with us, Gill, I hiss, out ter Arthur's village.

I've stopped whisperin and I'm waitin. Gill's lookin at the deck. I can see the odd gold strand of her hair, caught alight despite the dim. She says nowt. I start up again.

Listen. Dan Reid kem ter see us tonight, but me mam sent him away before he could talk ter us. He's bin round before but I didn't know till tonight. He knows Arthur, and Arthur's the only way he'd know ter come ter mine. D'yer see?

So yer think this Dan knows where Arthur is, then? says Gill, lookin up at us, summit in the sound of her voice gone glittery with the chance of it, like a single strand of her hair in the dark.

I say nowt. I don't move. A car crawls by, its headlights slicin close ter us as it gans. Fer every second that the skim of light shows both our faces, I stare hard inter Gill's shinin eyes, and then everythin's blackin out and gan invisible in the affterwards.

I spose we're out now, says Gill. We can't just leave it as it is and gan sneakin back in, can we?

Let's go, then, I hiss.

Gill sniffs. Yer know where ter find this Dan?

I reckon.

Yer reckon or yer know? Cus we're not gan unless yer sure, Christopher. Fuck, she says suddenly, slappin her hand on me arm. How're we gonna get out there?

Have yer got any money?

Yeah, course, she says, pattin her handbag.

We'll get the bus.

EIGHTEEN

I mek a show of squintin at the timetable, runnin me finger-tip down the days and times ovver and ovver, while Gill leans in the corner of the shelter. I can see her watchin us from the dark, the glint of her eyes. We were here before it was due so it must be late, I say.

We're not gettin back though if it comes, are we?

It doesn't look like there is one back, I mutter.

How can it gan out there and not come back?

I dunno, do I. Mebbe it gans on somewhere else, I say, lookin up the empty road, all the power of me lookin bent on squeezin a bus outta neewhere and round the corner.

They'll think I've bin kidnapped. Stolen outta me own bed. Abducted.

When we find Arthur—

Oh, Christopher, as if yer've got the first idea! I never shoulda come. Two more minutes. That's what I'm givin it. Two, and then I'm away.

I look up the road again. I know we're far out, the two of us, and who's ter say we haven't got through town fer nowt, sneakin up Scalegate Road, then fleein faster as we got further, past the shut corner shop on Millholme Avenue and ovver ter Currock Road, and then up Currock Road, past the dark glass swimmin baths on James Street, and onter the Viaduct, and then down the Viaduct Way, keepin ter the shadders, but only just, cus time was gonna mek all our sneakin useless if we ran out of it and missed the last bus. I'd felt the heat of every car, their headlights like cooker hobs as they passed. We'd given every pub a wide berth. And then we'd got ter Bridge Street, ter the stop I knew the buses passed on their way outta town, and it'd felt then that it'd be impossible ter walk back home. We had ter wait, even if we were waitin fer a bus that'd long gone, cus the waitin itsel was mekkin its pullin round the corner possible.

Thirty seconds, Christopher. Twenny-nine, twenny-eight.

I'm starin up the road as a familiar engine-sound grows, and now I'm scuttlin backwards inter the shelter, me heart fallin through us as a black cab sweeps by.

And now Gill's steppin out, and I think she's gan till I see she's jumpin, stickin up her hand. It's here! she's shoutin as she waves the bus down.

It swings through the night with me and Gill reflected in its black winders, our outlines doubled in the vibratin glass so each of us is sittin there, shivery-edged. I turn me face away from the glass. A can's clatterin along the deck under the empty seats, up twards the front of the bus, and now down twards the back again as the engine shudders inter a low gear and starts haulin us up a hill. The further we've got from town, the more level the road, and the longer the stretches when the can's just sat in one spot, rockin on its side. I tek a hod of the silver bar on the seat in front of us, long enough fer me hand ter warm the metal, then I tek me hand away and watch the mist shrivel off the surface. Down the corridor of yeller light, the one other feller on the bus is cavin further inter his donkey jacket.

D'yer think he's asleep? Me voice sheks with everythin else gettin shekkan by the revs.

Do I care?

I'm just sayin. He might miss his stop, mightn't he? I say as the can starts ter rattle in a long arc from one side of the aisle ter the other. The old feller jerks awake, then his chin straightaway starts ter sink again, lower and lower onter his chest, deeper inter the collar of his coat.

He looks like the tramp, says Gill, and I sidle a look at her face and see her wishin she hadn't said it, bitin hard on her bottom lip.

She unsnaps and snaps shut the catch of the handbag on her lap. I dunno how yer persuaded us inter this.

I say nowt. I turn ter watch the old feller again, me eyes on the greasy tangle of hair at the back of his head. I'm thinkin exactly what Gill's thinkin, wonderin if he's just gonna ride the bus ter the last stop and then stay on ter ride it whichever way it gans back, hauntin it all the way ter wherever it gans back to.

The bus groans and creaks. We pull through a scatterin of houses. There's a single streetlight passin on its orange tinge, like a sickness, ter the leaves of the tree it's stood under. There's a bare farmyard walled away in the darkness behind propped-oppen gates. The bus trundles beside a low-runnin plank fence, and a leafy hedge, and then the brief light's left behind and it's just me own face in the black winder, starin in at itsel.

It's not far now, I say.

Yer know why I'm doin this, don't yer?

I turn ter look at Gill. The tip of her tongue curls up fer a second and touches her top lip.

Aye. Cus yer heard em. Yer know we have ter find Arthur before they do.

No, she says, lookin at us, her mouth pressed inter a line. When yer cut yer own thumb today.

Yeah?

Did yer mean ter do it?

I'm frownin. The bus gans up a gear and the engine's let off. I can feel the twist of bafflement still in me face.

Yer dunno, d'yer? she says.

I shift on the slippery seat. Me kegs pull tight ovver the elephant in me pocket, that I wanna give back ter her, but can't. I scratch me forehead, ter cover me face, then I put me hand on the bar of the seat in front of us and close me fingers round it. The plaster on me thumb's tuggin at the skin it's stuck ter.

Sometimes yer do summit and yer dunno where it's gonna land yer, says Gill. Yer know when yer doin it that it's gonna change stuff. Yer know yer can't predict what's gonna come of it, and part of doin it is ter change stuff so much that yer don't know if yer'll recognise yersel down the line. But yer never know before it comes if it's gonna be a good change or a bad change. Yer just know that doin this thing'll change the most stuff round the most. See?

She looks at us. I nod slowly and say nowt. We gan round a bend and the empty can rocks in the aisle. When I think it's alright ter, I turn back ter me own face shekkin in the black glass.

We climb down at the crossroads and both stand as the doors slatter shut and the bus squeaks and shudders and pulls away. I watch the lit inside, the old feller zonked out in his coat, and then winder affter winder slide past. I'm starin affter the red lights at the back of it and then they're gone and I'm listenin ter the distance swaller the rumble of the engine till all that's left is enormous quiet. Not pure quiet, cus there's a *chirrup-chirrup* and a *plink-plink, plink-plink* and I look ter see moths flurryin about the head of the street-lamp stood at the meetin of the roads.

Where to, then, Christopher? Gill sings, bright and fake.

This way, I say, and I start down the village, across the crossroads and under the streetlamp, Gill joggin ter catch up and walk beside us.

It's spooky, she whispers.

It's just quiet.

I don't like it. It stinks of cowshit.

I look back, at the crossroads draped in light, and then ahead along the road. I can see another lamp up ahead, but inbetween is just the dim road and the houses set further back in the dark. I brush me hand along the cold stony wall beside us as I gan.

Suddenly Gill grabs hod of me arm, stoppin us both dead. What's that?

What?

There, she says, pointin ovver the road. Them lights. Oh, she whimpers, and then I see two discs of gold hoverin in the dark ovver the road, then suddenly swoopin round.

Don't say owt, I whisper, and Gill nods her head at me shoulder. As I watch, the gold rings blink out and then appear again.

Is it a ghost? hisses Gill.

No, I whisper. I dunno.

I'm strainin ter see inter the blackness ovver the road. I can mek out the wall in the gloom, but the blackness ovver the wall is no different ter the blackness of the sky, as if the whole black night's parked just ovver the road, beyond the wall. The trees are swishin. The gold rings veer suddenly away inter the dark, the air whitely flurryin, and nowt's left ter hear but the chirpin of crickets and me and Gill's breathin.

It's gone, says Gill. Is it gone?

I reckon it's gone, I say, and I let go of Gill's arm before she can say owt about us havin had tight hod of it.

It feels like it's gone, doesn't it?

Owl, I say. It was an owl, and me heart balloons at the certainty of it.

They don't exist anymore, whispers Gill.

Yer don't have ter whisper, I say in a normal voice, and of course they do. Out here they do.

It's pitch bloody dark, Christopher. Whisperin's exactly what we have ter do. We shouldn't be out here, should we?

No, I say, but I can feel the emptiness of the unbuilt fields all around and Arthur's village like a single nest high up in the night, and me own bed such a long way down. But I reckon if I can only keep climbin I'll be gettin closer ter Arthur, wherever he is in the dark.

Let's get outta here, says Gill, startin ter tug us along by me sleeve.

We hurry on, past a gateway set in a tall hedge, with balled gateposts taller than us at either side and the house behind it sleepin with all its lights crated up inside. On we gan, under a streetlamp where we look at each other's orange faces, only ter cross again inter the shadders.

The pub, I say, as we gan past, the unlit sign hung high on its pole and the front garden cluttered with the shadders of the tables and chairs. Me eyes're tryin ter peel apart shadder from shadder, ter mek sense of the hedges and the walls as we gan.

Here, I say, and we turn, Gill follerin us down the lane, the cobbles lumpin roundly through me trainer soles and the gloom gettin thicker. The lane levels and the yard oppens out, not ter me eyes, cus it's darker still, but ter me ears, cus I can hear the concreted emptiness of it. The farmhouse and the bothy're there, borderin the yard, and the blacker dark of the barns gapes beside em. Me and Gill're planted at the edge, neither of us ready ter start ovver twards the farmhouse door and the bothy door beside it, both of em shut fast.

I don't even know if this is where he lives, I whisper.

Oh, now yer tell us, hisses Gill. Well, if he's not in, someone will be and they'll know where he is, won't they?

Aye, I spose, I whisper, but I'm far from sure I wanna gan wakin strangers up. I keep peerin at the lifeless-lookin house-front. Summit shrieks suddenly from the dark, and red-eyed shapes gan wingin through me head. Gill grabs me wrist.

Looks like there's nee one there, I whisper, mostly so I can hear me own voice again out loud.

Doesn't mean there isn't. Go and knock on the door, whispers Gill, lettin go of me wrist and givin us a wee push. I rock on me feet but stay stood in the same spot. I've grabbed hod of the bar of the yard gate and click me finger-nails on it as I turn me face up ter the big night. It's deep in stars. I can hear the hiss of emptiness out here, away from town.

Yer've gotta getta hod of yersel. Yer know what's gan on now, don't yer?

Gill's got her face crammed up close ter mine. Yeah, I say.

So yer can do summit if yer'd just stop bein backward about it. Gan on, she hisses, and shoves us, harder this time so I trip forward onter the concrete.

Yer not comin with us?

Oh, Chris, she whispers from the shadders, and I turn away from her voice, cus there's nee other way, and start across. The yard's wide in the dark, with the night even wider all around us. I look up again at the stars and imagine mesel, tiny on a great empty square. Any moment, I'm expectin a light ter trip and freeze us in its blaze, me shadder jumpin clean out of us across the concrete. Me mind's pedallin round as I creep forward, and me dad's in me head tellin us how well I've done ter hunt down Dan Reid and find Arthur. Tomorrer in me mind there's nee hurry ter get ter school, cus everyone's waitin fer us there, fer me and Arthur. They're all lined up along the cloakrooms, teachers in all, sayin nowt, but smilin.

The dark's chirrupin around us and I can feel the quiet, how breakable it is, as if any second the weight of us might crack the yard like a sheet of ice and I've ter keep slippin across it softly before it does. Suddenly I'm at the bothy door and nee light's bin tripped.

I put me palms on the chill stone surround and lean in close with me head crooked, ter listen. There's nowt ter hear. I tek a squint ovver me shoulder twards the gateway, lookin fer any shadder that undoes itsel from the rest, but Gill's swallered there and the gloom's unmovin. I turn back and put me palm ever so gently ter the door. Flakes of door-paint crackle under me hand. I lean harder. I lean, and a rush heaves us forward, so hard I can't unlean cus I'm fallin inter the scorchin light let out as the door gives way.

NINETEEN

I see white or black, I can't tell which. I'm blinkin at the blurry deck, me breath bent inside us. I can't choke it out, cus I'm clamped around me neck, me head in a woolly vice, crankin tighter. I hear voices through the wool, but me ears're blocked by the enormous rasp of it and're gettin grated so hard they're singin with pain. I'm havin ter keep steppin ter stay on me feet as I'm dragged round, the oppen doorway fulla night passin blearily in front of me eyes, and now table legs, and now a pair of boots. I'm pluckin at the clamp with me fingers, tryin ter loosen it off, but me fingers feel brittle as twigs. There's smoke in me nose. The warm inside air's smashin ovver me face and me tongue's gettin wrung outta me head. Madly, I'm clockin the dents in the lino and the copper button on the jeans of the big legs locked inter step with me own. I'm hearin me own blood hoofin against me skull and a voice outta the blood roarin, WHERE YER BIN?

And then I'm let go of. I stagger once, twice, but stay on me feet. Me legs can hardly hod the loose load of us. I'm whoopin in great lungfuls of air. Me fingers gan ter me singin ears, which feel slippery, but there's nee blood when I bring me hands in front of me face.

Christopher! shouts Gill.

Oh ho! says Eggy, who's loomin ovver us when I turn, a

great blue cableknit jumper rolled up ter his throat and a hat pulled down ovver his head.

Who the fuck is this? says Dan Reid, who's stood at the door, watchin Gill step in from the dark. She glowers up at him, reachin behind her head ter tighten her ponytail, but he just scrapes the door shut and bolts it.

Yer fell fer the old oppen door trick, Dan says ter us, dustin off his hands.

Aye, fell all the way through, laffs Eggy.

The only way ter outsneak a sneaker, lad, and that's ter leave the locks unlocked and the latches off.

It's him, is it? says Eggy ter Dan.

Is it you? says Dan ter me.

Yer knocked at me house earlier. I'm Arthur's mate, I say, still rubbin me ears.

The wee fucker, says Dan.

It's him, says Eggy.

Aye, it's him. Chris isnit, the pisshead. And who's this? says Dan, noddin at Gill.

Is this him, Christopher? says Gill, ignorin Dan and shruggin off her handbag. She teks a cool gander round the bothy.

Dan, this is me friend, Gill. Gill, this is Dan Reid, I say, me face gan hot as I say it and feel stupid sayin it.

Ah do fuckin remember you, says Eggy, jabbin a finger inter me back. When that Grieve lad cut himsel that night, aye? You were with him.

The wee fucker, says Dan. Sneakin aboot, his sticky paws where they shouldn't be. Yer know?

I know, I say quickly.

Yer know? Then why've I bin draggin me arse inter town tryin ter tell yer?

Dan Reid's scrapin a chair round ter face us. I shut me mouth and try ter look as if I know less than nowt as he drops inter the chair, pincerin a fagbox outta the top pocket of his denim jacket with the thumb and one finger of his right hand. I snatch a glance at Eggy stood with his arms crossed. His big head's balanced on the cableknit neck of his jumper, like an ostrich egg in a woolly eggcup. I rub the hurt outta me own raw neck with me good hand. Dan strikes a match and hods it away from himself as it flares. He blows out the match with the first draw of his fag, then teks loadsa wee puffs till they're added up ter a haul of smoke he sucks all the way inter himsel.

He begged us, the wee fucker, affter I'd caught him, just like I caught you. I woulda sent him ter fuck—

Yer shoulda, says Eggy.

Aye, well, says Dan, and looks at his fag tip. I can hear the hiss of Dan's fag burnin in the quiet as we wait, but Dan says nowt else. I can't help gazin at the wrist wired with copper hair stickin outta Dan's denim cuff.

Where did yer catch him? says Gill suddenly.

Dan flicks his ash inter a saucer balanced on the arm of the chair. He looks hard inter the dead ends crushed there. I reckon he hasn't heard Gill's question, but when he looks up at us his grey eyes're slotted.

She speaks, but does she know?

Aye, she knows, I say.

What does she fuckin know? he says sharply.

I turn towards Gill. It seems ages since I've sin her in the light, and she's stood easily, her chin stuck out and her eyes, each one a splash of black lashes, unblinkin now she's outta the shadders and the dark. She's starin at us like I'm a spider in a plughole.

I turn back ter Dan. She knows Arthur knows. That's why we kem ter you, cus we figured you know where he is, and that's why yer kem ter mine.

I snap me head round ter see Eggy fold double, his hands slapped on his thighs, snortin. The three of us watch him gan redder. He throws his face up ter the low ceilin. I can see the silver in his teeth as the laffter barks out of him.

Oh, agh, phew-ee, he splutters at last. Did yer get that, Dan? We're all in the know, he says, before he's collapsin again.

Dan's watchin calmly, one side of his gob hitched up inter half a smile and bright white, unsunned skin showin like bone through the partin slashed in his red hair. Eggy's slowly gettin a hod of himsel. He sheks his head and swipes his knuckles across his face, as if he can smooth it blank and serious again with the back of his hand.

We're all in the know, says Eggy, gaspin fer breath and pointin between himsel and the rest of us, but nee one knows what anyone else knows.

He whips off his woolly hat, scrapes his hand behind each sprung-out ear and then pulls the hat ovver em again. He sighs, all the laffter blown out of him.

He knows about the murder.

Gill! I snap, but she's got her bright eyes narrered on Dan Reid. I look from her ter Eggy and then back ter Dan Reid. He's grindin his fag inter the saucer, the last of the smoke unwindin bluely out of it. I lift me right foot and the lino untacks from the floor. I gan as still as I can.

Put the kettle on, ey, Eggy, says Dan, and Eggy stomps behind us and through ter the bothy kitchen. I hear him gigglin before the tap rushes and watter rings inter the empty kettle.

Nee one knows yer out, d'they? says Dan, knockin another fag out of his box.

I shek me head. Gill doesn't move.

Then we'll get yer both back ter yer beds. I'll put a comb through me hair, and do me best fer yer if it comes down ter that, since I reckon this is me own fault.

I can hear Eggy oppenin cupboards, a lid gettin rived off a tin. Dan carefully lays his unlit fag on the top of his matchbox on the arm of the chair.

Yer don't know, I say, tryin ter keep mesel locked, eye ter eye, with Dan. He sits back in his chair, a big vein beatin in his temple. The quiet pools around us.

Yer right, lad, says Dan suddenly, his face brekkin oppen and a smile escapin across it. I divn't know what he's doin out there. But he was happy enough, happy enough liftin milk off the steps. But bacon outta the fridge? Money off the side? That was the decider, like. Eggy's right, fer once. I shoulda dragged him home then and there. Me own fault.

I can hear the kettle risin ter a boil.

There's people affter Arthur, I say slowly, as clearly as I can.

Dan stows away his fagbox and sits forward, jabbin his elbers out ter rest, one on each arm of the chair.

Cmon, lad, he says, and I can feel me eyelids flutterin as he pins us with another slate-edged stare.

Yer pal's tekkan himsel onter the marsh fer a few days with whatever nuddy-mags he could find stashed aboot the place. And my fuckin bacon, let's not forget, and quite cosy he was in all when I dropped in. I figured he'd be missin his mam soon enough, or his own stink'd bring him yam sharpish. Badgered us, he did, gev us yer address. I thought if the whole business could be left at your door, then so much the better. So the deal was done and nee harm in it, except ter yer pal, and nee chance I was gonna get dragged through his shite again. Once was enough – gettin the fuckin squeeze from his folks affter he cut his hand that time.

Dan leans forward suddenly in his chair and sweeps his finger between Gill and me. But just look who's turned up ter prove us fuckin wrong. Eggy?

Aye, says Eggy from the kitchen, and the clinkin of a spoon in a mug stops dead.

Do we deliver all three desperadoes or wat?

Ah dunno, Dan. We'd be at it all night.

Yer don't have ter do any deliverin, thank yer very much, says Gill, pickin paint flakes off her sleeve. Chris, you know where we're gan, don't you?

I gawp at her. I can feel me gob hangin oppen.

Yer don't know yer front end from yer arse end, d'yer, lad? says Dan. Oy, lass! Where'd'yer think yer gan?

Gill's grabbed up her handbag, turned on her heel twards the bothy door and is pullin at the bolt. Eggy appears from the kitchen with two mugs in each fist.

Yer can find him now, can't yer, Chris? she says ovver her shoulder.

Aye, I say, frownin, cus Gill's tellin us, not askin us, and I just can't tell her no. Aye, I say, but as I do there's a flickerin at the back of me mind. Summit's catchin alight, and I'm sayin, Aye, more certain now, cus me head's full of an idea, like a flame that's bin there all along, smoulderin in the crumpled-up ball of me brain. Aye, I say. He's gotta be at the bunker.

Well, that's where we gan, says Gill breathlessly, still tuggin at the door. We don't need owt else from these two.

I look from Dan ter Eggy. Dan's straightenin his fag where it's laid on the matchbox, as if it's a puzzle he's bent on workin out. Eggy's stood, a grin cracked inter his face. I gan up ter the door and Gill slides outta the way so I can put the flat of me hand ter the lug of the bolt. I start heavin at it.

Yer might need these two, says Dan Reid, pointin ter himself and Eggy, ter oppen the door fer yer. He sits back in his chair again and watches as Gill shoves us outta the way and teks another turn tuggin at the bolt.

Oh aye, there's a knack, says Eggy, squattin ter set the steamin mugs down on the deck at Dan's feet.

Aye, says Dan. The knack is not bein a bairn. Then it's easy enough.

Cmon, kids, I've med yer a cuppa tea, says Eggy, startin twards me and Gill.

I turn ter tug at the bolt once more, but me hands're as weak as watter, and then Eggy's crouchin down and me and Gill are squinchin with our backs ter the door as he stretches his arms out wide ter grab us both tight around our legs and lift.

Suddenly I'm kickin air, stood on nowt, and the sweaty wool of Eggy's hat's raspin against me face. I can see Gill shovin down with both hands on Eggy's clamped arm, as if it's a belt she might wriggle out of, but she's as far off the floor as I am and we're both gettin swayed unsteadily, high ovver the room, the lightshade moonin so close I have ter twist me head ter keep from nuttin it as we gan. I'm lookin down inter Eggy's glowin face, down his red throat, cus his head's thrown back as he laffs. The sound of it shifts about as I'm tipped, nearly head ovver heels, and get bounced inter Gill's knees and elbers, and now I'm starin at the bothy ceilin, the bedsprings still poppin and tremblin beneath us. I push mesel up on one unsteady hand. Dan's stood at the side of the bed, his top lip hooked inter that half grin, hoddin a Garfield mug out ter us.

Shall I read the two of yer a bedtime story before we gan?

Fuck off, says Gill from beside us, but she's reachin ovver and tekkin the hot mug from Dan.

There yer gan, he says, turnin ter fetch another. The mattress wobbles.

Watch it! I nearly threw this ovver yer, says Gill, but I've clocked Dan Reid halt with his back ter us, and Eggy clocked him too and stopped slurpin from his mug and turned quickly twards the door, hearin the same *clang* I did from the yard outside.

Eggy, Dan says quietly.

Aye, says Eggy, and turns ter me and Gill with a square-cut finger ter his lips.

Nee one knows yer out, lad? asks Dan ovver his shoulder.

No, I say. I trade looks with Gill, her eyes wide and the mug of tea fixed unsipped in her hand.

Dan Reid strides softly up ter the bothy door. With the toe of his boot he scoots Gill's handbag aside and listens, just as I did from the dark on the door's other side. Eggy lowers his mug slowly and leaves it without a sound on a ledge in the wall.

We told yer, says Gill suddenly, scrabblin up, hoddin her tea mug high as she clambers off the bed. I swing me legs off in all and stand.

They've follered us. They musta bin watchin and they've follered us.

Dan Reid's turned from the door and is starin at us. Gill's clutchin the edge of the bed, her face gone floury, bitin her lip.

It could be Bry, whispers Eggy.

We'd've heard him whistlin a mile off. Right. Tell us everythin, Dan hisses, either of yer.

But there's the sudden ringin out loud of summit metal hittin the floor of the yard beyond the door. The room gans rigid as we listen ter it jangle ter a stop. Me eyes're with every-one else's, locked on the door, but me mind's revvin so hard that nowt looks solid, not the white walls or the lino floor or the thick plank door itsel. I watch Dan turn ter Eggy. Eggy nods and Dan puts his hand ter the bolt while Eggy slips behind him ter stand flattened against the wall, his nose ter the doorframe. As I see Eggy's hand gan feelin ovver the wall beside him, I tek a last look at Dan's empty chair, the low table and stool, the steamin cups and the sink. I see Eggy's fingers find the lightswitch and then I gan pitchin headfirst inter blackness.

There's total silence, but I swaller and hear the incy tightenins of the muscles in me own throat. Me eyes're oppen, cus the blackness is bloomin in em. There's a *tink tink*, like a clock-tick, from the bothy kitchen, and I know fer certain it's the metal kettle coolin. I'm starin inter the dark till it seems ter lump inter the shapes of the bothy, and Gill beside us. I blink but the dark's nee different when I oppen me eyes.

They're outside, yer fuckers, Dan whispers from outta neewhere. I look twards his voice and keep mesel pointed that way.

Yer can't tell em, says Gill's voice, nearer ter us than I thought.

Shut the fuck up, hisses Eggy.

Say summit, Chris, she says. They can't tell em where Arthur is, and we can't either.

Lass, hisses Eggy.

Eggy, snaps Dan, let em speak.

They're gonna kill Arthur if they get ter him, I gabble, me voice like summit I've groped fer and found, familiar as a lightswitch. Arthur's a witness and they're the ones he saw. They think I know where he is, and now I do.

There's nee sound, not even the kettle tickin, fer long seconds. I put me hand up in front of me face, and see nowt. I waft it round, feelin fer anythin solid in front of us, but there's nowt.

Eggy, says Dan, the sound of his voice comin from inside us now that the dark and me're the same thing.

Aye, says Eggy, I'm with yer, Dan.

I bring me arm down, and summit grazes it. I flinch, but cool, narrer fingers search me fingers and then me hand's slotted inter, and suddenly me body's me own and the dark's outside of it, and I'm feelin Gill stood beside us, me fingers linked tight with her fingers. I know fer sure I'm stood on the solid bothy floor as the silence is scraped inter and a scufflin and breathin and budgin of bodies is in the room with us. The sound of the door crashin back on its hinges fills me ears and Gill's fingers're snatched outta me own.

There's a blast of fresh night. The slammed air shudders against us. Summit gans ovver and is crashed through with a splinterin of wood. I shuffle, stickin me hand out and meetin a wall. I flatten me back against it. The blackness is risin and fallin ter the sounds of gruntin and half-words, yelped from everyspot. I press me palms ter the cool, knobbly surface of the wall and start ter slide along it with babysteps, testin each step as I gan. Suddenly the space around us is swished and stirred, and I know through me skin that someone's close. I'm crouchin as a body bangs with an Oohf! against the wall on me right, and chunks of plaster rain down. Things're swingin invisibly past me face. There's the holler scrape of summit gettin slid off a wooden shelf, a gap of quiet it must be fallin through, and the smash. AH YER FUCKER! someone roars, and I feel the stampin of heavier feet, up through the floor, through the soles of me feet. A mug gans ovver, the *whish* of its spillin as plain as if I'd sin it. The pitch-black's judderin, every kick and punch sent in shockwaves through the air, and the air slammin us, but me left palm's on a corner's edge and suddenly I'm inchin around it, inter the lightless bothy kitchen, the grunts and the scufflin swingin away ter me right. I'm stood, breathin hard in the kitchen's pocket of stiller dark, as Booby's voice monsters around the bothy.

YER FUCKIN GREEBOS!

Eggy! hollers Dan Reid.

Aye, man, says Eggy, muffled-soundin and breathless. The wall at me back's fallen inter and I jump as it sheks. I hear a saucer land on the deck, but it doesn't brek. It's gan round and round on its rim, quicker and quicker, circlin at last ter a standstill just as the kitchen appears in front of us and I'm blinkin madly in the sudden yeller dazzle.

TWENTY

There's the battered kettle on the single gas ring in front of us. The whole kitchen's no more than a cupboarded aisle in the light. This is what it's like when me mam's caught us outta bed, when I've had me telly on too late and I've just knocked it off, but she's kem in and flicked on the light before I could get back under me covers. I'm on me own, hardly breathin. There's hardly any breathin from round the corner neither. Me hands're shekkin. I press me facebones against the wall that's stood between me face and whoever's on the other side. I'm hidden, starin at the narrer kitchen doorway as they all start yellin at once.

Dan! There's pure fear in Eggy's voice.

Gill! grunts the Black Hole, fer sure.

Leave it, Eggy, says Dan, his voice ragged, half-choked.

Shut the fuck up! rumbles Booby, and the room's dragged inter stillness affter him. Now I hear great gasps, drips drippin, and the fibres of summit brokken creakin further apart. Me nose is madly itchin, but I daren't move ter scratch it.

We're here now, Booby says calmly inter the stillness, and all I'm here ter ask is where he is.

The pause starts ter stretch, gettin longer on the other side of the wall. I'm lookin down me front, seein me own heartbeat under me jumper.

So where the fuck is he?

Fuck off, Carl, spits Gill. Geroff us!

Carl! growls Booby. Get ovver here and stop messin about with the fuckin bait.

Shadders in the doorway gan flickerin ovver the kitchen lino. I press me facebones harder inter the wall.

Easy, lass, it's alright, says Eggy.

Aye, it's alright. Yer've done yer bit, lass, but I'll not ask the rest of yer again. Where the fuck is he? booms Booby, his voice like rubble.

Put it down, man. There's no need.

Farm boy! roars Booby. Yer won't fuckin tell me what I can and cannot do!

I dunno who yer on about, says Eggy's voice calmly.

Gill, tell him who we're on about.

I dunno who yer on about, Booby, says Gill.

D'yer hear that, Carl? says Booby. The bait's a liar, from the fuckin inside out. She'll be swearin night's day, up's fuckin down – keep the fuck still! – but under the brass she fuckin knows.

Knows what, yer fuckin pig? says Gill, her voice jagged.

Lass, warns Eggy.

I said shut the fuck up, farm boy!

Yer a pig.

Gill, Gill, says Booby, tuttin. It's easy ter bleed yer heart out now, isnit? Look at poor fuckin Carl, mad fer yer, and yer tret him like a piece of shit. He's wronged, and when he's wronged, I'm wronged in all. Yer let us foller yer out here, and now yer can tell us where he is. Easy. Then we'll be away and let these lads git themsels mopped up.

Mal, yer've gotta kid with me fuckin sister, says Gill.

I know nowt, lass. Nowt. We're alright, you and me. He doesn't mean it, d'yer Boob? We're alright.

In the silence of nee one sayin owt, I tot em up – Booby, Carl, Mal – the three of em through there, on the other side of the wall. The three of em in on it. Me facebones ache, pressed against the stone. I'm swivellin me eyes desperately round the kitchen, lookin fer owt ter climb inter or under, owt ter hide meself behind.

Yer not fallin fer this, are yer, Carl? says Gill. Course yer not. Yer don't just do what he tells yer to do.

Lass—

I'll ave yer fuckin tongue if yer oppen yer mouth again, farm boy. Really I will. Now, yous two should mek up. If me hands were free, I'd be squeezin the two of yer together, properly givin yer what for, till yer were mended, the pair of yer. Carl, why don't yer, ey?

I lift me hand, me palm tacked with sweat so tight ter the wall it meks a suckin sound as it peels off. I'm strainin so hard ter hear if they've heard that me eyesockets hurt.

I dunno what the fuck yer on about, Booby, says Carl at last.

I mean, why don't yer mek the move, yer clammy larl shite? Yer ready, aren't yer, Gill? Ter kiss and mek up. Or mebbe yer just wanna tell us where the fuck he is.

Don't you fuckin touch me, Carl. Don't yer dare.

Don't worry, Carl lad. She says the same ter every feller who finds her spreadin hersel ovver a gravestone – keep fuckin still! I've fuckin told yer, says Booby, a struggle frayin his voice.

I'm warnin yer, Carl, says Gill, her voice tremblin.

That's it, lad. Get in there. Yer'll not be forgettin that yokel cunt so easily, will yer lass?

A scufflin of feet, sudden moves, a *screeak* of chairlegs as a chair's shoved ovver the floor – outta the way or inter someone's path, I think as I hod me breath.

Ow!

Booby, man. Cmon, Boob.

Are yer fuckin squeamish, Mal? says Booby, and as he does me guts somersault and I find mesel unpressin me body from the wall, me breath still held. Steppin forward's like risin ter the surface from underwatter, and now I'm risin all the way, clean through the kitchen doorway, inter the bothy, and me voice is burstin out of us.

I'm here, I'm here.

Faces turn but the looks on em mean nowt ter us in the blur of bein torn in two, one of meselves stood here in the wrecked room with nee idea, and the other still tucked safe around the corner in the kitchen. I'm tryin ter bring em together, the two of meselves, but like a transferred transfer and its backin, they won't be lined up and stuck back down.

Chris lad, says Booby. Yer a sneak and a half, aren't yer?

I say nowt, cus I've clocked the knife.

Look at us when I'm talkin ter yer, son.

I do. I look up from the knife at Dan Reid's throat, past his head clamped under Booby's arm and on up, ovver the slope of Booby's belly and up ter the tiny eyes, black as raisins, pressed inter his face.

And here yer are. Here he is, Carl, he says, beamin sweatily.

Aye, grunts Carl, and me eyes gan with Booby's eyes, ovver the upturned chairs and the smeary floor and the spindles of wood lyin about, ter spike-haired Carl, stood stock-still with Gill's wrists in his hands.

Yer led us a merry dance, but I think I know where we're all at now. Carl, I said, just watch em and foller them, and I knew he wouldn't have ter watch the two of yer fer long. His best mate and his bit on the side. Yer know who I'm on about, Chris lad? Don't fuckin move! he snaps, and I don't look twards Eggy, who I reckon dared ter move, but keep me eyes on Booby as he shifts his grip on Dan.

Dan's feet scuff the deck and he meks an *eck-eck* sound in his windpipe. Booby puffs and kinda shrugs his whole body and Dan gans stiff and still. I can see the silver huntin blade properly nippin inter the skin of Dan Reid's throat.

So what I was just askin the lads and Gill ere – well, yer woulda heard us, wouldn't yer? No? Well, I was just askin where yer man is. Yer know him and Carl've got history, and then yer mate goes and sticks it somewhere it doesn't belong, ey, Gill?

Yer a fuckin liar—

And now! Booby shouts ovver Gill. And now here y'are, the both of yer. What about that?

He glows, his face like ham, glazed and jolly. Nee one says owt. I can hear Dan Reid's breath raspin narrerly, in and out, and the *tap tap* of drips drippin on the lino. Mal Sharkey's still got his hand ovver the lightswitch on the wall behind Booby, his dead hair hangin ovver his eyes.

Yer understand, don't yer, Chris lad? I couldn't stand by. Yer mate and Carl need ter clear the air, the two of em, face ter face. But now Carl's probly thinkin the worst of you in all, lad. Aren't yer, Carl? He's just got one of them heads – a head fulla junk.

I look with Booby back at Carl. He's still got a hod of Gill by one wrist, but he's turned twards us. I can see the cords at full stretch in his neck. His gob's snarled off his bloody teeth.

So you, Chris lad, need ter let him know that disappearin off the Arches yesterday wasn't on account of yer knowin what Arthur fuckin Grieve was up ter with his mott. And then yer need ter tell us where Grieve is, seein as yer out ere in the middle of the night and I cannot see any other reason fer it but that yer a step ahead of us, clever little cunt that yer are.

They know nowt, says Eggy suddenly. They rolled up ere askin us cus they know nowt.

I turn twards Eggy, noticin his hand cupped under his nose, and it's the blood caught in his hand and drippin through his fingers that's *tap-tappin* on the lino, but as I'm realisin this Carl steps in from the corner of me eye and punches Eggy so hard in the face that I stick out me tongue and taste it before it dawns on us that it's Eggy's blood spatterin me lip and me chin. Eggy gans backwards, his bloody hand out behind him. Gill's frozzen, her white fingers clawed ovver her mouth. I watch Eggy in slow motion, kickin fer balance, blood scatterin from the fingers of his outspread hand, up the wall and ovver the deck behind him. Me own fingers gan ter the side of me mouth and I look at the blood-smear on the tips of em.

What d'yer say, farm lad? says Booby. I can hear chokin. I look from Eggy, who's amazinly kept himsel upright, ter Booby who's lookin down at the crown of Dan Reid's head. Dan's raspin summit and buckin under Booby's arm.

I can hear yer fuckin mumblin, says Booby.

The bothy's like an oven. I'm wonderin if it's the heat swelterin outta Booby himsel. Mal Sharkey's flattened himsel against the door. I look back at Eggy, his hand ter his face now and his fingers pinchin his nose, swayin with his two feet planted on the deck. Carl's squared up ter him, his fists balled and his eyes poppin. I catch Gill's shocked-white face as it flickers at us from across the room, behind Carl's back. She's on her toes, creepin. I look back ter Booby, lumped ovver Dan Reid, the tussle of em pressin Mal back against the bothy door.

I'll fuckin scalp yer, Booby's sayin softly. Don't think I won't.

This is trouble. This is trouble. The trouble I'm always waitin fer, lookin fer behind us, feelin in a fuckin point pushed inter the skin of me back, inter me spine. I can smell the fag ash, see the spilled tea mixed with it, and the blood smeared in dirty bootmarks ovver the floor. Trouble's here and I'm cramped in with it, every body here bigger than me own and the bothy too hot and too small fer their muscle and blood.

Gabble's wellin up in us again.

I know. I know, I say louder, so Booby'll hear us. His red face swings up and his black eyes steady on us. Me own eyes flick down ter tek in the blade, still locked at Dan's throat, and Dan's head wedged under Booby's other arm.

Listen ter the lad. He knows I'll fuckin scalp yer.

I catch the flutter of summit ter me right, and now Carl's howlin.

No, I shout ovver the howl and the sudden brekout of scufflin. I know yer killed the tramp. And I know Arthur knows in all. That's why yer affter him.

Booby blinks and swings his face left ter trade stares with a startled-lookin Mal. I flash a look the other way. I see Gill crouchin across the room right opposite us. I getta glimpse of Carl and Eggy fallin together, hoddin onter each other, an arm each raised ter the ceilin, fists on the ends, and their legs locked as they grapple back and forth, and now me eyes're back on the blade.

And Booby's suddenly loomin twards us, Dan's legs draggin behind him. He's a landslide luggin Dan, his body comin down on us, his face tippin ovver us. As I stagger back, Booby's grabbin a fistfulla Dan Reid's hair and yankin Dan's head up.

Dan's head, swingin by its hair in Booby's fist, looks twistedly at us.

I touch me face, checkin me fingertips fer blood.

I look back at Dan, dragged by his hair up onter his feet, the bright blade grinnin at his stretched white throat.

I knew you were fuckin trouble, Mister fuckin Trouble.

Booby's breath's in me face, a hot livery blast of it. I'm toe ter toe with Dan Reid, who's up on his tiptoes, hoddin his neck off the blade jacked up under his chin. Booby's tekkin a deep breath. The belly-wall of him presses in on us. I try ter catch some air before it's all pushed out of us, me hands flat on the wall at me back. Summit smashes ter pieces. The light's swingin, so Dan Reid's swingin and Booby's swingin, both of em washed ovver with shadder, then lit, their glarin faces slidin outta somespot hellish, which is here and me own spot too.

Shall I? Booby says, his spit sizzlin inter me eyes. Shall I bath yer in him, yer potter fucker?

Do it, yer fat cunt, rasps Dan, his voice strainin outta him.

Don't, I say, and the taste in me mouth, a coin's zingy taste, is the word that'd tell Booby about the bunker on the marsh. I swaller it.

Don't, says Booby in a mincy voice, heftin Dan Reid higher. I hear the bothy door get pulled in and chugged shut again, and Booby's risin from us, his great face shearin away ter look behind Dan in the direction of Mal and the door.

Where's he gan! asks Booby, surprised, as if me and Dan might be surprised in all. I look right and see Carl and Eggy wound together on the deck, each punchin inter the other, then I look back up inter Dan's eyes, both of em peeled ter the whites and starin at us as if I'm a long way down, at the bottom of a cliff. I've nee bright idea ter look back at him with. Booby's swingin his head ter his left. His belly's gan out and then in, the gap I'm squeezed inter tightenin and then lettin out. The lightshade's yawin less. I'm wonderin how many breaths I've bin in this spot fer, me arms pinned ter the wall, cus time's stretched the way the room is by the lightshade draggin it to and fro across itsel. I'm tryin ter see round Booby, ter see if Gill's crouched where she was, by the sink, but Booby's face is hovin round and down twards us, his fat lips twistin off his teeth.

There's nowt ter fuckin lose then, lad.

Dan's feet start ter desperately scuff and kick. His grey eyes bulge. Booby's belly's pressin inter us. The giggles are risin in us like bubbles and there's nowt I can do ter bust em before they hiccup out of us, cus I've madly wondered how many others there are who've got swallered up and find emselves in Booby's belly, crouched in a cave of stinkin bones and chewed-on shoes.

And he's laffin with us – a wet, wobblin laff that's slippin outta him and slitherin ovver me face.

But the bothy jumps suddenly – a room jumpin out of its skin – and I realise the light's bin smashed inter again, and the room's got kicked forward with us in it, and then I hear a grim, sure *crack*.

The blade in Booby's fist gans fallin away from under Dan's chin, the silver wing of it swoopin in front of me eyes. Suddenly I can breathe. Booby's heavy against us. I'm tekkin a deep breath. Me chest swells and I shove Booby Grove back, back till the room's oppened up and the deck's shekkin cus Booby's felled. Booby's down on the deck and his belly's like a world itsel, shekkin now as if he's laffin there, flat on his back. And Dan Reid's gone fallin away with Booby, but he hasn't gone down, and he's snatchin the knife up. I look past him at Gill stood ovver Booby, her handbag hangin off her hand.

Yer've knocked him out, I think, but me mouth won't work ter let out the words. The lightshade's still swingin, and Eggy's arm with it, his fist gan ovver and ovver again inter Carl's face, clamped there under his arm. I watch till his fist stops and Eggy lets Carl slither like a half-filled sack ter the floor. As Dan Reid squats at Booby's side and starts ter heave him ovver onter his front, Eggy stares at us, gaspin through a mask of blood, his nose split like a plum.

What the fuck've yer got in there? croaks Dan. Bricks?

Tins. Tins of beans, says Gill. Never leave home without em. Perverts everywhere.

Fuck me, puffs Dan as he flops Booby ovver and starts ter heft first one of Booby's big arms and then the other out from under him and behind his back.

Fetch us summit ter tie him with, will yer? Ovver there, says Dan.

Gill drops her handbag with a clunk and starts ter cast about the bothy. I'm tryin ter get me legs under control, cus everythin's wobblin while they're wobblin.

Aye, that'll dee, says Dan as Gill pulls a plug outta the wall and follers the cable ter a smashed radio she unplugs in all. She skips ovver ter Dan and he grabs the cable off her and starts ter cross it ovver and around Booby's wrists, Booby's hands floppin like dead things. I'm desperate fer a piss. I can taste blood in me mouth. A moan rumbles from Booby. I turn quickly ter see Carl stagger ter his feet and gan bargin inter Eggy from behind, knockin him onter his knees. Booby's startin ter wallow himsel around on the deck. Dan's hurriedly drawin the cable through itsel, and the bothy's fillin with movement that's too big fer it again. Gill's grabbin up her handbag, her face pointed at us, widenin her eyes. I stare back. Eggy and Carl're slippin redly together, the ovverturned chair skiddin with em, and trouble's pressin coldly inter me skin again. Gill jerks her head. She rolls her eyes, stamps her foot, and shouts, GO! and I'm at the bothy door, tuggin at it. I look back once at the faces, each fixed elsewhere, and then the light's let out across the yard, and it's easy ter pull mesel affter it, away from the noise, draggin the door shut and peltin inter the dark.

TWENTY-ONE

Me fists're swingin, grey in the ovver-hung lane, the cobbles rollin under me trainers. I'm snortin air, the pain of piss in us. Onter the main road where the dark's gettin edges before me eyes, roofs and trees scratched black against the bluer black, and stars pingin above and in front of us as they lift off the rooflines and chimneypots. The night's a cold crackle in me nose. I run on down the road, between the blank-faced village houses, me legs pumped full and frostburn in me lungs. The chill's clamped me forehead, crackin me skull, and before I've even thought ter turn, I've run off the road, inter the narrerness between black hedges. Under me feet the pavement's kicked ter dust, and the dusty track gans lumpy as the streetglow slips behind us. Hedges and tractor-ruts slide outta the shadders. Me ankles kill, but I steer meself inter the lane's flat middle where there's grass ter run on. The moon's sailin ovver. Me throat's shredded, but I'm away and the dark's got nowt ter scare us with affter the blade and the handfuls of scatterin blood and the meat of Booby's breath. I foller the curve of the track, slowin as I round the bend, and all I'm carryin away from the village are the sounds of meself – me gaspin and the scrapin of me jeans and me own voice as I pant, Okay, okay – and I stop and bend double, the air sawin in and outta me splinterin lungs.

Mister fuckin Trouble.

Okay, I say, ter shut out the growl of his voice in me head, so I can stand on me own with me own word in me ears, the fields scootin all around us, away inter the dark. I've nee breath ter spit with – I try but the gob just flusters out, stringin itsel off me bottom lip. I let it hang. I'm listenin ter the tide of tiny night flitterins, but there's not a footfall or single rumblin voice ter be heard. I drag the back of me hand across me mouth. I breathe. There must be so many fields between me and owt else that talks. I unzip me fly and fire a glintin twist of piss inter the dark. I breathe, the knot in us slippin undone, the heat of me piss risin off the floor.

Shall I bath yer in him, yer potter fucker?

Okay, I say. Okay.

Me right leg's shekkin. I plant me right foot firmer on the floor. I'm pissin it all out, the fear of the blade oppenin Dan Reid's throat all ovver us, and the crack Eggy's fist med on Carl's face, the crack an apple meks when yer throw it hard against a wall. I can hear me piss watterin the dust inter a puddle of mud. It's an age I'm stood, me face tipped back ter look at the stars and the sweat on us gan cold and silver-feelin, as if it's mercury rollin in beads down me spine, the way it rolled across the workbench the time Dennis the Menace spilled some out fer the class ter see. I put two fingers ter me scrawny neck and feel me own life beatin in us.

Don't worry, me mam always says, yer'll fill out. But I was never that worried, not like I was in the bothy, with me heart just under me skin and me growin bigger still ter do. Cus it was a man's arm Eggy had us clamped with, and Booby had hod of Dan Reid like a doll. Me own bones must still be soft, and the man I'm gonna be was nee use as Dan stared down at us ovver the blade. I'm breathin deeply now, deep enough ter squeeze everythin outta me head but me breath, and they're all gettin breathed away, their bodies boxed with the smoke and the noise in the far-off yeller-lit bothy.

I'm done and start walkin, still zippin me fly. The night's resealed itsel around us. I peer behind us inter the black. I can't be sin if I can't see. I'm tellin mesel I know where I'm at – in the same dark stretch Arthur led us through, pissed that night, and there's not a wall in it I'll find meself backed up against. I rub me arms, me left with me right hand, me right with me left, and suddenly I'm at the fork in the lane, cus the hedgerows have fallen away on each side inter nothinness, and I have ter choose.

There's a tree in front of us, its branches spread like blown ink up inter the night, and a gate beside it I gan up ter and touch. Its chain clinks and there's the faintest holler-soundin *bong* as it knocks on its post. I climb it gently, like a cold ladder, up ter its third bar, and stand starin at Scotland.

I'm nee distance from it in the dark – a sprinkle of street-lights that means houses and roads – and the black watter between it and the Solway marsh is just a flinty strip that all the humped and hidden miles of dark farmland run down ter. I lean me body against the top bar till the cold of the bar's glowin through me jeans. I swivel me head and stare straight inter the field in front of us. But in front of us is a darkness that's eatin out me stare. I jump back, rattlin the gate, and start ter walk, blackness gettin blacker as the lane drops away down the hillside under me feet. Cus it's down I'm gan, and I'll have ter keep gan, till I reach the flat marshland and the bunker.

There's the smell of mud and I know I must be passin close ter a watter trough stood on the trampled ground at a field's edge. The hedges loom on both sides. There's a lorry-rumble far off – a sound like the distant sea, or thunder miles above us.

I know the shape of these witchy trees twistin up against the night. I know em from the time Arthur brought us down ter the rifle range ter dig out me own bullet, and now I know fer sure I have ter foller the lane ter me left. So I turn, and wade through the ovvergrown grass, the yeller slice of moon swivellin ter me right, a beatin of wings and a *whoop-whoop* choppin down from the blackness ovverhead.

I start ter count me steps, ter know how far I'm gan, even if it's only in footsteps. Twenny steps, and there's lightness in the sky. I can see lumps of the land now, as if there's a stored glow leakin outta the grass. Another twenny, and I'm tekkin a deep drag of the night and startin ter count from nowt ter twenny again, walkin on inter the flatness. Now I can mek out the seam between the sky and the dense, darker level of the marsh, and I see standin up against the night's starry blue-blackness a black unstarry box that I'm draggin mesel twards.

I stop and crouch down ter touch a star at me feet, but it's a wee white flower. I pinch it between me thumb and finger, snuffin it out. Summit wilder than a dog is croonin across the dark fields at me back. I push mesel up and on. But now I'm stoppin again. It's the stars gan out at me feet that've med us wary. I check the position of the box, bigger now against the sky. I start shufflin twards it, steppin suddenly inter nowt.

One foot's wagglin in thin air where the deck shoulda bin, and I'm wobblin on the other, flappin me arms fer balance. Uh, uh, I say, me weight pitchin back and forth, me hands paddlin the air, tryin ter stop mesel keelin forward inter nothinness. Flap, flap, me arms gan, and I'm teeterin on the very edge of the earth, and then staggerin back and findin me two feet and standin, gaspin, not darin ter move.

I punch mesel on me thigh, cus I'm rememberin the marsh in the light, when me and Arthur kem down here, the skinny bridges of boggy turf between deep, collapsin canyons of shitty black watter and sinkin sand. Pain's bloomin in me thigh muscle.

Okay. I breathe.

I crook me neck and look up inter the night, at the spray of stars. I mek meself lift one foot, and then the other, startin ter foller the path of starry flowers, squintin now and then up twards the bunker on the skyline, keepin meself gan roughly in its direction.

I can mek out the mud that the turf's changin ter, and the roughness of the bunker's grey brick walls. It's colder now in the paler gloom without the thick night wrapped round us. The bunker's got its back to us, the turf dragged up around its shoulders. I can't see the slits in its face, cus its face is turned ter look out fer German u-boats in the Solway. Fear's fillin us as I mek me way around the box. There's nee livin sound, but the mud's squidgin and fartin under me feet. Suddenly I'm stood, eyein the black doorway and the black narrer winder-slit from side-on, and I'm certain now that I'm out here on me own – an idiot, miles from anyspot useful. I look up and down the silent length of the marsh. It's grown outta the dark weirdly flatter and emptier than it ever was in me head. I'm sure I'm gonna climb the concrete step inter a holler concrete room with straw on the floor and old feed bags and cans kicked inter the corners, and nee one'll be there. What'll I do then?

Hello, I say, and me voice gans featherin away inter emptiness. I rub the underside of me nose with the knuckles of one finger and stare at the chipped brick corner of the bunker till me eyes start ter sting. I look at the veiny-blue backs of me hands. I try ter tek a step, but me legs're driven inter the mud. There's a deep suckin as I haul one foot and then the other out. I put me palm on the flinty corner as I slide round it ter the bunker-front and stare inter the dark doorway. I can't see owt. Hello, I say, flattenin both hands on the brick doorframe and pushin mesel up inter the dark.

TWENTY-TWO

Chris, man. Oh thank fuck. Are yer okay?

I didn't even know me eyes were shut till I had ter oppen em. I've kem back ter meself from somespot, but where I've kem back from is just sick black wooze in me head. His candlelit face is moonin ovver us, lookin grubby, and I can smell straw and smoke and the grease in his hair.

I didn't mean ter – yer just fuckin appeared, yer spanner. Say summit, will yer?

I look past Arthur's face at the bare grey ceilin. Underneath us, the straw's cracklin like a fire. I kem down the lanes and across the marsh in the dark and now I reckon I'm on me back, lookin up at the ceilin of the bunker dancin in candlelight. I can feel me own head, huge in its case, and a black agony that's lickin at the path of stars and Booby Grove and the night, suckin em inter a corner fulla shadders. I lie, the straw cracklin underneath us, and let me body hang, as if I'm lyin on a straw-covered ceilin lookin down at a bare grey floor.

Me head, I say. I know I've said it, cus I heard me own voice and tasted it like a dead wire on the back of me tongue.

That's it. Yer alright, man.

They're gonna kill yer.

Yer alright, man. Tek it easy.

Me head. What's happened to us?

Arthur's face zooms away and disappears. I can hear him crunchin about on the straw, and see the bubble of light wobblin with him ovver the walls. I tek the weight of me body back from wherever it's bin hangin and try rollin mesel onter me side.

All that comes up is a string of spit, even though the great swollenness inside me head's heavin against me skull, squeezin tears outta me eyes as I retch. Me nose is streamin. The candlelight's drillin inter me face. I gag and gently put me head facedown in the crook of me elber.

Cmon, Chris. Sit up. Let's see yer.

No. Fuck off, I say inter the shady space under me arm.

Yer have ter sit up.

I can feel Arthur's hand a world away on me shoulder. The straw's pricklin me chin where me spit's stickin it. I don't have ter, I moan.

Yer do. So that I can see that yer alright.

I'm not alright, I say inter the straw. What've yer done ter us?

I know. I'm sorry, he says, and teks his hand off me shoulder. Then he puts it back again and starts rubbin. I sneak me own hand inter the space under me arm and put me fingertips ter me head through me hair, ter the place on me head that feels numbest. An egg is what I'm suddenly thinkin – how yer can have a lump like an egg on yer head. I try checkin me fingers fer blood by liftin up me face and bringin me hand in front of it. Me hand warps, or me head warps, or the whole bunker does, and I'm rememberin what it's like ter get welted, and this is what it's like, what I'm feelin right now.

Yer hit us. What did yer hit us with?

Cmon, says Arthur. Sit up so I can have a look at yer.

I push meself up off the deck, me left hand on the edge of the fencepost lyin in the straw beside us.

Did yer hit us with that?

I didn't mean ter. I didn't, says Arthur, his hand clamped ter me shoulder.

Aye, but yer did though.

I said I'm sorry.

Yer fuckin shouldn't ave, I say inter the dusty-tastin straw, knackeredness all of a sudden soakin inter us, mekkin us heavier than the floor I'm lyin on, sinkin us inter it.

Yer have ter get up, says Arthur, and I feel him gan behind us, and then his hands're gan slottin inter me armpits and he's givin us a heft. Yer can't lie here, man.

Me arm's still shadin me eyes, but he's dragged us half up, and I look down meself, at the front of me black jumper, straws clingin ter it here and there, and at me legs in me jeans. But I'm so tired and the floor feels so level and good as me own bed.

How many fingers am I hoddin up? Arthur says, comin round ter crouch in front of us again.

Do I have ter guess?

No, yer wazzock. Yer sposed ter look. Yer sposed ter look and tell us how many, and if yer get it wrong. Well, I dunno what it'll mean. But it'll be serious.

Is it? Is it serious? I say, me fingers gan straight ter me head again, cus me heart's gettin snatched at by the fear that Arthur can see the folds of me blue and yeller brain, oppen ter the air and stuck with bitsa straw.

No, no – I didn't mean that. Just tell us how many.

Three, I say, cus I've lifted me arm high enough ter see Arthur's hand with his dirty fingers held up, black rinds at the ends of his long fingernails.

Good, he says. It's not serious or yer'd see six.

Nee one's got a hand with six fingers on it.

Exactly, he says, grinnin at us. Now let's see yer on yer feet, he says, clappin his hands together, the crack clatterin from wall ter wall and boomin through me skull.

I put me palms on the cold deck and start edgin meself up on me arse. I'm waitin fer the retchin ter kick off, cus there's a ringin in me head again, like the ringin I've heard from the back of the telly when it's bin on fer hours, when I've looked down inter the back of it through the plastic slots and seen the hot orange coil where I reckoned the ringin was comin from.

Cmon, says Arthur. That's the way.

I feel like I'm pushin meself through the bunker ceilin and inter the sky, and now I'm as empty as the sky.

Whoah there, says Arthur, and I'm saggin on him, his arm round us, hoddin us up by me armpit.

I found yer, I hear meself say.

Aye, says Arthur. Jackpot.

We're stood in the middle of the bunker's gloomy room, the two of us. It's not yet that light through the door and the winder but I can see the dark gettin rinsed out and the grey estuary appearin like a rubbin in the doorway. I'm tryin ter turn, ter look around the room, but me brain heaves. I shut me eyes on the nest of straw and blankets in the corner and on the thread of smoke risin off the floor.

I've gotta sit down.

Okay, okay, says Arthur, and starts luggin us ovver ter the back wall. Yer alright, he says as he sets us down, me heels ploughin up the straw as I sink onter me arse. The wall's clammy on me back, but it's gan straight up and hods us upright enough ter mek us feel straighter. Arthur's stood with his hands on his hips. He's grey-faced and skinnier than a week agan, the knees of his jeans shone black from kneelin in dirt. He turns ter look outta the door, and then he's gan ovver and crouchin at the tiny heap of ash under the winder. I foller him with me eyes, me head like a washin-up bowl with too much dirty watter in it, sloppin up the sides. He blows out a candlestub planted on an old lid, and then teks the black stick leanin against the wall and starts ter poke the smokin heap.

I'm sorry, I say.

What yer sorry fer? he says ovver his shoulder.

I didn't know when I med yer gan down ter the park. I didn't, and then yer took off, didn't yer?

Arthur says nowt, his back ter us. I peer down at the grainy skin of me hands in me lap.

Is everyone lookin fer us? he says quietly.

Aye, the cops as well as Booby. Yer should of told us.

Why should I of?

Cus yer just should of, cus I'm yer mate.

Arthur jabs the heap of ash once more, and then he's standin and leanin the stick back under the windersill. I swivel me brimmin head, away from the scorched bricks behind the fire and ovver the unrinsed, milky-dull bottles lined up against the wall. In the corner opposite Arthur's nest, there's a scrowy mess of tins and blackened foil. I settle me eyes on it long enough ter clock a shrivelled plastic bacon wrapper.

I know yer didn't mean ter hit us, I say, cus Arthur's said nowt.

What yer gonna do? he says as he gans ovver ter the far corner, crouches, and starts ter ratch through his nest, tekkin a blanket and foldin it, draggin a satchel out by its strap and peerin inter it.

We'll wait till it's properly light and then gan back ter yours. I got away from Booby and them – they're up at Dan Reid's – but they're not gonna dee owt in broad daylight, are they? Gill's up there in all.

Gill?

Aye, Gill Ross.

Arthur says nowt, just keeps on sortin tins inter his bag with his back ter us.

Did yer do it? I say.

Arthur stops sortin, then swivels on his heels ter stare at us. I'm watchin one look hunt another ovver his face.

Does everyone know?

No, just me. Booby told us on the Arches.

Arthur's frownin at us. And yer told nee one else? His

eyes're feelin ovver me face, like a blind man's fingers, gan everywhere but me eyes.

No, I just went and asked her.

Asked who? says Arthur, still frownin at us like I'm the unsolved side of summit he thought he'd puzzled out.

Gill.

What the fuck're yer on about, Chris?

When Booby told us yer'd shagged Gill, I just went and asked her.

There's a pause, then Arthur's laffin a wild, gulpin laff, still crouched, but one hand keepin him held up by its strutted fingertips on the deck. It sounds like a laff uprooted and gettin dashed ter pieces on the bricks of the room.

He told us before I found out what they'd done, I say quickly. But yer can tell the cops what yer know now. Yer know Booby and them killed the tramp, don't yer?

Arthur stops laffin just as suddenly as he started. He pinches his nose, his face in his hand, then pushes himsel round on his toes, back ter his bag and tins and blankets, and starts ter sort through em again.

I never shagged Gill, he says ovver his shoulder. Booby was fuckin with yer.

What? Why? I say, cus if Booby was lyin ter us on the Arches, then I knocked at Gill's house fer nowt, and she's here fer nowt in the arse-end of the night.

Have yer got any cash? Arthur says suddenly.

No, but we don't need any. We'll just ring from—

Not a penny?

No. Nowt.

I watch the back of Arthur's shekkin head. What? I say.

Yer nee use, are yer?

We don't need any money, Art.

Yeah, I do, says Arthur as he stands and zips up his body-warmer. He pulls a woolly hat out of one of the pockets and fits it onter his head. It looks like work clothes he's got on, as if he's all of a sudden old enough ter slate a roof or dig up a road.

Yer've never bin any use, he says.

I just didn't bring any with us.

No, I mean ever. Yer nee use ter nee one, you.

Me head throbs. But I had ter come and find yer, I say. Once I found out.

Yer've found out nowt, yer prick. And don't fuckin look at us like that!

Arthur's voice rolls hollerly round the bare room and he's turnin, grabbin up his bag by its strap and slingin it ovver his shoulder.

I'm alright.

Do I give a fuck, yer baller? I'm gan.

I dunno if I can walk yet, I say, cus he can say what he wants and even if it's hurtin us I can't think badly of him, cus I know what he knows and has carried all this time on his own.

No, I'm gan. Not us. You can dee what yer want, he says, pattin himself down and castin one more look around the room. His white, sooty face won't settle on mine. I'm startin ter walk mesel backwards up the wall as he steps inter the grey doorway, me crusty trainers skiddin on the straw.

What yer doin? I say, planted squarely on me feet but swayin weakly, weightlessness fillin me legs. Art, I say, what's gan on? But he's peerin left and right outta the bunker. I start across the floor.

Yer shouldn't've fuckin kem, says Arthur, not lookin back at us.

Yer what? I say, me knees bucklin under us, me body swayin ter a standstill on the spot. I shouldn't've kem? But I fuckin have, haven't I? I've kem and yer just gonna fuckin leave us.

Sit the fuck down and stay down. Yer've brought them out here, haven't yer?

But Booby and them know yer know. They were lookin fer yer anyways, I say, startin ter limp twards him. It wasn't gonna be long till they found yer. But yer don't have ter gan, I hear meself shout from right up close ter the back of Arthur's head, me hand on the doorframe.

Arthur keeps lookin out, at the mist hangin ovver the marsh. I can see the white knucklebones through the skin of his tremblin fists. He sniffs.

Are yer alright? I say, more softly, ter his back.

I'm gonna leave yer here, he says. It's what I was gonna do anyways.

But yer don't have ter.

Arthur turns. I step back unsteadily, and I'm lookin straight inter his face, a face as brittle as ice on a puddle.

It's alright, I say, cus I reckon Arthur's there, just under the fear and the frozzenness, and I can reach him if I keep inchin carefully forward.

He's pullin off his hat and scrapin his hand through his hair.

Booby and them, he says, his eyes full on mine. They're only lookin fer us cus I'm not doin what I said I would do.

I tek a breath, ter say summit, but nowt's comin.

Your face, he says. Yer look like yer've just hatched.

TWENTY-THREE

The birds're singin like mad. I've snapped a brown, dried-out stick of cow parsley outta the lane's edge, just ter give mesel an excuse ter stand and catch me breath. I split it with me thumbnail and crack oppen the brittle tube. There're nee earwigs balled up in it, so I'm the first ever livin thing ter see the creamy inside of it. Fuck it, I say out loud, and I turn ter look back at the mist draped across the fields and the marsh down below us. I squint fer a long time at the strip of glittery mud the tide's left, but I can't mek anythin out, so I turn and gan on. The sky's streaked with pink and the dust of the lane's gotta pink tint in all. I'm ploughin me right foot side-on through the dust, ter scrape up a heap, but I'm doin it without brekkin me stride and the heap's left behind us as it's scraped up and I keep scuffin me way along, waitin fer the risin sun ter lay a slab of heat against us. I wannit like I never have – the sun leanin on me back and warmin us through me jumper – cus me skin's grey-feelin and me scoured head's fulla evil fumes.

I did it, Arthur said, back in the bunker, his fierce eyes on us.

Yer didn't mean ter.

I did. Yer can't say I didn't, cus I did. I don't wanna've done it now, but now's now, isnit? Now's not then, and then I put a light ter him. To his hair, Chris. I fuckin lit it, said

Arthur, his voice trailin off. Me throat was stingin, me eyes were blurry. I was stood there as Arthur sank down onter the bunker step, shruggin off his rucksack.

That was then, I'm thinkin as I kick up another splash of dust. And I'm thinkin of all the things yer don't see as they're gan on, cus yer somewhere else and gettin on with whatever yer gettin on with. Then, in the bunker, Arthur told us and I saw it all, and what I saw got inter me head and was sweatin through me skin.

The sky's ripped with pink. I'm lookin inter the hedgerows as I trudge, through the gaps in em and inter the fields beyond. Funny how the night gans and everythin rises outta the dark – the green distance and the backs of me own hands – but it all feels less than it was and emptier. The sky's got nee stars and it's strange ter see it so early, crackin up, but all this pink and blue's only coverin up the stars, so the day's a kinda lie, mekkin yer think that clouds and blueness is all there is ter see. Cus everythin's exactly how it is in the light and nowt's what it might be anymore.

The lane's curvin round, and here's the gate I climbed under the inky tree, rough-skinned and solid now I can see it. I turn down the lane ter me right, the mornin fresh in me nose, the grass wet and the dewy leaves in the hedgerows drippin. I'm gan past another gateway inter a field and I hear a swish and turn ter look, and a horse is stood there, its long, carved-lookin face juttin ovver the toppa the gate and its polished brown eyes gazin at us from under its eyebrows. I stare back. As it breathes, the horse's nostrils flare and clutch. A single muscle's twitchin in the slab of its neck, and I reckon its coat's buffed more perfectly than the bodywork of any black Lamborghini. There's nee sound but horse breath and the birds singin from every which way, and the horse leans suddenly and starts ter rub its neck on the bar of the gate. I put me hand twards its bowed head, pattin the bristly tousle of horsehair between its ears. It's alright fer you, I say, but the horse just snuffs hot breath at us and sheks its head. Don't shek yer fuckin head at me, I say, but the horse is swingin its face round and swishin its tail and sidesteppin two thumpin steps ter the left, as if shiftin its balance. I start ter trudge on down the lane again. I look back, but its long face is lost behind the hedge. I slot me hands inter me jeans. In one pocket me fingers find the elephant, and in the other the cold case of the Zippo.

I was leant against the doorframe of the bunker, suckin in clean air, choked suddenly by the smoke that was still tricklin from the wee fire under the winder. Arthur had dumped himsel down on the bunker step and started ter talk. I could see he was shudderin in his bodywarmer as he told us how he'd bin in town a fortnight agan, and he'd walked round a corner straight inter Booby and Carl and Mal Sharkey.

I hadn't sin em since that time Carl got tortured, when Booby got us the booze, so I shit a fuckin brick, he said. But instead of Carl startin on us, Booby's givin us a fag, and Carl's face is a fuckin picture, but there's nowt he can do but gan along with Booby, cus he's just ruled by the fat fucker, isn't he?

Arthur paused ter look out across the marsh. He was sat bent ovver his cupped hands, as if he was hoddin summit small and alive in em. He bent further and further inter himsel as he talked, his face filmed with sweat, a sweat I could feel filmin me own.

And me heart got squeezed, as if it was me heart in Arthur's hands, as he told us what happened.

Down ter the garage they went, fer a gander at the second-hand bikes, then ovver the road ter Talky. Mebbe it was the hot affternoon, Arthur said, but it was easy enough ter be kickin about with em, and he was lucky fer Booby, cus Booby was askin him which machines ter play, and then winnin. Carl had a can of hairspray and a placky bag. He got gigglier and gigglier, and Booby was rollin his eyes at the state of him, but Booby took a blast on the bag and then held it out and nodded, beamin down at Arthur.

Then it was evenin and Mal Sharkey went inter the offy fer a bottle and it got passed around too. They went under the echoin subway, the four of em, and Arthur wasn't bothered about gettin home. They were older and he was just thinkin the thoughts he reckoned they were.

It was all easy enough, or mebbe it happened before Arthur could've walked away.

No. He could've walked away but he wasn't himself. He was tryin on somebody else's skin while he was with em – while he was with Booby and them.

Carl was offerin this old giffer in the park the bottle. There was a dribble left in the bottom, but the giffer was just mumblin ter himself and lookin straight ahead. He was just plonked there on a bench on his own, and an odd-bod's not someone yer can gan past when there's four of yer, not without sayin summit or doin summit.

So Carl shoved this giffer. He shoved him then kem at Arthur and wiped the tramp off his hand on Arthur's T-shirt before Arthur could get outta the way. There was a yappin noise, med of everyone tryin ter say the smartest fuckin thing, and this giffer was in the middle of it. But he sat himsel back up on the bench and just looked straight ahead, noddin his head. Then Arthur went ter sniff him, cus Carl had wiped him on Arthur, and the foolin around was like summit they had ter pass between em. So Arthur went up close ter him and had a sniff. Arthur didn't know if the giffer stank or not but he said he did. Get a fuckin whiffa that! And Carl gans up ter have a sniff, and Mal does, and they're fallin about as if the giffer's stink is knockin em out cold.

D'yer think I wanna be fuckin tellin yer this? Arthur shouted suddenly, springin up from the bunker step, his face twisted, his dirty-white fists shekkin at his sides. Cus I'm gonna get told what happened, yer know? That's what'll happen, Chris. They're gonna sit us in a room and tell us what happened and that's gonna be the way it happened, the way they tell us it did, and I'll be fucked.

I was lookin past him, outta the doorway, at the light

comin up. I couldn't say owt. Then Arthur sank back down, the fury just snuffed out of him, and started rootin about on the deck fer a piece of straw ter split with his thumbnail. His voice was shekkin as he told us the rest, and I was picturin the daft unwindin of it, like I was there mesel.

Them old streetlamps were comin on, the boxes on poles stood on the path around the park, and the big flowers were hangin off the hedges, those big stinkin flower bombs. Arthur was warm enough in his T-shirt but this giffer was sat there in a big coat. That was wrong, cus Arthur was warm enough in just a T-shirt. The lamps were comin on and Arthur could still see the flowers glowin faintly as Mal stuck his arm through the giffer's arm and dragged him up onter his feet. The two of em were stood arm in arm, and Carl catches the giffer's other arm so the three of em were arm in arm. Mal and Carl start marchin along, the giffer limpin along between em. There're hoots, and Arthur's laffin in all. Booby's face is lit as he sparks up a fag and then his face gans out again as he flips shut the lighter and chucks it glintin through the dark, and Arthur catches it. A fag's chucked affter it, which is easy ter find cus it's a white line glowin on the cinder path, but Arthur lights the wrong end, dazzled by the flame of the Zippo. He tries again, the bitterness of the singed filter on his lips, and the park's black-dark as he flips shut the flame, and he's blinkin ter mek out any glow from the flowers, or the shapes of Mal and Carl as they march the giffer along. But Arthur blinks and starts affter them, cus he doesn't wanna be left outta anythin. Carl's singin we're off ter see the wizard the wonderful wizard of Oz because because because because.

Because what? D'yer know? Arthur said, lookin up from his split straw, his eyes wobblin. I shook me head and looked down at me own black hands.

It's bin in me head, he said, all this time, and I blinked mesel and swallered and blinked again.

Arthur had grabbed up the bottle off the bench ter swing as he went affter em. He'd turned back ter see Booby's shadder and the tip of his fag comin affter him. The fuckin size of him in the dark, just comin along, easy as yer like, and the tiny fag-tip bobbin about. Mal was draggin the giffer's coat off when Arthur got caught up. Yer not gonna try and fuck him, are yer, Mal? The giffer was stampin his feet madly, his arms stuck in his sleeves, and then Mal properly tore the coat off his back. Arthur watched as the giffer stood like yer'd stand and wouldn't move if there were dogs set on yer, and before Arthur could duck outta the way, Mal had chucked the coat ovver his shoulders. The weight of it was summit else, but Arthur did a twirl and it lifted – the weight of it lifted off him – and it was on Arthur ter do whatever was next. So he did the giffer, swiggin from the near empty bottle and staggerin under the weight of the coat.

He was a tramp in a tramp's fuckin coat, and Carl and Mal caught on straightaway and started bumpin him back and forth between em, not shovin him with their hands, but bellyin him, and Arthur went staggerin about, the park spinnin, the shaddery clots of trees spinnin and the lamps leavin trails of light behind his eyes. And then Arthur didn't wanna be a tramp anymore. He was brekkin away from Carl and Mal and shruggin off the coat and stampin it inter the deck, shit-scared suddenly. And he'd remembered Carl's undies hooked oppen and Carl screamin, and he knew he couldn't have the coat on a second longer cus it woulda stuck ter him and the stink of the giffer woulda got inter Arthur and they'd've had an excuse not ter tell the fuckin difference between him and the giffer.

He was stampin out the coat like yer'd stamp out a fire, but there was nee fire. So Arthur med a fire. He sprinkled the rest of the bottle inter the heap of coat, and then he crouched ovver it with the Zippo flipped oppen, fishin fer an edge that'd catch. There was justa blue fur at first that went ghostin up the sleeve. Everythin else was shut out of his head, cus Arthur's eyes were fulla the blue flame in the dark. He was crouchin face ter face with himself. That's how it felt. There was nee one who could get between him and himself. And then it took and he fell back from the yeller *whoosh*, feelin fer his eyebrows with his fingers as he went.

He didn't know how the giffer got ter be wearin it.

One of em musta grabbed the coat up by a bit that wasn't lit and slung it ovver the giffer. The flamin coat was in Arthur's eyes and then the giffer was wearin it and it was gan out as the giffer med off twards the river in the dark.

The coat was gan out, but it was easy ter foller the glowin of it through the dark. Arthur was laffin. He was. The giffer started screamin.

That's what yer'd do, isnit? said Arthur. Yer'd scream in all. I would. You would.

I couldn't look away from Arthur's face, so I smiled. I did. Summit warbled from the marsh beyond the bunker door, and I smiled a smile as empty as that passin lonely sound.

Carl med a flamethrower out of his can of hairspray. Arthur didn't reckon Carl even knew it'd work, but the Black Hole had caught up with the giffer and aimed the spray at a still-glowin bitta coat and the spray caught so Carl was squirtin fire out of his can. And Arthur was still laffin. The fire was drippin off the giffer onter the leaves and pitterin out when it hit the deck.

But then Arthur wasn't laffin anymore. The screamin was scarin him. It was too dark by the river ter see anyone's face. He wanted the giffer ter hush up, so he knocked him down and started stampin the noise out.

TWENTY-FOUR

There's nowt left inside us ter throw up so I swaller and taste me own sick. Nee one's up and about, but the birds're still gan, a fuss of em hagglin on the phone wires as I straighten meself up, hoddin me gut. Me legs're like cardboard, as if I'm propped on empty bog-roll tubes, but I mek em stump forward – stump, stump, stump – and I come out from between the hedges, off the rutted lane inter the village and onter the pavement. I look up and down the empty road. The mornin's so early it's caught the phonebox with its light on and the tree above it rustlin like brown paper. I turn and start up the village. There're curtains drawn in the winders of the houses as I scuff past, and soon enough I'm slippin past the beer garden, the grass spiked with dew and the benches stacked on top of each other like climbin frames, and then a car's creepin up on us from behind, its revs kept low, and the shock's got us retchin again.

It's passed us before I've had time ter force the fist of me heart back down me throat, and now I'm gawpin at the smoke from the exhaust and the number plate and the misted-up back winder as the car rounds the corner and the mornin's unbrokken again. I turn ter lean on a wall, the red stone cold under me palms. I let me head hang down between me arms. I spit and breathe. I'm thinkin back ter yesterday when I cut me own thumb on Michael's fuckin sword. It feels a week agan.

Where the stones of the wall meet the pavement, there're weeds and grey-headed dandelions growin outta the cracks, shovin through between the tarmac and the stones. I stare at em as hard as I can, and at the grit I would never've noticed if I hadn't stopped and wasn't starin so hard at one stupid spot. I've ended up here and these chips of stone have ended up here and now I'll remember these weeds and these specks of grit and this view between me own arms of a wall meetin a pavement and mekkin an angle the old dandelions have squeezed emselves through. And what's the use of it?

I push mesel off the low wall and carry on up the road, knowin now that the world didn't get emptied in the night. Cus that's what I'd bin thinkin as I walked back across the marsh and up the lanes. I'd bin waitin fer the sirens ter gan off, hopin this place'd be all mine, with the sun in the sky and nee one left ter catch us where I shouldn't be.

Me heart's flurryin, cus here I am, staggerin along the pavement in Arthur's village on Monday mornin, and the night's changed nowt. Back at home, me bed's empty, and at Gill's, her bed's empty in all. I'm movin me feet fer summit ter move, hurryin up the road, which is a road that another car's sure ter come along sooner or later, and now I'm joggin across the road and off it, down the turnin twards the farmyard and the bothy.

I creep along the cobbles, the shadders of the branches ripplin ovver me feet. I watch em in a daze, these dark reflections of the trees above us. Me heart slows now I'm under cover, but I can't lift me face ter look up at the real branches and leaves cus there's a thick murk sloshin in me skull, threatenin ter tip us backwards inter blackness if I look ter the sky. The cobbles end at the gateway and the farmyard oppens out, empty and glarin white in the mornin, and I stare across it at the shut bothy door.

I crouch at the gatepost, tryin ter work out what time it is. It seemed so long on the marsh in the dark, long enough fer the world ter empty and then fill again, and fer today ter seem like Sunday carryin on. I'm feelin too tatty fer the new day. Me own tongue tastes mouldy and fur's grown on me teeth. I'm countin me breaths in and countin em back out, and then I'm up on me toes, nearly turnin ter flee, as the door starts ter oppen.

Eggy, I say, me voice croakin, cus it's him who's stepped out, pullin his elbers behind him in a mornin stretch. Me body slides ter the floor. I lift me arm, a ton weight, but he's stood lookin across the yard, inter a corner I can't see inter. He's puttin his hand through his hair and then pullin his hat outta the back pocket of his jeans, shekkin it out and yankin it onter his head. Eggy, I'm croakin ter meself, Eggy, but me mushy bones won't hod the weight of us. Hand ovver hand I haul mesel up the gatepost. Relief's what it is. Relief's floodin through us and me skeleton's gone soggy. Eggy's shadder's stretched out on the white yard, a skinny stain that's tricklin away from his feet. His bloody face snags on mine and his body turns as he starts ter lollop, his shadder runnin twards us ovver the yard, and then I'm shuttin me eyes that're meltin out.

A dry hand's under me chin. Me face is tipped up ter his face, all its redness shinin down.

Yer alright, lad, he says, and I'm lifted up.

TWENTY-FIVE

The first sip of tea burns all the way, between me lungs and inter me empty gut, but it's like gettin scrubbed on me inside till I'm glowin and awake.

Slow down, lad, says Dan Reid.

I don't drink tea, I say ovver the rim of the mug.

Yer coulda fooled me.

He's leant forward in his chair. Everythin in the bothy's turned right side up again, but one arm of his chair's hangin off. He's got his fagbox sat on the other. I look around us, clockin the frayed white of splintered wood, the crookedness of shelves. There's a pile of legs and a tabletop propped against the wall. The stains on the lino have dried ter rust. Bry's tryin ter get a spindle fitted back inter the seat of the upturned stool on his knee. He looks up, glowerin, and sheks his head at Dan.

One fuckin night I get lucky. One. And I come back ter this mess.

He sheks his head. Dan looks at him and says nowt. Nee one's sayin owt. Dan's face is bruised and shiny. His eyes're bloodshot and swollen, as if he's bin cryin. But I don't reckon he's bin cryin. Gill's drummin her fingers on her sleeve, her lips pursed.

Worth it though, Bry, says Eggy, who's peerin at his split nose in the tiny mirrored lid of a mek-up case. There's a ripe purple swell half-shuttin his left eye. Ach, he says, suckin air in sharply. Fuckin listen ter this. Listen. He turns, bringin his face down ter Bry's ear. He's got the bridge of his nose in his fist and he's wobblin it.

D'yer hear?

Bry sheks his head, and Eggy swings ovver ter me. The mug's breathin heat inter me face. I gan still as a gristly *snick-snick, snick-snick* sounds in me ear.

Yer hear that? says Eggy.

I nod. I wanna be outta the dim bothy where everythin's cracked and headachy and stale. I'm thinkin of school, of walkin inter me form room and havin the tide of chatter meet us. The girls'll be sittin sidesaddle on the lids of their desks. The lads on the back row'll be on two legs of their chairs, leaned back against the wall, their arms crossed, while others're twisted round in their seats ter talk ter them. Every-thin'll be the same but the sameness'll be new again. Behind Cannonball-nostrils even the blackboard'll be bright black from bein washed ovver the summer. I wanna be sat down at a desk, and ter answer, Here! when me name's called, and then have the name affter us called and then the next, leavin us in me place, me exercise book oppen ter a dazzlin clean page.

Yer didn't find him? Gill says again, her hands on her hips. Eggy's snapped the mirror shut and is hoddin the case out ter her. She doesn't move, starin straight at us.

I told yer. He wasn't there. What yer gonna do with them outside? I say, turnin back ter Dan.

We're still thinkin about that.

I tek another sweet sip of tea. I look at the shut bothy door. Booby's and Carl's eyes had follered us as Eggy lugged us across the yard and up ter the door. I couldn't see their mouths under the tape, but they were still, the two of em, propped up in the corner of the yard. I could see the hair in their laps and clumps more of it blowin gently about em on the yard. The gaffer tape med em look like sacks of silver, an enormous sack and a smaller one next ter it, their two pairs of ankles wound round and round. Bloody nicks showed all ovver their shaved blue heads.

Well where is he, says Gill, and what happened ter yer?

I dunno Gill. I told yer. Nowt happened, I say, starin her out. I went down ter the bunker. He wasn't there, so I kem back.

We've gotta get home, she says, snatchin the mek-up case off Eggy and startin ter pace to and fro. If yer haven't found him, we've gotta get home. There's no gettin us outta this now. And you brought us out here, she says, stoppin and pointin a shekkin finger at us, black smudges under her eyes.

It's alright, lass. We'll get yer back, says Dan. There's time enough, int there, Eggy?

Aye, plenty, Dan, says Eggy, his fingers still on his nose.

Bry's shekkin his head. He tosses the bits of stool clatterin onter the floor at his feet. I jump. Dan Reid doesn't even flinch.

We'll get yer back and nee one'll be any the wiser, he says.

Who's gonna pay fer me fuckin stuff? says Bry.

Dan just looks at him, a matchstick poked between his fingers.

If we could find their fuckin car, says Bry.

Aye, well, says Dan. There were three of em. We'll get summit outta those two taped up in the yard. He turns his battered face ter me. Yer mate was there when I went down two days agan, he says, steadyin his grey eyes on us.

Aye, I know.

So where d'yer reckon he's gone?

Mebbe he's gone home, I say, me palms shiftin round me mug.

Would you gan home?

No.

Nor me, says Dan, nibblin on the dead end of the matchstick. He's still lookin at us, and I see him again with the knife at his throat, not wantin ter die. I reckon his grey eyes can see clean through us, as if me face is shaller watter with me lie trapped in it, flickin its tail. I look down inter me steamin tea.

They'd watched us, Booby and Carl, as Eggy lugged us ter the door, but I couldn't steady me eyes on em the way Dan's steadied his on me now. I couldn't stare em down, cus now I'm carryin that night in Bitts Park in me head, just the same as they are, and I can't get rid of what Arthur's med us swaller down. I can't spit it out, the smoke and ash of it, not ter anyone, and it's gonna be here ferever at the back of me throat.

D'yer wanna fag? says Dan, grabbin his fagbox.

No, I say quickly, and I don't.

Right, then, he says, pushin himsel up from the creakin chair, careful not ter put any weight on the wonky arm. Yous two get yer arses inter gear. Eggy, what time is it?

Five-summit, Dan.

Me dad's in at six, I say.

Gill's lookin furiously at us as I drag mesel onter me feet, her jumper hangin off her, as if she's shrunk ovvernight.

It's not my fault he wasn't there, I say, pretendin ter look fer somewhere ter put down me mug.

She huffs at us and grabs her handbag up outta the corner. Dan pulls oppen the bothy door and light swarms in.

Sorry about yer stuff, I say ter Bry. He's sat on the edge of the bed with his elbers on his knees. He just sheks his curly head. I put the mug down at his feet, and turn. I blink as I walk twards the door. Eggy's stood waitin outside. He walks beside us on me right, shieldin us as I start across the yard. I don't look back at the two of em in the corner.

Dan leads us up the lane and onter the road. We tek a right and troop along the verge, and then tek another right, and walk down the side of a white house ter a parked white van. Dan's fishin in his pocket and then countin fer a long minute through the bunch of keys he's dragged out. Then he tries the handle on the passenger side.

Oppen anyway, he says, grinnin a grin at us that's missin its two front teeth. He pulls oppen the door, then he's gan round ter the driver's side.

Cmon, cmon, says Eggy, hustlin us round the oppen door and inter the van. There's a bitta old carpet on the floor. We're all four of us squashed onter the front seats. Eggy slams the door and then budges against it, mekkin sure it's properly shut. The van stinks of dog. I look at Gill, squashed up beside us. She's starin, rock-faced, through the windscreen. Dan teks the steerin wheel and I see his skinned knuckles, then I clock the dented dashboard and the well at our feet, where a gutty tangle of wires is hangin outta the doorless glove compartment.

Don't worry, says Dan, fiddlin with his keys in the ignition as he gets comfy in his seat. Yer look worried.

The van fires up first try. He revs it too hard. As the engine dies back down from a rattlin scream, he cranks the gearstick. The van judders, and we're pullin outta the lane, then turnin onter the road twards town. I press mesel inter me seat.

The last white house of the village is gan by, and now the hedges're gettin higher, like shaggy green walls we're barrelin between. I'm concentratin on gettin carried along, off me ankles and sore feet. I sneak a look at Gill, her handbag on her lap and the handles looped ovver her wrists, her face fixed on the grey road gettin fed under the wheels. I glimpse a gang of big black birds at the side of the road, hoppin up onter the verge. They look too clever by half with their wings behind their backs. I count the bug splats on the windscreen, lookin at the glass and not at the countryside gan by. Then I look through the glass and ovver the fields, at the woods that're smearin past, too fast ter peer inter, too fast ter see what might be hidin away inside em.

I press mesel further inter me seat. Gill twists as me leg pushes against hers.

Ow, she says. What're yer doin?

Nothin, I say ovver the engine, the noise of it louder now the van's sped up.

Yer pokin us, she says, twistin round. What yer pokin us with?

Eggy's lookin ovver, his head gettin juddered cus he's restin it against the side winder. Me skin's gone clammy.

Aye, says Dan Reid, what yer pokin her with, lad?

Eggy laffs. The two of em are grinnin. There's a crackle comin off the two of em, off their skinned knuckles and split lips. Dan's turnin his face from the road twards us and then back again. Yer carryin a poker in yer pocket, or wat? he says.

Yer properly spiked us, says Gill ovver the two of em. She's squirmin round on her seat, her handbag tippin off her lap and inter the well.

It's nothin, I say, but trouble's chilled me spine.

I'm fuckin sure it isn't, says Eggy, and Dan hoots and slaps the steerin wheel.

Gill's gropin around under me leg and I'm tryin ter twist away in me seat. All of a sudden she's stuck her hand inter me pocket.

Gerroff us!

He's not used ter it, lass, says Dan, chortlin away.

Her hand's wormin about, but I feel it stop when she gets a hod of the elephant. I gan still, ready ter shrug and say it's nowt.

Aye, he thinks yer should buy him summit nice first, says Eggy.

Dan's dartin frownin looks between the road and us. We've kem down a hill and now we're windin through a cluster of houses huddled under shady trees, their leaves dyin already in big yeller licks. Eggy's peerin round Gill and inter me lap, his face gettin whipped ovver by the tree shadders. We come out from under the shade just as Gill tugs her hand outta me pocket and hods the elephant up ter the windscreen. She's just starin at it in the full glare. I'm starin at her.

He wasn't pleased ter see yer, says Eggy. He just had an elephant in his pocket.

Him and Dan Reid cackle and hiss. Gill's frownin and smilin at the same time, as if she's pleased that what was in me pocket was just this wee yellery-white elephant, its trunk raised and its foot stampin. She turns it ovver in her hand. We're out from under the trees but I can see thoughts whip-pin ovver Gill's face, like the shadders of branches. Dan's steerin us round a blind bend and then gan up through the gears again now we're on the straight. Eggy's leant the side of his head back against the judderin winder. And now I see it, the exact second Gill realises where she's sin the elephant before. Her face sets suddenly, cus there's nee decision fer her ter mek between frownin and smilin. She's turnin ter us, and I'm ready ter start denyin everythin, but she just beams, reaches inter the well fer her handbag, pops it oppen and slots the elephant inside. She latches the bag shut again. Dan slows right down ter ease ovver a bridge that gives us a view of the scrappy with its towers of flattened cars and heaps of rusty exhaust pipes. Eggy's bruised eyes're shut. Gill's suddenly squeezin me hand where it's stuck with sweat ter the vinyl seat cover. Her hand's cool. She looks at us and smiles again, as if she's just unwrapped a present. I can see the city comin twards us, rank affter rank of red-faced houses lined up on the outskirts.

Yer on yer own from here, says Dan Reid, leanin across the seats ter speak ter us through the passenger side. I don't expect the hornies ter come knockin at me door, no matter what. D'yer foller?

He doesn't wait fer an answer. As he pulls himsel back upright behind the wheel Eggy swings off the kerb inter the van, yawnin. He slams the door. The van roars away and we're stood watchin it gan.

Yer a liar, says Gill, cuffin me shoulder.

What d'yer mean?

Yer said yer didn't find him.

I didn't. Cmon, we've gotta get in.

I start off round the close twards Gill's house, leavin her stood on the kerb. I want rid of her, before she grabs us and finds I'm shiverin, shiverin even though me throat's burnin and me mouth's fillin with all I'm dyin ter tell her and can't. I'm rememberin me sister. She watched us sneakin ovver the dark landin through the crack in her door, and when she shut the door so softly on us it was a kinda promise. She'd looked right at us but she hadn't med a sound, as if fer once me and her had a secret between us and she was gonna keep it. There's a traffic rumble in the distance. I can feel the city around us draggin itsel awake.

He gev yer it, didn't he? says Gill catchin up and nippin in front of us so I have ter stop. I know he did.

I dunno what yer on about, Gill.

She's ratchin her handbag oppen, plungin her hand in.

Arthur, she says, hoddin up the ivory elephant. He took this from me gran's, didn't he? And he gev it ter you when yer found him last night. Ter give me. Yer can't lie ter us, Christopher. He's done it so I'll know.

I didn't find him.

I look straight inter Gill's face, at her pale mouth and smudgy eyes. I can nearly see through her skin.

I knocked him down cus he was a noise scarin us. In me head, Arthur's voice is as flat and cold as the Solway in the grey light.

I turn away, brekkin the look between us. I can smell the graveyard from where me and Gill are stood, a green and earthy chill seepin from ovver the wall. Me heart feels blown loose.

I knew yer'd found him, so yer can tell us what he said now, says Gill, comin round us, tryin ter lock eyes with us again. He's gan ter the police, isn't he? He's gonna tell em what he saw.

She's beamin.

How could he have given us that? I say, waftin me hand at the elephant she's still got held up.

He musta tekkan it from me gran's, when me and him were there.

She waits, watchin us.

Don't look so shocked, Christopher. I woulda told yer.

So it's true about you and Arthur?

Course it is. Didn't he tell yer?

I can smell the smell of the bunker, and hear the straw cracklin under us. I'm watchin Arthur's back as he packs his rucksack. When he looks ovver his shoulder at us his eyes're like the reels of a bandit, waitin ter get spun.

I never found him, I say. I took the elephant from yer gran's yesterday, when I went upstairs. I dunno why I did. I shouldn't have. Arthur never gev us it cus I never found him. I just didn't want yer ter find out I'd nicked it from yer gran's. Sorry.

You took it?

I've just told yer.

I hear the crack before me face starts ter sting. Gill's turned and is stridin away. Me hand's gone up ter me cheek. I can hear the pain of the slap more than I can feel it, but me hand's up automatically, ter cup the warm spot.

Gill! I say, me voice too loud. I'm sorry. The houses're watchin us now. Their winders're tekkin us in, the redness that's glowin outta me face, outta me whole head, like a beacon at a crossin. I'm stood with me hand on me face, me trainers crusted with dry mud, before the day's even got gan.

Will yer give her it back? Gill! I hiss at her. Gill.

She doesn't even look back.

TWENTY-SIX

There's black under me fingernails. The plaster on me thumb's unstickin and grey. I stamp me feet and some of the dry muck cracks off the bottom of me trainers and lies brokenly about on the pavement. There's grey mud spat up me jeans in all. Me dad's cab's not here and I'm tryin ter get all me noise outta the way now, before I have ter creep in the back door. But if me mam's up, what'll I say? I'll say I woke up early. She'll probly buy it cus of the cops last night. I'll say I couldn't get back ter sleep, so I went out inter the yard.

But yer filthy, she'll say.

I'll just shrug, I reckon. I'll shrug cus it's best ter not even try ter explain. She'll just mek her own sense of it then, which'll save us tryin ter tell her summit she won't believe, cus she'll believe whatever sense she meks of it more easily than she'd ever believe me.

Get up there and inter the bath, then, fer goodness' sake. At least I'm not havin ter dig you up out of yer pit.

She'll shek her head, so her bird's nest wobbles, and pull the pink strings of her dressin gown tight. Okay, I'll say, and start fer the stairs.

As I gan I might tek another peep ovver me shoulder through ter the kitchen. Me mam'll be reachin up ter oppen the top cupboard where the cereal boxes are. She'll feel us peepin and turn and smile at us, just the kinda smile yer give when someone's caught yer when yer thought yer weren't bein watched. I'll smile back at her, and I'll know she believes I've bin in the yard, kickin a ball or kneelin and watchin the ants march along between the grassblades. And that'll be that.

I look at me house, but there's no tellin if anyone's up. I can hear a sheet of plastic on the site gettin flabbed in and out by the wind. It's breathin the way a placky bag does when someone's suckin one in and out. A shiver scurries down me back.

But me mam might just ask, Is everythin alright? which'll really be her askin us if I couldn't sleep cus of Arthur.

Yeah, I'll say. I'm fine.

You don't have ter tell me if you don't want to, me mam'll say, smilin at us again from the doorway. We've all got secrets.

It's not a secret, I'll say, which'd probly be the wrong thing ter say.

But we've all got them. I'm just sayin you don't have ter tell me, just because I'm yer mam.

Okay.

Okay, she'll say, turnin back ter the kettle, but flickin us another wee smile ovver her shoulder, as if she doesn't actually believe us, but doesn't mind much anyhow.

I stamp me feet once more. I start across the road, comin at an angle twards me house, gettin ready ter crouch in close ter the mouth of the cut, ter keep mesel outta sight. I hear the wee electric zip of the milkfloat and the clear, pure jiggle of the empties as they're shuddered along another crescent outta sight. It's a sound from somespot between sleepin and wakin up, and now I'll have ter get up without ever havin gone ter bed, and I'm wonderin as I crouch here how I'm gonna see the whole day through at school. If I can just get through ter dinnertime, and if the sun comes out, then I can lie on the playin field with me arm ovver me eyes, chewin a piece of grass till me spit gans green. That'd be okay. I'm peerin round the cement fencepost planted at the mouth of the cut. It's pitted like the moon, but me dirty fingernails're against it, mekkin it nowt but grey cement. Suddenly I know summit's behind us, and I try ter look round, but too late.

Yer took yer time, says a voice inter me ear, and fingers're pullin me hair back and the achin egg on me head's gettin yanked up by the roots. Me wrist's grabbed and me hand's shoved up between me shoulderblades.

Stop it. Don't squeal, wee man, or I'll brek it fer sure.

Mal's sour breath is in me face. I try ter lean mesel away from him, away from the pain shootin from the joint of me shoulder down me side.

You and me, dead simple, like. None of this crashin about and kickin doors down. Git yersel turned round – that's it – and we're away.

He's swivelled us round, away from me house and back down the cut. I stumble but he keeps us pulled up on me feet by me bent-back arm.

Stop snivellin.

Where we gan?

Just somewhere outta the way, wee man.

He's changin his grip on me wrist and puttin his arm around me shoulders, like a fake mate, and squeezin hard.

There's a black cat ahead of us, sat rubbin its eyes beside the fence.

How long've I bin waitin fer you? says Mal.

I dunno.

It wasn't a fuckin question, wee man. Yer think I'm a fuckin gowk, he says, and twists me arm again. I told em not ter gan pilin in, but nee one listens ter Mal. D'yer? he snaps, diggin his fingers inter me ribs.

No, I say.

D'yer think I'm a gowk?

No.

But yer musta done yesterday when I was stuck there and yer went through me fuckin pockets. Yer musta thought I was a gowk then, he says, and pokes us. Did yer?

No, I say through me clenched teeth.

Same as yer pal, that skinny tapped bastard. Yer know where he is, don't yer?

We've stopped and Mal's shekkin us till me teeth chatter and me head pounds.

Don't fuckin bother, he says inter me ear. Save yer breath fer when yer really need ter tell us, wee man. Cus yer will really need ter tell us. It'll be the thing yer most wanna fuckin do, I'm tellin yer.

Above us, the lecky wires're swingin gently in a wind that's hardly any wind at all. There's a waft of burnt toast that woulda told us where I was if I didn't know already.

I can't sleep, says Mal. Yer know?

I say nowt. His breath's on the back of me neck. The black cat's watchin us, its paws on the floor, ready ter scoot.

He wouldn't be stopped, yer pal, and we fuckin tried. I shut me eyes and see that giffer's fuckin face, says Mal. Me shoulderblades grate together as Mal shoves me arm higher.

I was wrong, I say through me teeth.

I shouldn't even be doin this, he says, as if he hasn't heard us. He should be tekkin responsibility. Yer can't fuckin expect us ter shovel the shite. Yer know?

He's gone.

What d'yer mean he's fuckin gone? Mal says suddenly, shekkin us.

I yelp in pain. The cat teks off down the cut.

What yer fuckin sayin, wee man?

Look in me pocket, I say, me voice judderin.

Mal stops shekkin us.

In me pocket. He gev us it and told us what happened.

His grip gans still on us.

I was wrong, I say. I thought he hadn't done owt, but now I know and there's nowt I can do, cus it was him, wasn't it?

Mal's shiftin behind us. His fingers're loosenin on me wrist.

Give us it, he says. Gan on.

I bring me arm from behind us slowly, wincin at the stiffness in it. I slot me hand inter me jeans. Mal's got us clamped by me upper arm, his fingers diggin inter me muscle. I close the Zippo in me fist and pull me fist outta me pocket. Mal sniffs, but I hear him tekkin an excited, ragged breath.

When the tide's out, yer can walk across, Arthur had said.

All the way?

Aye, all the way ter Scotland. Then he turned and went.

I stood in the bunker and watched him gan. The mist rubbed him fainter and fainter, and then I thought he'd mebbe turned back and I stepped off the deck of the bunker and started across the mud. But me eyes had tricked us and he hadn't, and I stopped. I didn't wanna step back inter the grey room with its straw fulla the stink of old fires and sleep, so I started back across the marsh, back the same way I'd come in the dark, not lookin once ovver me shoulder.

Suddenly I'm fulla silent madness, beatin in us like great white wings, but I turn calmly, bringin me fist round and hoddin it out ter Mal Sharkey. I can see his eyes watchin it. His fingers've slackened off me arm. I start ter oppen me fist, the silver bright in me palm, and as I let the Zippo drop, I feel Mal's hands fall off us ter snatch at it, and I kick at him hard.

Me foot meks solid contact with bone. There's a surprised *Ock!* sound, but I'm already twistin round, the silver case skitterin on the deck. And there's nowt to us. I'm light enough ter fly, pushin mesel between him and the fence, me eyes on the mouth of the cut as me trainers grip and I tek off. Mal's a scuffle. Cunt! I hear him spit, but I'm away and swingin round the fencepost, outta the cut, twards me house. The wings in us are beatin. I know there's nowt in us that can be held.

Acknowledgements

Trinity College, Cambridge, generously welcomed me as a Fellow Commoner in Creative Arts, 2005–07: to the Master and Fellows and to the members of the College, I extend many thanks, as I do to the Civitella Ranieri Foundation, who granted me productive time in beautiful surroundings, among great company. I would like to thank my dear friends Dr Richard Thwaites, Ian Fenton and Janni Howker, who read versions of the book and thoughtfully gave invaluable advice. Peter Straus and Jenny Hewson provided me with much encouragement and practical help: I am most grateful to them and all at RCW. Over the years, Sam Humphreys and all at Picador have been extremely patient and supportive, and I owe them, and Andrew Kidd, many thanks. Charlotte Greig has been a challenging and scrupulous editor; the book has benefited greatly from her patience, and I deeply appreciate all her work. Sarah Hall has been a steady reader and a mercurial inspiration, a feat she achieves, as she does many more miraculous feats every day, with jaw-dropping ease.

Climber, author and film director Graham Hoyland was the fifteenth Briton to climb Everest and during one of his nine expeditions to the mountain was responsible for the discovery of George Mallory's body. He worked as a BBC producer on programmes such as *Dragons' Den*, the *Today* programme and *Around the World in 80 Faiths*. He is the author of *Last Hours on Everest*, *Walking Through Spring* and *Yeti*.

Praise for *Merlin*

'To get deeper into the nuts and bolts of aviation, Graham Hoyland spent a year taking apart the story of the Merlin and putting it back together in a form that roars beautifully from the very start'

SIMON CALDER, *Independent*

'A stirring account of how these hand-wrought machines, geared for speed and encased in elegant airframes ... delivered us in 1940 ... *Merlin* depicts a heroic age of smashed land, air and water speed records ... and the extreme bravery of those pioneers, who incurred many fatalities. Hoyland marries the drama and excitement with a clear focus on the technical: he puts you in the cockpit and into the very guts of the machines ... Anyone with a serious interest in engineering will find much to enjoy and appreciate'

COLIN GREENWOOD, *Spectator*

'*Merlin* paints a finer, more detailed and complete portrait of the aero engine and the people who made it than almost any other single volume on the subject ... Illuminating and entertaining'

Pilot magazine

Praise for Graham Hoyland

'Illuminating and entertaining'	*The Times*
'A towering work full of twists and turns'	*Independent*
'Richly enjoyable'	*Daily Mail*

ALSO BY GRAHAM HOYLAND

Last Hours on Everest
Walking Through Spring
Yeti